I0535456

WARRIOR
BOOK 1 OF THE VUKASIN SAGA

B.D. Snowden

GEEKY GOTH PRESS

DEDICATION

This book is dedicated to all of my friends who kept my
spirits up when I felt like quitting

ACKNOWLEDGMENTS

I couldn't have finished this book without my support system. I am thankful to my beta readers. The men and women of Books, Booze and Betas are an awesome group of people who love books as much as I do.

CHAPTER ONE

The sun was shining and the breeze gentle. There was just enough bite in the air to let one know that colder temperatures were on their way. It was a fine day for most anyone else, but Megan O'Connor wasn't paying attention to the day.

Her eyes were fixed straight ahead on the path. It was like she could block out the orderly platoon of white marble grave markers if she didn't look at them. Megan hated this place. She hadn't stepped foot in the Veteran's Cemetery for over a year. Not since they laid Richard to rest here.

He was supposed to have been home by the end of that month. He had promised it would be his last deployment. Megan blinked back the tears that threatened to fall at the memory. Richard had been right. It was his last deployment; but thanks to a roadside IED it was his last everything.

Megan didn't want to remember Richard in

the casket. She wanted to remember his laughter and his smiles. That was why she avoided this place.

This place just reminded her how alone she was in this world. Her parents had passed away years before, so Richard and his military unit became her family. With the loss of Richard, Megan also lost the tight-knit supportive community that once surrounded her. She had been forced to leave base housing, and her friends and neighbors trickled away. She couldn't really blame them. Megan had become a reminder that their loved ones may not come home, and as a military wife, you just didn't think about that, not if you wanted to keep your sanity.

"Momma…where's daddy?" The gentle tug of her daughter's hand brought Megan out of her self-pity. This was the reason she was here today: Abigail Lindsay O'Connor, the greatest gift Richard ever gave her.

Megan felt like she was struggling alone in the world since Richard's death, but it wasn't all about her. She had to be here for her daughter, even if that meant doing things she would rather not, like come to the cemetery. Abby had wanted to show her daddy her new princess Halloween costume that Megan had made for her.

The grief counselors the military made them see had warned Megan that she would need to allow Abby to grieve and process her father's death in her own way. Being in this place hurt Megan's heart because she missed Richard so much, but she would suffer through anything for the sake of her daughter.

They neared Richard's gravesite. His grave was at the back of the cemetery near a thick hedge of cedar trees. He was buried under one of the few pecan trees in the cemetery. It was a rather nice place as far as gravesites go. There was a stone bench next to the grave under the pecan tree. Squirrels scurried around, collecting the nuts for their winter stores. Birds could be heard chirping in the trees. Megan tried to pretend they were out in the park rather than the cemetery.

Megan laid her hand on the cold white marble inscribed with the name of her beloved husband. "Here's your dad, Abby. You talk to him while mommy goes and sits on the bench."

Megan sat down while Abby chattered away at the stone. She wasn't sure that her five year old fully understood the implication of talking to a grave stone. Megan wondered if part of her daughter was still waiting for Richard to come back from his deployment. Megan consoled herself with the observation that Abby seemed to be a happy child, despite losing her father.

"Look, Daddy....Mommy put ruffles and sparkly ribbon on my dress. And I'm gonna get a crown and everything." Her daughter's happy chatter lightened her heart a little; maybe this wasn't such a bad idea after all.

*****

"Banji, Akia…you have your assignments?" Reijo of Clan Tiaret surveyed this last two-man team with a critical eye. Like all men from Vukas, they were very tall and muscular. The rigorous training they received in their warrior's den had sculpted their bodies into something solid and deadly. The pair were twin brothers and one of the best warrior teams he had. He had always wondered if the fact that they had been together since the womb was one of the reasons they coordinated so effortlessly.

"Yes, *Kijani-a,*" they answered simultaneously.

"I have arranged for you to be sent to an area with few life signs, but within an easy run to a populated area. Do not draw attention to yourself. This is a raid, not an invasion. Find a lone female. Do not take a female that has the smell of her mate. You are the last team for this assignment at this time, and I cannot stress how important it is for you to come back successful."

The twins exchanged glances. While Akia's stoic expression betrayed nothing of what he was feeling, Banji's grin let everyone know that he was looking forward to the adventure.

"You don't have much time: a single sun cycle. So do not dawdle," Reijo said more for Banji's benefit than Akia's.

Reijo turned to the console next to him and laid his palm on the flat surface. The cool crystal heated with his touch as the matrix scanned him. When it finished the recognition program, various symbols illuminated the surface. Reijo punched in codes and coordinates and turned his attention to the two pillars towering above them.

The interstellar transport facility was housed just outside of the capital city. It was a much more complex version of the travel slip streams used to transport goods and people around the planet. It had mostly been used to travel to worlds in nearby solar systems; the destination for these soldiers was at the very edge of its capabilities. Of course it came as a surprise to everyone that their possible salvation was found on a tiny planet in the most desolate galaxy they had knowledge of. Up until just a few years ago it was thought that particular galaxy was devoid of sentient life, and then a lone specimen changed everything.

Lightening arched between the pillars as space and time folded in on itself. The wall behind the pillars visually distorted and a wind howled through the chamber. Reijo and the slip stream attendants latched on to hand holds to keep from being pulled in. With a final check of the coordinates, Reijo waved Banji and Akia on. The pair nodded and released their holds, allowing the stream to suck them in. A pop of displaced air could be heard and felt as they passed the event horizon. Technicians monitored the readouts until it showed the pair had been thrown clear of the slip stream, and then they shut it down. At this time tomorrow they would open the slip stream once more in the reverse direction. If all went well, the men would return home with their quarry and there wouldn't be any accidental passengers on the return trip.

*****

Megan smiled as Abby twirled on her father's grave. Just a few more minutes and she would pack her daughter up to head home. She almost missed the shadows of the two men approaching her and her daughter, but they didn't miss her. One elbowed the other and pointed in her direction. She saw his head snap up to attention. The men were strangely dressed in what appeared to be some sort of uniform. It wasn't the army uniform she was used to seeing around this area; in fact, she would think it was a couple of single soldiers out participating in some cosplay party if their hair had been buzz cut.

Megan was on the verge of real anger at the thought that some local college kids had decided to party at the military cemetery. That anger boiling up quickly dissipated as the men drew closer and she realized these weren't some college kids, but battle-hardened men. Maybe they were ex-army, she thought.

They seemed in no rush but kept their eyes on her as they approached. Megan's heart rate increased as she realized just how large these men are. She would swear they were close to seven foot tall. She could also tell that they were definitely related, most likely twins since they looked almost identical except for different facial expressions. As they neared, she could hear them speaking to each other in a language that she couldn't understand.

Megan stood and walked over to Abby. "Time to go, sweetheart."

Abby looked to her mom and then over to the men her mother was watching. Megan could tell that Abby thought the men were scary too. Abby held her mom's hand tightly and didn't argue as Megan pulled her away from her daddy's grave.

*****

Akia grumbled about how this had to be an over-sexed society because despite the countless females they had encountered, every one of them carried the scent of a male on them, with the exception of the two females whose blatant display showed them they were obviously mated to each other.

Both Banji and Akia felt the weight of their failed mission pressing down upon them. The people of Vukas had only a few generations at best before they died out completely if more compatible females were not brought home.

The pair was headed back to the slip stream coordinates when Banji spotted her. She was a tiny thing, but filled with luscious curves. Her hair was the color of flames hanging down her back. Pair that with her fair skin and she seemed to glow in the sunlight.

Banji elbowed his brother to get his attention. "Akia, we may not have to go home empty handed after all."

Akia raised his head and scented the wind. A delicate, sweet smell drifted toward him. The scent was decidedly feminine, though there seemed to be a note of someone else.

"I don't scent a male near her, but…." Akia sniffed again.

Banji's eyes never left the woman as he too inhaled her scent. "She doesn't carry the smell of a male. I don't even scent any recent arousal. She has no mate, Akia."

As they neared the woman, she rose and walked a short distance, taking the hand of a small child. She eyed the men warily, moving to put herself between them and the child that was most likely hers since their coloring was similar.

Banji heard a hiss from Akia as he drew in a breath. This woman had obviously whelped, but she carried no markers that would show she was mated. What kind of man would leave a woman and her offspring defenseless?

"She has no mate, Akia…. We must take her."

"You would leave the young one defenseless?" growled Akia.

"Of course not; we would bring it with us."

"We are not authorized to bring whelps, Banji. If we break protocol it could go very bad for us."

The pair paused to study the two humans as they walked closer. Banji and Akia were between the human and the exit of this area. As they get closer it became clear that the little human was female as well.

"The little one will grow into a female that can be mated; I do not think that *Kijani-a* Reijo would punish us too harshly for that, especially since it would be the off spring of the woman."

"I don't know, brother…." Akia never broke regulations, but this mission was different from any other assignment, and they were running out of time.

"Well, I'm bringing them back." Akia sighed

because once Banji decided on a course of action, there was no swaying him away from it.

*****

Megan tried to skirt around the mountainous men in her path. Something about the way they stared at her while speaking in their strange language sent up red flags in her mind. Experience had taught her to listen to those red flags.

Megan kept sharp eyes on the men as she ushered her daughter towards the parking lot at the front of the cemetery. She briefly wondered where they were from since their language was nothing like she had ever heard before, and after nearly a decade as a military wife she was familiar with most of the language families from around the globe.

Their language was very guttural, with what almost sounded like growls, but it didn't sound like it was similar to German. The dark hair and complexions of the two men had her briefly wondering if they were of Mediterranean or Middle Eastern descent; but again their words didn't sound like anything from any of those areas. She puzzled if she should report the suspicious men to the caretaker.

Megan and Abby were coming level with the two men when a gale force wind kicked up. For a moment Megan wondered if they were going to be caught in a sudden fall storm. Central Texas was fairly well known for unpredictable weather after all. But she looked up and the skies were still bright and clear. The windy disturbance seemed to be localized to only the cemetery.

It was in that moment of distraction that Megan felt a large hard body tackle her to the ground. Abby's hand was jerked out of her grip and Megan heard her daughter screaming. Megan twisted, trying to get leverage against the large man who pinned her down.

"Get your hands off of me!" Megan heard a whoosh of air from the lungs of her assailant as she elbowed him. "Abby!"

"Mommy!" It ripped Megan's heart to shreds to hear the terror in her daughter's voice. Megan twisted and squirmed until she was half free of the man who held her down.

"Mommy!" Abby's screams increased to a panicked wail. The little girl cried out an indistinct sound of pain and then was terrifyingly silent.

Megan couldn't see her daughter in the position she was pinned in, but her daughter's silence broke something inside of her. Any sense of self-preservation was gone. Her only thought was to get to Abby.

Megan twisted herself free of her attacker's grip when he released one hand to reach for something. In the few seconds of advantage that gave, Megan was up on her hands and knees scrambling away.

"Abby!" Megan rushed towards her daughter's prone body, not knowing if these bastards had killed her. Her fingers could almost reach out and touch Abby when Megan felt a prick in her arm and the world faded to black.

The two men picked up Megan and her

daughter. One cradled the child like a baby. The other slung Megan over his shoulder. After gathering the two unconscious people up, the burly men walked into the eye of the howling winds. A pop, a mild concussive whoosh, and all four people disappeared from sight, leaving the cemetery caretaker to wonder in the morning about the lone car abandoned in the parking lot.

CHAPTER TWO

Banji and Akia were spit out of the slip stream. It was only their years of experience at such travel that kept them from falling. As it was, Banji stumbled, nearly dropping the woman he carried on his shoulder. Akia caught him and kept him upright since neither one wanted to injure their precious cargo. One technician raised a brow when he saw the child Akia carried, but they knew better than to question or interfere with anything the warrior class did.

The slip stream was shut off and the brothers decided to head towards the palace. The women brought back were currently being housed there, and it was a safe bet that Reijo would be there as well for them to debrief their mission.

As they stepped into the sunshine after leaving the transport facility, the child in Akia's arms began to stir. The drug they had used to knock them out was wearing off quickly.

"Banji, what should we do with the whelp? Youngsters have never been allowed in the palace proper."

Banji looked over at the child. "She looks old enough to have been weaned. So I would think that putting her in the hands of the royal school would be best."

"But she is female and so much more delicate than our own kind."

"If the way the mother struggled was any indication, I have a feeling that little one would surprise you."

Akia shifted the child to a more comfortable position but said nothing in response to his brother. He knew Vukasin boys were a rowdy lot and the schools instituted a rough discipline to keep control of them. Akia wasn't convinced that taking the little girl to the school would be the best solution.

The stoic brother looked up to see the walls of the palace courtyard ahead. If he was going to find another solution, he would need to figure it out fast, especially since his small bundle was beginning to stir more and more. Akia reasoned with himself that even if he couldn't figure something out he could always visit the school to check up on the child.

The little girl woke up entirely about the same time they entered the courtyard. With a nod, Banji headed towards the building housing the women they had brought back, while Akia turned in the opposite direction to head to the royal school. The child's eyes widened as she realized that she was going to be separated from her mother.

Akia watched in horror as the child's face turned nearly purple. He had been prepared for some tears since this was a strange new place, but he had not reckoned on the ear-piercing wail that erupted from the child. The volume was improbable; it wasn't possible for such tiny thing to make such a loud noise. The obvious distress caused a few of the phased ceremonial guards to come running.

The sight of the phased guards doubled the volume of the child's screams and changed them from simple distress to downright terror.

Banji stopped and turned to see what was wrong with his brother. Akia shrugged as if to say he didn't know what to do, which caused Banji to chuckle. His laughter didn't last long, as his own charge shifted suddenly, her knee connecting forcefully with his chin.

*****

Megan's head ached as the blood pounded in her ears. It took her a moment to figure out that she was hanging upside down, which was why all of the blood was rushing to her head. She tentatively opened her eyes. She knitted her brow in confusion at what she saw. Why the hell was she hanging over someone's ass? Granted it was a nice, shapely ass: very muscular, just like she liked them. As she watched the ass in question, she noticed that she was bouncing along. As the fog cleared from her mind she realized that she was being carried like a sack of potatoes over someone's shoulder.

The humid atmosphere let Megan know that

they were no longer in the cemetery, and even though she wasn't sure how, she was fairly certain they weren't even in central Texas anymore. Megan tried to take in their surroundings without alerting the man who carried her to the fact that she had regained consciousness. She could hear the two of them speaking in their strange language. Other voices nearby seemed to be speaking it as well. This made Megan wonder just how long she had been unconscious. Surely it had to be days to get to whatever country this was. And why were all the voices she was hearing only masculine?

She pushed the puzzle of where they were aside in her mind. She was still worried about what happened to Abby. Finding out what happened to her child was her top priority. Her last recollection was of Abby's prone body in the cemetery. That was why when she first heard Abby crying. Megan was afraid it was just wishful thinking, but as the wails grew stronger, she breathed a sigh of relief that at least Abby was still alive.

The man holding her stopped and turned, laughter rumbling through his chest. Megan was considering her next move when her daughter's cries turned into screams of terror. Megan lost all thought save one…get to Abby!

Without thinking, Megan's body sprang into action. She had never been more grateful for the decades of martial arts training her father had insisted on. She used the man's own body to leverage herself up. She planted her knee square in his chin and then flipped away from his falling body.

Megan sprinted to the second man, who held her daughter. Without pausing, she did a side leg sweep and caught the man right behind his knees. The force of the blow caused his knees to buckle, and a fighting Abby kept him off balance until he landed flat on his back with an "oomph."

Megan scooped up her daughter and hugged her tight. For a moment she forgot she was in a strange place, until several shadows loomed over her and Abby.

"What the fuck?!" Megan looked up and saw these huge humanoid creatures advancing on her. Each carried an ornate spear. At first Megan thought they must be men in costumes because they looked like what most people would describe as werewolves. They were enormous, the smallest standing at least six foot tall. Their bodies were covered in fur. Their snouts were elongated and filled with wicked-looking canines. The only difference from the Hollywood werewolf was what looked like bony bits of armor along the arms and top of the head.

Megan stood and placed herself in a fighter's stance. "Abby, stay behind me, baby. If I tell you to run...you run and don't let them catch you, ok?" Abby nodded, her tiny body trembling and her eyes wide.

One of the creatures reached out to grab Megan, growling at her. Megan shifted and grabbed his wrist. Using an aikido throw, she flipped the much larger beast over her shoulder. The rest of the pack, Megan counted four more, stopped dead. They seemed shocked that such a tiny woman managed to get the better of one of them. Megan didn't give them a chance to recover from the shock. She twisted the arm of the beast she had just flipped and stomped on his other hand, which held his spear. She caused enough pain that his grip loosened from the shaft of the spear. Megan snatched it up. Her training had never covered spear work, so she used the weapon like a staff instead.

The creatures advanced on her one by one. Megan was so busy defending their advances that she really didn't stop to think why they didn't rush her and overwhelm her with numbers. But then, her sensei did always say she lacked strategy.

Megan spun into another attack, adding momentum to the end of the spear. Her blow landed on the side of one creature's head. A satisfying crack and the creature dropped at her feet. The next one she knocked the wind out of with a blow to the gut. Megan kept the fallen creature in her peripheral vision as she turned to face the third assailant.

This one had seen her take on his two comrades and approached her with more respect. Soon Megan was engaged in a one-on-one battle straight out of a kung-fu movie. If this had just been sparring at the dojo, she would be having a blast. But this wasn't for fun. If she lost here it could mean the lives of her and her daughter.

The creature was not used to fighting an opponent so much smaller than he was. He was finding it difficult to counter training that was ingrained for similar sized adversaries. So when he threw a block that was too high, Megan used her diminutive size to get under his defense and land a blow on the back of his head.

Megan was spinning to face another when she saw one of the men who brought them here grab her daughter. Abby screamed, kicking and thrashing against the man who had her. The little girl was squirming so much that the man tucked her under one arm like a football to keep a grip on her. Megan was thankful that it left his body open without having to worry about Abby getting in the way. She let out a war cry and rushed the man who held her daughter, the spear held in front of her like a jousting lance.

The head of the spear impaled the man through his shoulder. When Megan felt the contact, she gave the spear one last shove, sending the man to his knees. As he fell, Megan let the spear slip from her fingers and ran up the length of it, only pausing to pick up her daughter.

Megan franticly looked for a means of escape. The altercation had gathered quite an audience, and everywhere Megan looked there were more men speaking in that same strange language. She didn't stop moving but kept her eyes peeled for a way out. Finally she found an open gate in the tall walls that surrounded them.

Megan changed course midstride and headed for that gate as fast as her legs could carry her. She ignored her shortness of breath and the stitch that was cramping her side. Her only thought was to get out of that gate.

A bellow echoed through the courtyard. Even though Megan couldn't understand what it had said, the sound rang with authority. So it shouldn't have been a surprise that all of the men dumbfounded by the display they had just witnessed suddenly sprang into action.

*****

Reijo was watching for Banji and Akia from the balcony that overlooked the courtyard. Thanks to a concerned slip stream technician, he knew that the twins were bringing more than just an adult female to the palace compound. He hadn't expected the show he was now witnessing.

Reijo watched as Akia headed off towards the royal school. In Vukasin society, children are raised in communal areas by those who society deems best to teach them. Even their few females were taught in this manner, though their education wasn't centered on the arts of war like the male education was. This human child became distraught over leaving its mother. Reijo figured it was just the shock of a new environment and that the young one would adjust eventually. Reijo thought he would have to answer questions for the female regarding the welfare of her offspring. He was not prepared for the human female's actual reaction.

His jaw dropped as this tiny little female laid Banji flat with a well-placed blow. While shocked that she could get the drop on such a seasoned warrior, Reijo was fairly certain it was a lucky shot. After all, every warrior knew that experience can sometimes be felled by luck. But that reasoning melted away as he continued to watch her.

She faced five phased soldiers. Reijo knew that nothing like the phase existed on the female's planet. He fully expected her to scream in terror, because from her perspective they would be monsters. But she surprised him again. She shifted her body subtly, but even from the balcony, Reijo could see that she had put herself into a trained fighter's stance. Perhaps there was more to this little female than he first thought.

His respect for her increased as she fought off the guards. She was easily half the size of any of the men down there yet she was holding her own. Of course it helped that his warriors hadn't ganged up on her, since they had no wish to harm her. But even a Vukasin warrior would be hard pressed to win when outnumbered seven to one.

Reijo winced as her spear cracked the back of one of his men's skull. He stopped one of the servants passing by.

"Please have a medic dispatched to the courtyard immediately." The servant bowed and scurried off to carry out the orders he was given.

"There seems to be an interesting show going on in the courtyard."

Reijo turned and bowed before the stately man who was both his king and his cousin. "We have had an unexpected development, *Khalon* Ghaleb."

Ghaleb snorted, but smiled. "How many times have I told you that you do not need to address me as *Khalon* when it is just us? We shall always be friends and family, Reijo." He looked over the balcony and studied the tiny female in the middle of the fray. "Unexpected indeed. It looks like you might have a bit of a ghost lioness on your hands." The *Khalon* smiled, tapping his fingers against the balcony wall in thought. Suddenly Ghaleb pushed away from the wall, his mind jumping to some other task or train of thought. "Well I must be off. I'll leave you to sort this," he waved in the general direction of the courtyard, "mess out." Ghaleb turned and walked away, whistling as he went.

Reijo eyed his cousin. He had been around the man long enough to know that his mind was forming new mechanizations. Ghaleb liked to use people like chess pieces, getting them to move just the way he wanted; and Reijo had a sneaking suspicion that the royal house just took an interest in their newest female acquisition.

The shrill cry of a child brought Reijo's attention back to the drama in the courtyard. He watched as Banji grabbed the child while the mother was occupied with one of the phased soldiers. Reijo hoped they would get the woman back under control before someone was seriously hurt. Just as he finished that thought, Reijo watched as the woman took off with the spear at Banji. Reijo watched in horror and respect as she stabbed Banji before picking up her child and fleeing. Banji was still moving, so at least the blow didn't seem to be fatal, but he was still impressed that she showed no hesitation in her attack. He didn't want to admit it but he was looking forward to learning more about this strange female.

Reijo watched her a few more moments as she evaded the men in the courtyard. The medic had arrived and was treating the wounded she had left in her wake. He saw her intent when she found an opening. If she made it through the palace gates, they would have a hell of a time finding her and he couldn't assure her safety. This was, after all, a planet filled with sexually frustrated males.

The men of the palace seemed almost afraid of approaching her. Reijo chuckled. Considering the damage she had done to some of their best warriors, perhaps the men had cause to be wary. But he couldn't let her escape.

"Enough!" he bellowed to the crowd below. He took charge and started barking out orders. Obeying orders was so ingrained in the men that it didn't take long for them to cut off her line of escape. When she was surrounded, she fought like a wild cat, leaving numerous victims bloodied, but overwhelming numbers finally allowed them to pin her down. It was kind of comical to see four huge men holding down one tiny female.

Reijo quickly made his way down to the courtyard. When he passed by the medic, he grabbed the injector that would implant a translation device under the woman's skin. Reijo was fairly certain that he was going to have to do a lot of explaining. Hopefully the woman would listen long enough to calm down.

CHAPTER THREE

The men surrounded Megan and her daughter, shoulder to shoulder in a tight formation. All avenues of escape were cut off. Megan turned slowly within that circle, looking for even the tiniest opening. Unfortunately, once the men decided to coordinate, Megan could see she was outmatched. But she wasn't an Irishman's daughter for nothing, and she wasn't going down without a fight.

One of the men took it upon himself to snatch Abby from Megan's arms while the others bum-rushed her. Megan threw every punch, kick, and block combination her years of martial arts training ever taught her. When exhaustion and sheer numbers finally bested her, Megan was on the ground with four separate men, each holding her down by an extremity. But still she twisted and fought like a cat that someone was trying to bathe.

The men around her held her fast, grumbling to themselves. Those that weren't trying to hold her down were wiping blood from noses and split lips.

At least Megan got a few good hits in, and that thought made her smile.

Megan turned her head trying to scan the crowd for Abby. She finally found her being held under the shade of a nearby tree in the arms of the other man who had brought them to this place. For the moment, the man didn't seem like he was going to hurt Abby, but Megan's chest constricted at the look on her daughter's face. She had never been faced with this much violence in her young life, and she didn't know how to process it. Her wide blank stare told Megan that her daughter was most likely going into shock. *Damn it!* She hoped these men would let her have her back soon.

Silence descended on the gathered crowd, and Megan shifted as best she could to see what had everyone's attention. Stalking–you couldn't even call what this man did walking—towards them was the biggest most beautiful man Megan had ever seen. He was taller than any of the others gathered, which had Megan estimating from her position face down on the ground that he had to be almost seven feet tall. His skin was a similar bronze color that many of the men here seemed to sport. His hair was dark, almost black, in places but had lightened to a warm caramel color in the sun. But it was his eyes that snared you. They were a bright blue that seemed almost electric when paired with his dark coloring. If Megan had dreamed up tall, dark, and handsome…then the man now standing over her would have walked right out of her imagination.

He knelt down and was talking to her, but she

couldn't understand what he was saying. Even without knowing what the words meant, Megan could tell that his voice had been pitched to be soothing, like one would do when trying to calm an angry animal. Megan just glared at him. She wasn't about to relax with someone who was part of whatever group had kidnapped her and her daughter. Her own blue eyes blazed with defiance.

When the man raised his hand and Megan saw what appeared to be a gun held there in; she renewed her struggles. *Fuck!* She was going to die here and Abby was going to see it. At the very least her daughter would know that she fought to the bitter end. The man placed the gun at the base of her skull and Megan thought that at least she wouldn't suffer when the end came.

But the end never came. When that man pulled the trigger, Megan heard a pop and felt a sharp sting at the back of her neck. The man said something to the ones holding her down and Megan found herself released. She quickly stood upright, ready to defend herself from this new threat.

Megan shifted to the balls of her feet and lowered her center of gravity, when she was knocked to her knees by what felt like an electrical bolt that started at the base of her skull and traveled down her entire body. The man with the startling blue eyes continued speaking to her in his strange guttural growls, his brow furrowed with concern.

Megan didn't know what was going on, but she knew that they had done something to her. That was why when the man reached for her she smacked his hand away and glared at him. She wasn't able to stare at him long enough to intimidate because another shock wave forced her eyes shut, while she tried to compartmentalize the pain. And still the man continued to talk.

Wait a minute…Megan could have sworn she heard "It will pass" in a deep gravelly voice. But no one had spoken English since she had arrived in this strange place.

"What did you say?" Megan eyed the man warily. It was quite possible that they had fried her brain with those electrical shocks and she had fully lost it.

"…good the translation (guttural language growls)…soon we can talk." The longer he talked to her the more clear the blue-eyed man's speech became.

"I promise we have no wish to harm you."

Megan snorted, "Yeah right."

"It is right…you are an honored guest here." The blue-eyed man offered his hand to help Megan up.

Megan didn't move to take the offered hand. "Give me my daughter back, now." With a nod from the newcomer, Abby was released and rushed over to her mother. Megan enveloped her little girl in a quick hug before holding her at arm's length to check for injuries. "Did they hurt you, Abby?" Hands went up and down the little girl's body, looking for any injury. There were no obviously broken bones, though a few places were going to be bruised from the men trying to keep a fighting little girl in their grasp.

Keeping Abby in her arms, Megan stood to her full five foot two height. "Why did you attack us?"

The man with blue eyes crossed his arms and chuckled. His smile was filled with humor, but somehow looked unused, like he didn't normally smile much. The quirk of his lips revealed a dimple in his cheek. Megan loved dimples, and she caught herself staring at it. God, he was beautiful, and she couldn't help thinking that he had enough muscle that even with her ample curves he could pick her up and…shaking her head, she refocused on his eyes, demanding an answer with her own. Now was not the place to lose her rational mind to her libido.

"My lady, it was you who attacked my men, not the other way around." Megan wasn't sure if this was true or not; she just remembered reacting because Abby had been frightened.

"I am *Kijani-a* Reijo of the Clan Tiaret."

"Megan….Megan O'Connor." She didn't understand why she was giving this man her name, except that somewhere deep inside she wanted him to know her. Megan didn't understand what was going on. She hadn't been attracted to anyone this whole past year and here she was suddenly getting wet over a strange man who was part of some sort of kidnapping plot that she and her daughter got tangled up in.

She really didn't understand why these men would want her anyway. She had no family. She didn't come from money. So ransom was out of the question. She supposed it could be some form of human trafficking, but that wouldn't explain the fanged and furry in this bunch. Megan cringed with her next thought...perhaps they were going to be experimental subjects. She really didn't want fur of her own.

She took a deep breath, ready to launch herself into demanding answers when she felt Abby crumple beside her. Megan looked down to see her little girl collapsed unconscious on the ground next to her. Her concerns about their situation were forgotten.

"Abby! Oh, baby, please be ok." Megan knelt beside her daughter and gently pushed the little girl's tangled red hair away from her face. Megan was relieved that Abby seemed to be breathing normally, but she was extremely pale. Dark circles under her eyes stood in sharp contrast to the rest of her complexion.

Large, bronzed hands reach down and picked up the tiny bundle. Megan tried to stutter a protest when blue-eyes stalked off with her daughter. Jumping up, Megan jogged after them.

"Where are you taking my daughter?" She grabbed his bicep to get him to stop. "And could you slow down? My legs happen to be a lot shorter than yours."

Reijo paused and looked down at the little woman with flame-colored hair. "I'm taking her inside, out of the heat. I'm also going to summon a medic."

"I won't leave Abby. I'm going with you."

"As you wish." Reijo headed towards the palace. He caught himself a few times forcing Megan to jog to keep up with his long strides; he decided to try and engage her in conversation so perhaps he wouldn't keep taking off at his military pace. "The little one's name is Abby?"

"Abigail Lindsay O'Conner." Megan reached over and touched Abby's face; it felt a bit feverish to her and that had Megan worried.

"O'Connor? This is your clan name?"

Megan shrugged, "At one point in history, I suppose it would have been…but now it is just a family name."

"O'Connor is your family name? Your parents also had this name?"

This was such a strange conversation to be having. It was like this person didn't know how surnames worked. Megan looked at the sky; she saw the outline of the moon even though it was still daylight. Her dad used to say that was good luck. Thinking about her dad and family, the cultures she experienced being stationed in other countries made Megan remember that not every culture was the same. She knew she wasn't in the United States, let alone Texas anymore.

"No…my family was the Fitzpatricks. I took the name O'Connor when I joined my husband."

Reijo whipped around and leaned down to look her in the eye. "You have a mate?" He growled at her.

Mate? That's kind of a weird way to put it. "I did have a husband; but I don't anymore…not that it is any of your business."

Megan stalked off towards the door of the palace. She had no idea where she was going, but that man's attitude kind of pissed her off. This whole day had been rough, and all she really wanted was a good book, some chocolate, and bed. Besides, she figured his legs were long enough that he would catch up before she even made it to the door.

And she was right; Mr. Blue eyes was beside her in a moment, though he thankfully remained silent. *Well, at least he isn't an idiot,* she thought.

*****

As they neared the palace doors, Megan noticed that men scrambled to open the doors and bowed as they passed by. The man holding her daughter seemed to take it as his due. Evidently he was fairly high up the food chain in this strange place. She filed away that bit of information for later.

Since she had no idea where they were headed, Megan just followed. After what seemed like a maze of passageways, they arrived at a room that seemed to be some sort of study. Directly opposite of the doors, one wall was taken up with a massive window. There were no curtains, but stained glass designs of what looked to be a giant panther flanked the window on either side. The two remaining walls were covered floor to ceiling with shelves. Many of these shelves contained books and scrolls. Others held displays of different weapons. Here and there a bit of art was placed. There was a daybed near the window with two large chairs in a comfortable seating arrangement. Megan looked at her 'host' and his enormous size. Scratch that, not a daybed…mostly likely just an oversized (from Megan's perspective) loveseat. A table or perhaps a desk was tucked away in one corner.

CHAPTER FOUR

Reijo gently laid the child down on the couch. He wasn't sure why he had brought the pair to his personal quarters. The logical thing would have been to take them to the women's wing where the other earth females were being housed at the moment. He reasoned that Megan's warrior-like personality would stir up the women, making them more difficult to deal with. At least that was the reason he would give Ghaleb if asked. The truth was he didn't want to let them go. This fire maiden...ha, that was a good moniker...had sparked his interest.

A palm placed on a crystal console summoned a servant, quickly emerging to find out what the *Kijani-a* required. Reijo asked that refreshments be delivered and that the royal physician attend him here in his study.

"Royal? What are you, some sort of prince?" Megan had sat down on the couch and placed her daughter's head in her lap. The adrenaline had left her blood stream, and without it bolstering her energy Megan felt very tired; but she had caught the word royal and was curious.

Reijo laughed. It was a rumbling sound, like thunder across the plains back home. Megan liked the way he laughed; it was comforting just like home.

"No, I'm not a prince...it just happens that the closest medical professional is the royal family's."

"Oh." Megan stifled a yawn and was thankful when a servant entered rolling a cart laden with what appeared to be food and drink.

Reijo dismissed the man with a wave and turned to Megan, "Would you like some refreshment while we wait for the medic?"

"What I would like is to go home and take my daughter with me," Megan huffed.

"This is your home now. It would be easier on you if you accept that."

Megan gathered Abby closer and glared at her captor.

Reijo sighed. He knew it was unreasonable to expect her to accept this situation. They had forcibly taken her from her life and home planet. Reijo couldn't do anything about the circumstance that brought her here. The fact remained his people needed her and her daughter. So he pushed the cart so it was within easy reach of the woman. At least he could be kind to her while she was here. To put her at ease, he fixed himself a cup of raija tea. Most of his people didn't like the bitterness of the drink and would sweeten it, but Reijo was a soldier, and camp habits die hard.

He sat back and took a healthy gulp of the bitter tea with a satisfied sigh. When he looked over at Megan, he saw her eyeing the offerings warily. Reijo sighed; he was a poor host. He should have known Megan would be unfamiliar with the food of his world.

"Sweet? Savory?" He pointed to different foods as he asked.

Megan reached for one of the sweeter choices, which looked like a small fruit tart. She bit into it, surprised that it had a flavor similar to peaches and strawberries despite being bright green in color. Satisfied that the food was safe to eat, Megan tried to shake Abby awake; but all Abby did was moan and shift in the seat. Megan laid a hand on her daughter's brow and was alarmed at how hot she had become.

A knock sounded at the door and a servant entered and announced with a bow, "The Royal physician, Hikmat of Clan Tanis, shall attend you with his second, Elod of Clan Tiaret." With his proclamation finished, the servant turned to leave and was almost flattened by a large, rotund, bald man whose wrinkles created great jowls that reminded Megan of a bulldog. He was followed at a more sedate pace by a kind-looking younger gentleman who sported blue eyes like Megan's host.

Megan assumed that the fat man was Hikmat because he seemed to like to declare his importance in the way he dressed and acted. The man practically tripped over himself to ingratiate himself to Mr. Reijo, which just confirmed to Megan that he was some sort of big wig after all. The other gentleman stood quietly off to the side, obviously used to these displays. He looked at Megan and offered her a small smile and slight shrug at his colleague's behavior. Megan smiled back.

It wasn't until the fat man's voice rose in disgust that Megan turned her attention back to him.

"*Kijani-a*, I am the head of the royal family's medical staff. You can't expect me to treat these…. They aren't even Vukasin." The man waved a dismissive hand in Megan and Abby's direction.

"They are here at the request of your *Khalon*. And I would be careful whom you insult, Hikmat, because one of these outsiders may one day end up being your *Khala*."

The bulbous nose on the end of Hikmat's face turned an alarming shade of purple as he spat and sputtered his displeasure, but he moved towards Megan and Abby under the dangerous glare of Reijo.

Hikmat sneered at Megan. She supposed it was meant to be a reassuring smile, but it just made him look like a used car salesman who just smelled that he stepped in dog shit. Megan had dealt with her fair share of half-assed medical professionals going through the base hospitals. And she had already decided to watch Mr. Hikmat like a hawk since she didn't much care for his bedside manner. However, he lost that chance when the man jerked her daughter's arm. Megan didn't know if he was trying to get the child to sit up or take her pulse; but it didn't really matter which it was because she wasn't going to let that man touch her daughter again.

Megan smacked Hikmat's hand away from her daughter. The idiot glared at her and reached for the child again. Again Megan slapped his hand away.

"You will not touch my daughter," Megan said through clenched teeth.

Hikmat sputtered, "I am the personal physician to the royal family...."

"I don't give a rat's ass whose doc you are...because you won't be mine or my daughter's."

Hikmat started to shake in rage. How dare this nobody, this female, speak to him in such a manner? Megan noticed the change in the man's body language and stood, placing herself between him and her daughter.

"You insolent female." Hikmat raised one ham-like hand to strike Megan. She raised her fists and shifted so that if the physician attempted to strike her she was going to lay him flat on his pompous ass.

Unfortunately, Megan didn't get to open her can of whoop ass on the good doctor because Reijo had crossed the room during Megan's exchange with him. As Hikmat swung at Megan, it was Reijo who blocked the blow.

"Hikmat, you were called here to give a medical opinion, not to abuse our guests." Reijo's voice was calm, but held a hint of iron beneath it.

Hikmat visibly paled. He swallowed and

nodded. Once more he approached Abby, but Megan still stood in his way.

Megan crossed her arms. "No."

Reijo turned to Megan confused, "No?"

"No. That man will not be touching my daughter."

"Be reasonable, Megan O'Connor. Your daughter still sleeps after collapsing in the courtyard. A physician needs to examine her."

"Fine. He can do it." Megan pointed at Elod, who had been quietly standing off to one side observing his superior's interaction with the patients.

"But he's just an assistant! My underling," Hikmat practically wailed.

Megan pointedly ignored the man and spoke directly to Elod. "Have you completed your medical training?"

"I have completed the schooling, but I am to remain apprenticed to a master physician for seven years, M'lady." Elod spoke calmly and without pretense. Megan liked him more than Hikmat already.

"How many years remain in your apprenticeship?"

"Two, M'lady."

"So you have the knowledge to treat illness and injury, correct?"

"Yes, M'lady."

Megan smiled, "Perfect.... He can stay." Megan pointed at Elod. "He can go." Megan waved a dismissive hand in Hikmat's general direction.

Hikmat's voice rose in outrage. "You have

no right to dismiss me. I'm the ro—"

Megan rushed the fat man. Despite his girth, Hikmat was still very tall, as it seemed most Vukasin men were. Reijo and Elod found it rather comical to see this tiny woman who was just a little taller than Hikmat's generous waist back the man up against the wall with a finger in his face.

"I don't know how things are run in this place, but where I come from the patient always has the right to dismiss the physician. It is my child that is to be treated and I…let me reiterate that…only I will be the one who decides who her medical professional is. If you try to take that choice from me, I assure you that you will not like the consequences."

Reijo chuckled behind her. "I would listen to her, Hikmat…. She just fought a half dozen of the palace guard and won. In fact they should be heading to the medical wing for treatment as we speak."

Hikmat's eye bulged and he flinched when Megan removed her finger from his line of sight. Megan turned and walked back to the couch where her child lay. Hikmat tried to regain his composure.

"I will be informing his majesty of this incident." Hikmat huffed as he walked towards the door. A servant opened it before he could even reach it.

Megan called after him. "Please, do tell his royal high and mighty of this incident, because if you are an example of his decision-making skills, then he and I need to have a serious talk." Hikmat gasped and scurried out of the room as quickly as his fat legs could carry him.

Elod burst out laughing after his master made his hasty exit. "I pray you are chosen for us, M'lady. I've wanted to deflate that blowhard for years." Elod was much friendlier once Hikmat was no longer in the room. He turned to Reijo and gave the man an affectionate hug. "Hello, Cousin. How fairs it with you?"

"Ghaleb keeps me busy, but it is a good life. But let us focus on the little one first."

"Of course." Elod smiled as he passed by Megan, giving her shoulder a comforting squeeze. "We'll soon get her up and running about." He pulled out a metallic disk with a series of crystals embedded into the face. He held it over Abby and the entire thing began to glow.

"What is that? What are you doing to Abby?" Megan's normally strong voice cracked slightly on her daughter's name. It was the only outward sign of her strain and the worry she had about these strange men treating her daughter medically.

Elod showed Megan the device in his hand, "This is simply a medical scanner, and it will allow me to understand her symptoms fairly quickly."

"Wow! That is kind of like *Star Trek*. You know you could make a fortune exporting this technology."

"What is this *Star Trek* you speak of? And we don't export off world," Elod stated quietly as he examined Abby.

"Off world?"

Elod looked over to Reijo. Reijo simply

shrugged. With the drama in the courtyard, he hadn't had an opportunity to explain the situation to Megan yet.

"Has no one told you, M'lady?"

"Told me what?" Megan's alarm was rising. She was fairly certain what she was about to be told, and honestly it would explain the strange creatures she had fought earlier, but her mind just couldn't process it.

"You are on a planet called Vukas."

Oh god. They never would have gotten away even if she hadn't been defeated in the courtyard. No matter where they had run, they would never have been able to go home. Megan sank into the cushions of the couch, her mouth gaping open. So many questions were swirling around in her head. Why had they brought her here? What was going to happen to her now? What would happen to her daughter?

"All done…."

Elod's pronouncement cleared some of the haze of Megan's mind.

"I see no permanent damage; I believe the fever was stress induced. There are no viruses or bacteria present that would cause illness."

Reijo walked up behind Megan, putting a hand on her shoulder to offer comfort. He wasn't sure why he did it, other than she looked like she needed reassurance and he felt a compulsion to give it to her.

"But why hasn't she woken up?" Reijo asked quietly.

Elod sighed. "I'm not going to lie to you…. I

am not sure. If she was Vukasin, I would say that her brain scans show that certain areas of her psyche have been over stimulated and the sleep is a coping mechanism while the mind processes everything that has happened. But I would just be guessing here. I don't have enough baseline data on the off-world females to be certain."

Megan picked up her daughter's hand and caressed the palm with her thumb. "So what should we do?"

"I've given her something to reduce the fever. Other than that, my advice is to just watch her. I will come again in the morning. Hopefully by then she will have awakened." Elod packed up his supplies and stood to leave. "If she is still not awake by tomorrow then we will discuss what to try next."

Reijo brought up something that he had wondered about since learning that a child had been brought back. "Is the translation device safe for one so young?"

Megan's eyes widened as she rubbed the back of her neck, "Are you talking about that thing you stuck in my neck that hurt like hell?"

Elod answered for Reijo. "Yes, I'm sorry it caused you pain." Elod gave Reijo a bit of an evil eye as he continued. "Normally it would have been implanted while you were still unconscious; that way the fusing to your neurological system wouldn't have been painful. As far as it being safe for the child, I would assume so. Its systems would grow and change just as hers would. Even adults create new neural pathways. No mind ever stays the same permanently. But I would recommend implanting it before she regains consciousness."

Reijo spoke to Megan. "The choice is yours since she is your child. But I do think that perhaps she wouldn't be as frightened when she wakes up if she can understand what the people around her are saying."

Megan took a moment to think about it. She honestly didn't like the idea of some alien implanting something into her child. Yet, to be fair, Megan and Abby were actually the aliens in this place. In the end she had to make the best decision for Abby. Abby needed to know if someone was going to harm her, especially if Megan wasn't with her. Megan nodded.

"Alright...but do it now."

Elod took the gun-like device while Megan turned Abby over so he could reach the base of her skull. A few seconds after the translator was implanted, Abby's tiny body seized and then was quiet again. Still she hadn't woken up.

Elod scanned Abby one last time after they implanted the translation device; as far as he could tell everything was fine. He stood and gathered his supplies. He said his farewells to Megan with the promise of visiting in the morning. Reijo walked Elod to the door.

"Reijo, I was honest with the woman, but I would keep them isolated from the other off-world females just in case. And be careful, cousin; that woman may have made a powerful enemy in Hikmat. You know that his clan has been pushing for these women to be used in a breeding facility and the council is still considering that option."

Reijo considered Elod's words. He knew of Clan Tanis's proposition. At one time he had even considered supporting it as it seemed an efficient way to preserve a semblance of their race. Yet, after meeting these females…especially the two now curled up in his study… Reijo just couldn't bring himself to simply think of them as experimental subjects.

"I know, Elod. I will keep a watch out. If you hear any rumblings in the medical sector, let me know." With a final hug farewell, Elod left Reijo's study.

Reijo ran a hand through his dark hair. He needed to speak with Ghaleb. This whole operation was turning into an unnatural mess. Reijo wanted to believe that his own sense of right and wrong brought him to that conclusion, but he knew it had everything to do with the spit fire of a woman now in his study.

He turned back to speak with Megan; maybe she could provide an insight he hadn't thought of yet. It was funny how after such a short acquaintance he respected her opinion as a fellow warrior, and being female she would offer a unique perspective on things. Reijo wondered if she would ever bore him, but doubted that would be possible.

"Megan…." In the short time Elod and he had spoken, Megan had fallen asleep on the couch, her arms protectively wrapped around her child. The quiet scene made Reijo's heart stutter and constrict in an unfamiliar way. He knew that Megan was capable of protecting herself and her daughter, but a voice in the back of Reijo's mind told him that he should be the one to keep her from harm.

He called the servants to fetch a couple of blankets. He didn't want to wake the pair. While he waited, he openly studied the woman. Her coloring was striking compared to what he was used to. Vukasins tended to be a dark people. In fact the blue eyes of the Tiaret Clan were considered unusual. But both the woman and the little girl had blue eyes. Maybe they were meant for the Tiaret Clan; Reijo smiled at the thought.

Megan was so fair. Her skin was practically white and her every thought flashed across it in various blushes. It wouldn't be difficult to learn to read her thoughts just from that alone. She was so tiny. Reijo could have easily tucked her under his arm when they were walking. She brought out a protective instinct he didn't know he had. Despite her childlike size, Reijo marveled at the wealth of womanly curves she carried. She should have been soft and fragile, but her strength and courage had blown him away. She was a woman that any man would be proud to call mate. But being a mate wasn't possible for these women. They were here as tools to be used by Reijo's society.

A servant entered bearing the requested blankets. Reijo took them and dismissed the man. When he left, Reijo locked the door to the study. He walked over and gently placed a blanket over the sleeping pair. Megan stirred briefly before snuggling deeper into the covers, a satisfied smile on her face. Reijo hoped she was dreaming about him.

By the two moons, he had to stop this attachment to this woman and her child. Otherwise, when she was handed over to the clans for breeding, knowing that other men would have her would kill him.

Reijo situated himself in one of the arm chairs, draping a blanket of his own across himself to spend an uncomfortable night. He tried to convince himself that he was just doing his duty, making sure the woman didn't escape, but it sounded like the lie that it was even in his own mind. With one last longing look, Reijo closed his eyes and drifted off into a troubled sleep. His last conscious thought was disgust at what his people were about to do.

CHAPTER FIVE

Megan was woken up by tiny hands shaking her shoulder.

"Mommy, I'm thirsty...and I don't feel good." It took a moment for it to register that Abby was awake. When Megan finally emerged from her half-asleep state, she grabbed her little girl and hugged her tight.

"Oh baby girl, I was so worried about you."

"Mommy! Too tight!" Megan chuckled but eased her grip. She kissed her daughter's forehead, noting that her fever seemed to be down, even if it wasn't completely gone.

Megan looked around and couldn't find Mr. Blue eyes; the cart containing the food and drink from last night had disappeared as well. The thought of food made Megan's stomach rumble loudly, causing Abby to giggle. If Megan was hungry, even after last night's snack she knew that Abby needed food since she hadn't had anything since breakfast the day before.

Taking her daughter's hand, Megan walked to the study door. It was locked, but she quickly found the latch to unlock it. She opened the door a crack and peered out. She stopped short when she saw one of those fanged creatures standing guard just outside of the door. The creature looked over when the door opened. His lips curled up in a way that seemed to be kind of a smile. In that moment this creature kind of reminded her of the goofy mutt that had become a neighborhood dog at their last duty station.

"Do you need anything, M'lady?" Megan blinked. The words sounded unnatural, as if it was difficult to speak when the mouth and vocal cords are shaped differently, but she very clearly heard him, at least she assumed it was a him, ask her a question.

"Um…I'm looking for either food or that Kijani fellow."

The creature laughed, though it sounded more like a breathy pant, "*Kijani-a* is his title…. His name is Reijo. As for food, the kitchens are on the lower level." He pointed down a staircase to the right.

Megan smiled and gave a little wave before tugging her daughter along down the stairs. As they descended, Abby gave a little tug on her mother's shirt. Megan leaned down so Abby could whisper in her ear.

"Mommy, the big doggy man is following

us." Megan looked over their shoulder and, sure enough, the guard that had stood outside of the study's doors had followed them down the stair. Megan slowed down their walk and their guard slowed down as well, keeping the same respectful distance. Abby pulled on her mother's arm and they sped up; so did the guard.

Abby and Megan suddenly stopped at the foot of the stairs, which opened into an enormous room, and the guard almost fell trying to stop at his respectful distance. By this time Megan was fairly certain that the guard had been given orders to follow them. She looked down at her daughter and saw the same mischievous grin that was mirrored in her own face. Without a word Megan let go of her daughter's hand and they took off in opposite directions in the great hall they found themselves in. Megan trusted that her daughter wouldn't leave the room in this impromptu game of tag.

Megan was half way around her side of the room when she chanced a look at the poor guard. The poor creature was dithering back and forth still, not sure which of his charges to pursue. Megan was laughing and smiling brightly but not paying attention to where she was going when she ran into someone. They tangled together and fell into a heap on the floor, with Megan still laughing hysterically.

She sat up to apologize between bouts of giggles when her daughter's squeal caught her attention. She unceremoniously shoved herself up to find Abby, shoving her poor collision victim back into the floor.

Megan relaxed noticeably when she spotted that it was Reijo who had caught her daughter and was in the process of tickling her as he walked toward Megan. Megan's heart stuttered a little because his hold on Abby seemed so natural, like the child belonged there. She couldn't help but notice that Reijo seemed to be having as much fun as the child was.

"When I saw them bring you in, I figured you would be stirring up trouble in my household."

Megan's attention was snapped back to the poor man she had knocked down. While his tone of voice could pass as harsh, the twinkle in his eye and the smile on his face belied any upset over being bowled over.

Megan reached out a hand to help the man off the floor. "I'm so sorry…. Abby and I were playing a game of tag."

"Am I to assume that your poor guard had been elected as 'it' without his knowledge?"

As Megan helped the man off of the floor, Reijo came up to them. He suddenly put Abby down, snapped his heels together and gave a slight bow. "*Khalon*, I am humbled that you would choose to visit the Tiaret wing."

Megan gathered Abby to her and looked the new man over again. He was as tall as Reijo, which from what she could tell was tall even for the people here. But where Reijo's body was broadly muscular, the new man seemed to have more of a swimmers build. He was still very fit, but came off more the pretty fit than battle-ready fit. It was like the

51

difference between a movie star and a navy seal.

"*Khalon*? Is that your name or your title?" Abby blurted out her question, remembering what the furry man had said when her mom asked about someone.

Megan tried to shush her daughter. She knew enough from Reijo's reaction to know that he was a man of some import on this planet.

"It's quite alright," the man assured Megan. He then did something unexpected; he kneeled down to the child's level to answer her question. "It is my title…I think in your home you would call me a king." He looked to Megan to confirm he had the word right. "My name is Ghaleb."

Abby held out her tiny hand, so different from the shy, scared girl she was yesterday. Reijo was surprised at the change, but Megan was just glad to have her normally gregarious daughter back.

"I'm Abigail Lindsay O'Connor…but my friends call me Abby. Are you my friend? This is my mommy. Her name is Megan…. My daddy's not here anymore; mommy said that the angels needed him to help guard heaven."

"That's enough, Abby." Megan's sharp reprimand was spoken quietly, but Abby immediately stopped and looked down at her shoes. Megan hadn't meant to hurt her daughter's feelings, but she didn't feel comfortable with all of the strangers learning their life story, which Abby would tell them the entirety of from her child perspective.

*****

Ghaleb smiled at the tiny child; both mother

and daughter were as bright as their coloring. It had been a long time since anyone had heard laughter ring through these halls, and Ghaleb found he rather enjoyed it. He could see why Reijo had come to him early this morning with concerns about the breeding program plans.

Ghaleb had made a point of not meeting any of the off-world women simply because he didn't want to view them as people. The council of clan elders had made the decisions on how to organize the distribution of females. Ghaleb had never really liked their plans because they were cold and calculating and would only work as long as females were considered property without freewill.

Ghaleb was in a moral quandary. He knew that there were times that leaders of a society had to make decisions that were morally repugnant for the good of the society as a whole. However, Ghaleb seriously doubted that the current choices the council was making would save their society. In fact, Ghaleb worried if it might not be the final death knoll should they go through with it.

The problem lay in his position. While he had vast powers at the ruler of this world, his will wasn't absolute. There were certain laws and traditions no one was allowed to circumvent. But his more immediate problem was the checks and balances that allowed the council to overrule him as they had done with the breeding program. He could stall the distribution of the women for a little while, but not indefinitely. Yet, any opposition couldn't appear to come from the royal house since the council had made its position crystal clear.

Perhaps the solution lay in this very unconventional female before him.

Megan shifted under Ghaleb's uncomfortable gaze. She felt almost as if the man were trying to peer into her soul with the intensity of his stare. So she decided to break his scrutiny.

"I have a bone to pick with you, Ghaleb," Megan announced, frowning.

Ghaleb raised one elegant brow and directed the fiery woman towards a solar that offered more privacy than the great hall of the Tiaret wing. Yes, this woman would do nicely. Now, how to maneuver her into position?

CHAPTER SIX

Ghaleb and Reijo remained in the solar after Megan and Abby headed off to the kitchens for some food. Megan's discussion of Hikmat proved that she was both passionate and compassionate when it came to how others should be treated. If she proved to have the strength of perseverance that Ghaleb thought she had, this plan might actually work.

"I know that look, *Khalon*. What are you planning?" Reijo leaned back in his chair to eye his cousin thoughtfully.

The wiry king pushed himself up from his seat and began pacing. Reijo had never seen him this agitated before.

"Cousin, I can't talk openly here because I never know where the various factions have their eyes." Ghaleb turned and met Reijo's eyes. There were shadows under Ghaleb's eyes that Reijo hadn't seen before; things must not being going well with the council.

"I want to check on Megan and Abby. Why

don't you walk with me; then we can go to my study. I can assure you in short order that we will not be overheard there."

Ghaleb nodded absently. He was lost in thought trying to figure out just what he was going to tell Reijo. It wasn't that he didn't trust the man. In fact, Reijo was just about the only person Ghaleb did fully trust. But things needed to appear to have come about outside of the royal house. It could cause a civil war if the council knew that the *Khalon* was moving against them.

*****

Reijo and Ghaleb first went to the kitchens in search of the mother and her child. They soon discovered that the pair had finished eating and had decided to explore. They had heard that other women from their home world had been brought here and they wanted to see them.

At the doors to the women's wing, the two men heard raised voices. It sounded as if an argument was occurring on the other side of the door. Reijo sighed. This must be Megan's doing because the other women had been rather docile after their arrival.

"Shall we go see what is going on?" Reijo shook his head at Ghaleb. The man seemed to be enjoying this. Of course other than briefly watching her fight in the courtyard, Ghaleb hadn't witnessed the true force of Megan's personality. Reijo chuckled as he remembered the look on Hikmat's face as that tiny little woman had backed him up against the wall.

Upon opening the door, the yelling became more distinct. Evidently word of the council's plans for the women had somehow made it back to them. Someone had passed this information along to Megan. What surprised Reijo was Megan's raised voice. She was defending him.

"I can see some of the pompous asses around here trying to pull something like that, but I just don't see people like Reijo allowing it." Reijo could see Megan pacing in front of another woman; this one was tall and willowy, her height more reminiscent of the Vukasin people. Her hair was short and tightly curled. Her skin was a rich dark brown, as were her eyes. Her arms were crossed across her chest and she had an angry glare. She didn't seem intimidated by Megan's bluster, and the way the other women had crowded behind her it was fairly clear that she had assumed the position of de facto leader.

"You can believe what you like, but you and one day your little girl are going to be handed over to numerous men as breeding stock. Frankly, it doesn't surprise me this place hardly has any women when we are treated like nothing more than cattle."

Reijo cleared his throat to bring attention to the fact that he and Ghaleb had entered the room. Most of the women shrank away, but Megan and the tall woman did not. There was also a third who stepped forward, placing herself defensively in front of the others. This one was taller than Megan but didn't have the height of the dark woman. Her hair was silky and black with blue highlights, contrasting sharply to the paleness of her skin. She somehow seemed both delicate and strong at the same time.

Reijo hadn't been to the women's wing because honestly he didn't want to think of the females brought here as people. They were supposed to just be a means to an end. But Megan changed that. He took the time to look each woman over. They were all so very different: different heights, different coloring, different demeanor. He was amazed at how unique each woman was. There was some variation among his own people, but there tended to be a general norm that could identify most as Vukasin. If he had been presented with these women without knowing they all came from the same planet, he would have sworn they were found in different places.

"Is this true?" Reijo was knocked out of his thoughts by Megan's irate voice.

"Is what true?" Ghaleb answered calmly.

"Are we to be handed over to various men to 'breed' with no choice in the matter?"

"Well…um…it's a rather complicated question," Ghaleb tried to hedge. Reijo watched as every woman, even little Abby, mirrored the same cut the bullshit stance that Megan went into. Ghaleb may not realize it, then again he might, but he was about to become the enemy.

"It is a yes or no question," Megan said through clenched teeth.

"You have to understand, we are trying to save an entire species here."

Reijo had trained many fighting teams; there

is always a moment when individuals coalesce into a single unit. He watched as the group of women stepped forward. No longer were there those who held back.

"Yes or no?" Each woman echoed the question after Megan. The women came together into a solid wall of femininity. Despite their fragile appearance individually, as a group they had quite an intimidating aura.

"Well technically, those are the bare bones of the council's plans to save our ra—" Ghaleb didn't even get a chance to finish the sentence before Megan's hand made contact across his face, silencing him.

If it wasn't for the fact that an assault on the royal person was a serious offense, Reijo would have been hard pressed not to laugh at Ghaleb's shocked expression.

"How dare you!" Megan's blue eyes flashed and anger practically vibrated her short little body. Reijo was almost surprised when her fiery hair didn't actually burst into flames because her emotion was that palpable.

"We are not possessions; we are not tools….we are human beings with our own minds and free will. How dare you try to take that choice from us?!" Megan poked Ghaleb in the chest, backing him up against the wall just as she had done to Hikmat. "You better find a way to fix this, you royal ass! Because I am telling you here and now that I would rather die than allow you to take my choice from me or my daughter." The rest of the women muttered their assent.

"Know this," Megan continued and nailed Reijo with a hard glare, "I would rather die, but I will inflict as much damage as I possibly can before I go. And you haven't seen half of what I am capable of."

With that all of the women turned their backs on the two men and walked away. Reijo watched them, hoping that Megan would turn around to see him one last time. He almost wished that he hadn't because when she did turn, all he saw in her eyes was disappointment, and that hurt worse than any wound he had ever received in battle. In light of this new development, he forgot the conversation he and Ghaleb were supposed to have in his study.

*****

"What do you mean they are refusing food?" Reijo roared at the cowering servant.

"They said it was a hunger strike. They said they won't eat until they are either sent home or at the very least allowed to decide their own life choices." The servant cringed. This was the third day, and after each report, the *Kijani-a* had become more enraged. When the servant was dismissed, he swore that someone else could come with the dinner report.

Reijo stormed his way into Ghaleb's private quarters. He was the only man allowed such a privilege in the entire palace, a fact that had earned him more than one enemy. As such, he rarely utilized it, but today he didn't give a damn about the political machinations of the palace. His focus was solely on the human women, two in particular.

He didn't know why he had grown so attached to Megan and her daughter, but he had. Since their confrontation a few days ago, Reijo had wondered what his feelings would be if his own daughter was expected to do what they wanted these women to do. That had Reijo wondering what a daughter of his would be like; his agitation only grew when each time they looked like Abby in his mind.

Reijo finally came to the conclusion that for better or worse his heart was claiming Megan and Abby as his own. He only had his own species to go by but he knew that the women had only a limited amount of time before lack of food could become deadly, which was why he was here; Reijo would make Ghaleb take some sort of action even if he had to take on the council himself.

Ghaleb looked up from his book as his cousin barreled through his door. He had already heard of the women's hunger strike and had been expecting Reijo to come to him for a few days now. Laying his book aside, Ghaleb smiled.

"It took you long enough."

Ghaleb had already confided in Reijo that he felt that what the council was trying to do was morally wrong. Yet, as per their governing documents, he was tied to the will of the council as long as they choose to override his decision, which they already had.

"*Khalon*, I know you and I have discussed certain matters, but I need to know when we are going to move forward." Reijo went to Ghaleb's side board and poured himself a stiff drink.

Unbeknownst to Reijo, the reaction of the human women was exactly what Ghaleb had been looking for. He, even as *Khalon,* couldn't stop the council, but after some intensive study into their laws and histories, Ghaleb had discovered that the women themselves might be able to. Or he should say, more specifically, Megan might be able to. However, she had to come to this conclusion herself, but that didn't mean that Ghaleb couldn't nudge her in the right direction.

"Reijo, I have already been informed of your concerns and I think I may have a solution." Ghaleb considered his next words carefully. If all went according to plan, Megan would be in great danger. This had to be Megan's choice and she would need some strong allies. Thankfully she already had one in Reijo. Ghaleb smiled. He found it amusing that his greatest warrior was felled by a tiny slip of a woman.

Reijo crossed his arms and eyed his cousin. They had been raised together and he knew the man well enough to know when he was plotting something, like he was now. "Go on, I'm listening."

"I think it would be in the best interest to break up the women. Perhaps if they were on their own we would better be able to persuade them to take care of themselves."

"An interesting idea and it would possibly help to win a few more over to their point of view," Reijo conceded. "But you would have to be very particular which households you placed them in;

many within the Tanis Clan want them viewed as no more than property. That clan has many powerful friends. It would be political suicide to exclude them."

"You are correct, but I already have the households I think would be best…including one within the Tanis Clan." Ghaleb tapped his book thoughtfully on his knee. "My contacts have found that not everyone within the Tanis Clan is as enthusiastic of the clan head's choices."

Reijo set his glass down. "Megan and Abby are coming with me."

Ghaleb schooled his features to keep Reijo from noticing that this was exactly what he wanted. "That is not your decision to make, cousin."

"I don't care. Make it happen, *Khalon* Ghaleb." Reijo emphasized Ghaleb's title, effectively telling him he better throw some royal weight around to get it done.

"Fine, take those two; but I ask a favor in return."

"What?"

"Remember Kavi?"

"Is that old buzzard raptor still alive?" Reijo wrinkled his nose. Kavi had never been one of his favorite people. The problem stemmed from the fact that the old man had been one of their teachers, and while Ghaleb had excelled at law and history, Reijo was more warrior than scholar.

Ghaleb laughed, "You know very well that he is one of our greatest law keepers. But the summer heat is getting to him. I thought you might take him with you to your stronghold. The cool forests would do him some good. Plus he might be useful as a teacher for young Abigail."

Reijo didn't relish the idea of old Kavi tagging along, but if that is what it took to make sure he was the one caring for Abby and Megan then so be it.

"Fine. Make your arrangements. I want to head out as soon as possible." With that statement Reijo marched out of Ghaleb's room to make preparations for the trip.

Ghaleb smiled. Now to talk to Kavi about what he needed him to do.

CHAPTER SEVEN

The door of the women's wing crashed against the far wall, leaving a dent in the plaster. Reijo had snagged Akia on his way. The *Kijani-a* stalked into the area like the commanding general he was, Akia followed silently behind. After searching numerous rooms, the two men found the women all gathered in this wing's solar.

Reijo's crashing appearance startled the women, but once their initial shock passed, each turned to glare at the men. The hostility that faced them actually made Akia back up a little. But when he saw Reijo standing his ground and glaring right back at them, Akia straightened his shoulders and tried to hide the fact that he was intimidated by these females.

"Megan, Abby, pack your things. We are leaving!" Reijo barked at the group of women. "The rest of you prepare for your own journeys. Your escorts will come for you later."

Megan stood, calmly laced her fingers

together in front of her and raised a single brow in challenge as she looked Reijo in the eyes from across the room.

"For one, as you can see, we have nothing but the clothes on our backs."

Reijo looked around at all of the women who had been here for nearly a week and was horrified to realize that Megan was correct; every woman was wearing the same set of clothes they had been brought to the palace in. By the moons! His people really were asses.

Megan continued, "However, it wouldn't matter if we had trunks of items to pack because we are not going anywhere with you."

"Akia, get Abby. I will handle Megan."

Before Megan could react, Reijo dashed across the room and slung her over his shoulder. Remembering her display in the courtyard, Reijo locked one strong arm around her knees, preventing her from gaining any sort of leverage, which left her blows across his back ineffectual.

Reijo loved the feel of Megan's soft curves in his arms. If they hadn't had an audience, he would have demonstrated just how much he enjoyed them. As it was he had to subtly arrange himself to be able to walk comfortably out of the room.

He was distracted with thoughts of what he would like to do to Megan's luscious body, so he was slow to react to Akia's warning, allowing Megan to land a solid blow with her elbow right into his neck. It hurt like hell and staggered Reijo a bit, but like a true warrior he remained upright.

But as payback, he spanked Megan's backside hard, causing her to cry out a bit.

"Behave, or I will have to punish you." Reijo meant to say it as a threat, but his voice lowered and it came out sounding more like a promise for later.

Megan snorted. "That'll be the day."

She wouldn't admit how turned on she was by this display of alpha male. But she didn't have to admit anything. Vukasins have a heightened sense of smell, and Reijo had his nose practically buried in her sex with him carrying her over his shoulder. He could scent her arousal and it was playing havoc on his composure.

Reijo could have sworn he heard female laughter as they left.

*****

Megan was thoroughly embarrassed as Reijo made arrangements for their departure. He still hadn't put her down. She tried to comfort herself with the fact that Abby seemed to view this as an adventure. Megan recognized the man who was carrying her as one of the two that brought them here. If she recalled correctly, Reijo had called him Akia.

Akia had placed Abby on his shoulders and was hopping around like a bunny, bouncing the little girl until she was giggling. If Megan wasn't so cross with Reijo at the moment she might have even found the sight of such a large muscular man playing with a little girl amusing.

So far they had informed other military officers of their new job assignments in Reijo's absence. They had stopped servants to pack his things and arrange for transport. He even stopped in the kitchen to ask the cooks to prepare food for the journey. From Reijo's instructions, Megan had been able to glean that he was taking them to his personal stronghold up in the mountains.

Megan knew that they hoped that splitting up the women would break their rebelliousness. But each woman had pledged that they would continue fighting until they could go home—or at the very least had the right to decide their own fate.

One of the women, Himeko, was a lawyer from Japan. She was the one who suggested that if they could find a way to study the law and history of this place that they may be able to use it to their advantage. So this separation may actually be a blessing in disguise because it would allow them to eventually get access to the information they needed. Megan was fairly certain that alone and away from that retched council that she could convince Reijo to help them. Her gut was telling her that he was a good man, and her gut was rarely wrong.

*****

Megan bounced on Reijo's shoulder as he descended a set of stairs. She wasn't familiar with this part of the palace, though that wasn't saying much since she never had the chance to really explore. This area seemed to predominately be decorated in a double moon and single sun theme. She had figured out that Vukas had two moons, one of which was in such close orbit that it could be made out even during daylight.

Reijo's wing had a large cat-like creature as its motif. He had said it was the Tanis Clan wing. Maybe each clan's wing was decorated with a particular symbol. Megan wondered which clan they were visiting.

It didn't take long for Megan to find out. Reijo entered a room and Megan heard its occupant respond. She knew that voice…. That arrogant ass, Reijo, he brought her in front of their ruler thrown over his shoulder like a bag of potatoes. Megan's face colored in both anger and embarrassment.

"I see you wasted no time, Cousin," Ghaleb chuckled at Reijo as he entered with Megan thrown over his shoulder.

"*Khalon* I have a serious matter to bring to your attention." Ghaleb could see a muscle twitching in Reijo's temple. Most people would miss that subtle tell, but they had known each other far too long for Ghaleb to miss it. Ghaleb nodded for Reijo to go on.

Reijo finally set Megan down on her feet in front of him, but he did not relinquish his hold.

"Ghaleb, what do you see?"

The king's eyes widened at Reijo's question, not quite sure how he should respond to such a query.

Ghaleb cleared his throat, "Um, well I see a lovely female with an enticing figure despite being so short. Her fairness is quite unique on our planet…."

Reijo rolled his eyes at his cousin. "By the moons, man! Look at her clothes!"

"Well, they aren't to my taste, but—" Ghaleb replied.

"You know, Ghaleb, there are times you are an idiot." Reijo sighed exasperated.

"He's a politician. It comes with the territory," Megan muttered under her breath. Both Reijo and Ghaleb stared at her a moment before bursting out laughing.

"M'lady," Ghaleb motioned for her to take a seat near him, "have I told you how positively refreshing you are?"

"Refreshing enough that you would send us back home?" Megan batted her eyelashes at Ghaleb, starting another round of laughter.

"Alas I cannot. But even if I could I would still endeavor to keep you here to entertain me." Ghaleb opened the full force of his charming smile on Megan.

A possessive hand came to rest on Megan's shoulder, and she looked up to see Reijo staring down at her before he turned his attention back to Ghaleb.

"If you are quite finished flirting, Ghaleb…I didn't come here to ask your fashion advice, but to point out that Megan is still wearing the clothes that she was brought to Vukas in. In fact, all of the women are." Reijo gave his cousin a pointed stare with that last statement.

Ghaleb looked genuinely confused when he turned to Megan. "Why are you wearing the same thing?"

Megan looked up at Reijo as if to ask if

Ghaleb was normally this dense. Reijo gave a small nod and an eye roll that conveyed that yes, often Ghaleb was. Megan would examine the fact that she and Reijo were in tune enough to understand the exchange without saying a word.

Megan faced Ghaleb and in her typical sarcastic voice said, "Well it is rather difficult to change when you have nothing to change into."

Finally the light dawned on Ghaleb's face. "Damn it! We did haul them here with just the clothes on their backs. Why has no one brought this to my attention before?" Ghaleb demanded.

Megan stopped Reijo before he could answer. "Your Majesty, no one is going to concern themselves about the welfare of chattel." Contempt dripped from Megan's lips. "We are property according to what you have told me, so why would anyone else here view us differently. Furthermore, until were are handed over to whatever owner is decided upon for us, they assume you own us, so logically you would provide for us how you deem fit. Whose place is it to question that?"

Ghaleb groaned. The woman had a point. If there was to be any hope for his race, this game he is playing had better pan out.

"I will provide for Megan and Abigail," Reijo announced. "You need to make sure the other women are provided for as well, Ghaleb."

"Of course. The houses I have chosen will be more than happy to acquire anything that they may need." Ghaleb raised a hand when both Megan and Reijo would interject, "but I will make sure that they do."

Reijo took Megan's hand and pulled her to her feet, "We need to get going. There is still much to arrange. I'm afraid that new clothes will have to wait until we reach my home, since female fashion is rarely needed these days."

"When do you plan to leave, Reijo?" Ghaleb inquired.

"We leave with this evening's slip stream. We will stay at an inn in the main village for the night and travel the rest of the way on the morrow."

"Safe journey, Cousin."

CHAPTER EIGHT

"Horses! Sort of..." Megan gasped.

Megan was shocked when Reijo led her and Abby to what appeared to be carriages pulled by creatures that resembled the horses she loved back home, the difference here being that the colors leaned more towards earth tones and there was a spiny ridge that covered much of the neck. Reijo place Megan and her daughter into a carriage hitched to a matched team of green and black mottled beasts.

"Your technology seems so advanced; I kind of figured your transport would be more advanced as well," Megan said to Reijo as he situated himself next to her in the carriage.

"These are just to get us to the slip stream depot. We use advanced technologies to travel great distances, but our society finds that pack animals are the most ecological solution for short distances. In fact, the journey from the main Tiaret village to the stronghold is probably one of the furthest non slip steam journeys most would take. And that is mostly due to the terrain," Reijo explained as the carriage lurched into movement.

"Momma, are we going swimming?"

"No, sweetheart, we are just traveling."

"Then why are we going to the streams?" Megan laughed and hugged her daughter. This was the first time they had left the palace grounds since arriving, and even then the majority of their time they had been confined to a single wing. Megan had never enjoyed being cooped up for too long. She laid a hand on Reijo's knee and smiled up at him. Even though she knew she should be angry, she was too excited to have a bit of an adventure.

She let her eyes wander across the sites of the village as they made their way through the streets. It was bustling with activity, but she did notice a decided lack of women and children. When they rounded a corner, Megan saw that they were in what people on earth would have described as a red light district. Here there were women, but of obviously different species, there were also men and boys dressed as women.

Reijo saw Megan staring at the neighborhood they were passing through.

"This is where the comfort women live," he explained.

Megan's eyes snapped to his and narrowed; Reijo was sure that he had somehow upset her with what he said.

"Tell me one thing, Reijo.... This thing," Megan tapped the back of her neck, "it tries to translate not only the words but the concepts as well, correct?"

Reijo looked and confused and answered warily, "Yes…."

"So you are telling me that the brothels are government sanctioned?"

"Yes."

"Did the women choose to be there?"

Reijo shifted in his seat uncomfortably. He knew Megan wasn't going to like the answer he gave her. To be honest he couldn't blame her. Everyone, including himself, had turned a blind eye to the morality of the choices they were making.

"Some did."

"Just some…where did the other women come from then?" Megan leaned back in her seat and crossed her arms, symbolically separating herself from the closeness she had offered Reijo earlier. Her eyes held a glare that could make the most seasoned warrior think twice about crossing her.

"We tried to find genetically compatible females from many of the nearby solar systems. Unfortunately, we were unsuccessful until we stumbled upon a human woman. Many of these are the women from those experiments."

"So let me get this straight," Megan ground out through clenched teeth, "You kidnapped, raped, and then forced these women into sexual slavery? What the hell do you do to your own women?"

Reijo coughed, stalling for time. "Um…Vukasin women are allowed to choose what man they will be with; however…." Reijo stopped not sure how to continue. By the moons, he was a battled-seasoned warrior who had faced speaking before his entire government. Why was explaining this one aspect of their reality to one tiny woman so difficult?

"However?" Megan prompted.

He knew that what he was about to say would hurt Megan. That was the crux of his difficulty, because somewhere along the line she got to him. He didn't want to hurt her. He wanted to make her laugh and smile so he could see that radiant sparkle that only she seemed to have.

"Once a child is born and weaned, she would leave them behind and move on to another house and clan to start the process over." Reijo rushed though the explanation in a single breath, refusing to look Megan in the eyes.

Megan was silent. Reijo ventured a brief glance at her and saw that she was open mouthed with shock. He watched as she shook the shock off and allowed it to be replaced by righteous anger.

*****

"Your own women?" Megan was shaking. She wanted to reach over and slap some sense into Reijo and then proceed through the rest of Vukas's male population. Megan tried to calm herself by rationalizing their actions through the film of desperation of a dying race; but even then she couldn't fathom how a society could give up something as fundamental as a happy family. These people had chosen (at least the males did) to give up any hope of that any longer. They were fighting to save their race by giving up the very thing that would have made it worth fighting for. Megan just shook her head in disbelief and sulked in her little corner of the carriage. Well, she was going to show at least one of these stupid males the errors of their ways.

Megan muttered, "It is no wonder your gods took away your women, considering the fucking way you treat them."

"Mommy, you're not supposed to use the 'f' word."

*****

The carriages pulled up in front of enormous building that looked more like a temple complex than a transport station to Megan. It was stately and built of the same gleaming white stone as the palace had been. Statues depicting a half dozen various animals, most of which looked like predators, flanked the entrance.

Reijo helped Abby and Megan down from the carriage. His heart seized a little when Megan withdrew her hand at the first opportunity. Considering her reaction in the carriage to the Vukasin treatment of women, he really shouldn't have been surprised. He even tried to rationalize to himself that it would be for the best to not get too close to her because even if she had the rights of a native woman he wouldn't get to keep her for long.

But Reijo couldn't lie to himself no matter how much he wanted to. He wanted Megan in a way he never thought possible. The Vukasins had a rich society before they started dying out. Ancient poets and philosophers spent much time talking about the bonding of body and soul and love that could transcend time and space. Reijo had always believed that such things were merely fanciful tales, but now he wondered as he watched Megan and her daughter walk into the slip stream depot.

"Mommy…." Abby's voice quivered with uncertainty as she clung to Megan's leg. Everyone was staring at them as if they were some sort of exhibit in a zoo.

Megan decided to pick her daughter up both to comfort her and to keep her safely nearby.

"Women are a rare sight, and you and your daughter are doubly unique given your petite stature and striking coloring," Reijo whispered in her ear.

The sudden voice so close to her ear startled Megan, and without thinking she tucked Abby protectively against her body and dropped into a leg sweep, knocking Reijo on his butt. The crowd of gawkers started giggling at the sight of such a famous warrior being knocked down by a tiny woman. Reijo glared them into silence before turning his glare towards Megan.

"You shouldn't sneak up on me," Megan sniffed disdainfully and turned to walk away, not even knowing which queue she needed to head to.

She was a beautiful sight. She gave off the aura of regal nobility packed in her tiny frame. Reijo picked himself up off the floor and allowed his longer stride to quickly catch up with her without seeming to chase after her. He grabbed her elbow and gently turned her towards a line of travelers to their left.

"We need to go here. The luggage should have already left and will be waiting for us on the other side," Reijo explained.

Reijo looked to make sure their entire party was ready to depart. While it would be a few hours until sunset here in the capital, the sun would already be starting to set near the stronghold. He wanted to get them settled in the inn before darkness fully descended, so he did a head count: Megan, Abby, Akia….Banji would be joining them later once his wounded shoulder healed a bit more. He had also brought four of his warriors to act as guards in addition to Akia, who was assigned directly to Abby's protection. Reijo had assigned himself to Megan's. They had everyone except for that old buzzard raptor Kavi. If the man didn't get here soon, Reijo was going to leave without him, Ghaleb be damned.

They waited a few more minutes before Reijo decided to proceed without his old instructor, when suddenly a very old man came huffing up to their group. He was skin and bones with a whitebeard that hung down almost to his waist. Time had stooped his shoulders to the point that he had to walk with a cane or fear tipping over. On his back was a pack stuffed to the brim with books. It was quite probable that the pack weighed more than he did. But despite his frail appearance, the man's eyes were bright and lively.

"We had to wait for you to pack your books didn't we? And why didn't you send them with the cargo?" Reijo threw his hands up and muttered, "I should have just left him here."

"You always were an impatient ghost lion cub, Reijo. You know I wouldn't risk losing such precious history." He frowned sternly at the big man and popped him in the shin with his cane. "And do not even think about leaving me here."

Megan had to suppress a smile because Reijo looked like a chastised school boy as he muttered introductions.

"Megan, this is Master Kavi of the Long Scroll, formerly of the Clan Nardo."

Master Kavi barked a loud laugh. "So you were the one who started that title." Kavi turned his inquisitive eyes on Megan and her daughter. "And who do we have here?"

"Master Kavi, may I present M'lady Megan O'Conner and her daughter Abigail." Reijo continued, "Now if we could please get going?"

The old man smiled at Megan and she found herself smiling back. Kavi kind of reminded her of her late husband's granddad. It was comforting.

The queue moved forward and Abby stared wide eyed as the people in front of them disappeared into a whirling wind with a poof.

When it came their turn Abby was terrified to disappear, and Megan was having no luck calming her when Kavi leaned over to the child and whispered, "It's ok, Abigail. It's just magic. You like magic don't you?"

"Are you a wizard? Can you do magic?" the little girl demanded through teary eyes. "You kind of look like the wizard in the book mommy reads me sometime. But we don't read here; she just sings instead."

"Well, if I look like a wizard in your book I must be a wizard then," Kavi smiled and took Abby's hand. "Would you like to do some magic with me?"

Abby nodded and scrambled out of her mother's arms. She held tightly to Kavi's hand as they approached the pillars where the slip stream would manifest.

Kavi said, "With this spell I will take you from here to there."

"Where is there?" Abby asked.

"You will just have to see when we get there. Now repeat after me and then jump. 'Over hill, over dale; take me now through the veil.'" Abby repeated after Kavi as the slip stream activated, and when they jumped, the pair disappeared, followed closely by the rest of the party.

CHAPTER NINE

Reijo took Megan's hand as they stepped into the event horizon of the slip stream. The simple touch made Megan's heart race and she wondered if he noticed. Megan knew that she had no desire to stay in a place where she and her daughter were valued only as breeding stock, but a part of her wished that things were different—that she had met Reijo in some other place.

If Megan was honest with herself, her reaction to Reijo scared her a little. No man had stirred her desires since her husband. She had loved Richard with all that she had to give. Their love had been a sweet, comforting love, a solace from the difficulties of life. When Richard wasn't deployed, their home had been filled with love and laughter. She missed him still. But even her beloved Richard had not stirred such a powerful animalistic want in her.

Megan's musings stopped as she felt her body being pulled and stretched, like she was salt water taffy, through the slip stream. Colors, lights, and sounds swirled around her in a discordant cacophony until her stretched body suddenly snapped back together, shooting her from the slip stream into recognizable reality like a rubber band gun. She nearly fell flat on her face, but strong familiar hands steadied her, pressing her against Reijo's sculpted stomach and chest.

"You get used to it after a while." His voice rumbled through his body and into hers. The sensation pooled in her lower body and her womb clenched with want. God, she really needed to get laid.

Megan looked up through lowered lashes, blushing at the stray thoughts that ran through her head. She noticed Reijo's pupils had dilated as he stared down at her. He took a deep breath, as if he was trying to memorize her scent and groaned quietly. Megan would have missed it if she wasn't still wrapped around his frame because she felt it more than heard it.

Reijo suddenly straightened and put her at arm's length, awkwardly patting her shoulder.

"Well, we had better head to the inn; night is already beginning to fall here. We will continue on with first light."

Reijo turned and walked away with the rest of their party following behind. Megan watched his toned backside and let her eyes wander over the rest of his shapely frame. There was no denying that he was the most physically compelling man she had ever met. A night of unadulterated sex with him would probably be amazing. But would it be enough?

*****

Megan gawked openly. When Reijo had said they were staying at an inn, she had pictured a quaint little bed and breakfast type of set up, but they were now standing in the lobby of a place that would have rivaled Earth's five-star hotels. There was stained glass and sculpture everywhere. Most of it portrayed the large cat-like creature she saw in the windows of Reijo's study. She had since come to learn that each clan had a specific animal they used as their clan symbol. The Tiaret Clan's symbol was something called a ghost lion. The large, cat-like creature reminded Megan of a black panther from back on earth, except it had two tails that Kavi said were prehensile. It also had strategically placed bony armor along its neck and spine, a feature that many of the native animals shared.

Megan was admiring a particularly realistic sculpture of one of these cats when she felt Reijo take her elbow to guide her to the stairs. If there was any doubt in Megan's mind of Reijo's status in this society, it faded quickly once she realized that their "room" was a suite that covered the entire top floor of the inn. Every person had their own bedroom, even Abby. She was touched that Reijo had placed her and her daughter in rooms that connected by a shared bathroom.

Everyone went about the business of settling in. Reijo ordered a meal to be brought to the suite directly instead of having everyone gather in the dining room downstairs. Reijo made it clear that Megan was to eat, and if she did not he would force the food down her throat. Megan nodded; she had planned on breaking the hunger strike now that they had been separated from the other women anyway. She was Abby's only protection, and she needed to be at full strength just in case the council decided to try and take her daughter from her.

The group ate in silence until Akia blurted out a question, "Are the females of your race always so sexual?"

Megan nearly choked on the bite in her mouth, "Excuse me?"

"Well," he said in between bites, "when my brother and I were searching for unmated women, we could scent their men on just about every female out in public."

Megan laughed, "Well, that is probably because you had poor timing...but a man's scent isn't an accurate measure of whether or not a female is 'mated,' especially in that area."

Akia and the rest of the men stopped eating to stare at Megan.

"I don't understand," Akia questioned.

"You really have no idea about where you took me from do you?" Megan was surprised. She had assumed that they had done at least some basic research on her home world.

Reijo answered for the group. "Your planet is at the limit of our current capabilities of travel, and in fact we thought that sector was devoid of life. If one of your females hadn't gotten sucked in during an experiment, we wouldn't even have known you existed."

"Would you please tell us about your home?" Kavi asked. Megan looked around the table, and all of the other men seemed just as interested. Megan figured that the more these people knew about her, the more she would be regarded as a person, maybe even a friend, which would be better for her than always being viewed as a brood mare.

Before Megan could start, Abby yawned and laid her head on Megan's lap. It had been a long day for the child and she was tired. Megan shifted to take Abby to bed, but Reijo stood and picked up the little girl.

"You continue. Allow me to see to Abby." Megan watched him cradle Abby tenderly to him as he carried her to her bedroom. The thought crossed Megan's mind that Reijo would make a good father one day.

Turning back to the other men, Megan asked, "So what do you want to know?"
*****

Megan spent the next few hours describing how on Earth there were numerous governments and cultures. The men seemed fascinated by the diversity. Kavi was especially interested and even began jotting notes down and asked permission to speak with her again later if he came up with other questions.

Then the conversation turned from the general to the more personal. Akia was curious about the city he and Banji had been sent to.

86

"So earlier you said that scenting a male might not have been a good way of deciding who had a mate or not. Why did you say that? I would think that mates would want to be together regularly," Akia asked.

"Normally you are correct, but the city where you found me and Abby is tied to a military base. Just about everyone in that community has connections to the soldiers there. The reason it seemed like so many had recently had sex was because they had. We had just had a large division of men and women come back from deployment," Megan explained. "The spouses, mates, and our soldiers often can go a whole year or more without being in each other's physical presence, which is why scent isn't a good way to decide who has a mate or not."

"Why would your females not just find another mate to take care of them during such a long separation?" Reijo asked, truly curious.

Megan wasn't sure how to answer that question because she wasn't sure they could understand the concept of love and commitment. "Women in my country are not passed around like brood mares. We choose whom we wish to be with…and that choice isn't made lightly. Because when we make that choice we promise before all to be together until death do us part. Besides, sometimes it is our men who are waiting for their women to return from war."

A male whose name Megan couldn't remember gasped. "Your world allows its females to be soldiers?"

"Not every culture allows it, but in my country a woman, or a man for that matter, may choose to be whatever they want to be. Any job that a man can do, so can a woman."

Akia laughed, "Are you one of these women soldiers? Is that where you received your warrior's training?"

A shadow crossed across Megan's features and she looked down. "I was not a soldier. I learned to fight for an entirely different reason." With that, Megan got up and left the room. The men watched her leave, confused about why her mood had shifted so suddenly.

*****

"Her mate was a warrior who was lost in battle. In fact, Akia, she was visiting his grave when you and Banji found her," Reijo said quietly after Megan had left. He didn't really think that was the reason she had left the room, though he did know that she mourned her mate still. He would find out later what had truly upset her.

"She mourns him still?" one of the guards asked in surprise.

Reijo swirled his glass of wine, wondering just how much to tell these men of the conversations that Megan had had with him that first night. He wondered if knowing that these women were capable of such love and devotion would do more harm than good because eventually even if they were allowed to mate with one of these women, if the council had their way, the men would eventually have to give her up. It was a shallow future to be sure, but he was unsure how to change it. But then again, perhaps knowing something better could give the men the fortitude to help make changes in the future. Too bad such changes would most likely come before it would do any good for him and Megan.

"He fell in battle over a year ago according to what Megan told me." Reijo set his glass down.

"And she has not chosen another?"

"No, her bond was very strong with her mate. Her heart still hurts at his absence. She still loves him."

"I wonder what it would be like to know love like that," Akia said wistfully, and the rest of the men murmured their agreement.

Reijo looked toward the door of Megan's sleeping chamber. He had wondered the same thing himself, but he was slowly beginning to realize that he didn't want to know just any woman's love; he wanted Megan's.

"I wonder, indeed." Reijo stood, dismissing the rest of the men. They left the remains of dinner for the staff to clean up later.

Reijo walked past Megan's door, heading to his own sleeping chamber when he stopped. He thought he heard someone crying.

Reijo gently opened Megan's door. The sight that greeted him twisted his heart. In the dim light he could hear Megan's sobs and see her tiny body trembling with the effort of trying to hold in her sorrow. It shook Reijo to his core to see such a strong, feisty woman breaking down. Truthfully, it wasn't seeing a strong woman break down; it was seeing his strong Megan break down.

His Megan? When had he decided that? But the thought felt right. She was his, or she would be eventually. He just had to figure out how to keep her; but that is a worry for the future. Right now he needed to stop her tears and understand why she was so upset.

"Megan?"

"Go away." Her voice was muffled by the bedding.

Reijo almost turned to leave. This was new territory to him; he wasn't sure what he was supposed to do. Then he heard Megan crying into the coverlet and he knew that he wouldn't be going anywhere.

He crossed the room and sat down next to Megan on the bed. He really wasn't sure what to do next. In the end he needn't have worried because he soon found Megan wrapped around his neck, her tears soaking his shoulder.

Reijo said nothing for a moment. He just wrapped his arms around Megan and gathered her close. He gently stroked her hair and back, hoping to sooth the hurt from her body. He was fascinated by her hair. It was so soft and shined so brightly against his dark skin. It was as if Megan was the light to his darkness. It took every ounce of willpower not to fist a handful of her hair and bring it to his face so he could inhale that scent that was so uniquely hers. She smelled like a spring day after a rain had cleansed the land.

Reijo was so lost in the sensation of Megan being in his arms that he hadn't noticed that she was no longer crying. Megan was watching him, and Reijo could see the emotions battling inside as they crossed her expressive face. He reached up and tenderly cupped Megan's cheek. His thumb wiped away the last of her tears and he swore to himself that she wouldn't cry again if he could help it.

"Tell me, *jinaria*, why the tears?" Reijo called her his beautiful treasure in his own language, and she was. Megan was something beautiful and rare.

*****

Megan clung to Reijo. Too much pain and hurt were bottled up inside her. She had thought that she was over this—that she wouldn't have to face it again. But being here on Vukas she was forced to face the possibility that not only could she suffer through her worst nightmare again, over and over, but her daughter may be condemned to the same fate.

She should hate Reijo; by all accounts he should be her enemy. He had taken her and Abby away from everything they had ever known against their will. She tried to fight the draw that she felt, but it was useless. This was the first time she felt alive since Richard's death. She had a purpose besides just living day to day. Somehow she had to find a way to give hope to the women who would come after her; to give hope to her daughter.

Megan heard Reijo's request. She had never talked to anyone about what had happened to her so many years ago. She buried it deep inside because she wanted to forget. Destiny had other plans, however. It had been almost twenty years, and here she was faced with the same demon again. The only difference was this time was that she had been warned and she knew it was coming. She hoped that somehow that would make a difference for them all.

*****

Megan shifted away from Reijo and he watched as she withdrew into herself. Every instinct within him wanted to gather her up in his arms once more. He didn't do it, though he wanted to. This wasn't about him and what he wanted; it was about Megan and what she needed. So Reijo sat patiently while Megan decided how much she would let him into the wall she built around herself.

"Akia asked about me being a 'warrior.' I am assuming that he was referring to my fighting skills." Reijo nodded, afraid to speak lest she didn't continue her tale.

"I did not learn to fight by joining the military. I learned to fight so no one could hurt me again."

Again? Reijo felt rage bubble up from someone deep within himself. He couldn't understand how someone could intentionally hurt the woman before him. Yes she was feisty, but she was also generous and caring. She put the needs of others before her own.

Megan continued. "When I was a teenager, a child about to become an adult in a few years…a man raped me."

Reijo frowned. His translation device surely must be mistaken. What kind of man would force a child to do that.

It was as if Megan was reading his mind. "My age doesn't really matter; no person...male...female...young...or old, should be forced into having sex against their will."

Reijo cringed at her words because that was exactly what the council had planned for these women. In that moment, Reijo made the decision that he would fight for Megan and Abby. As long as he drew breath they would not be forced to endure such treatment.

"Tell me all of it Megan. I need to understand," Reijo growled.

"I was walking home from school. I cut through a park near my house, like I normally did. A group of seniors from my high school were hanging out in the park and started harassing me. I tried to get away, but they thought it was funny to frighten me. Soon I was trapped, and that was when it happened." Reijo could see Megan retreat into herself again. The events she was relating were obviously painful for her. She went on to detail how this group of males beat and abused her until she was incapable of movement. In the end, the leader of that group of males had taken her innocence.

Anger and hate surged through Reijo's mind. He was losing control of his emotions, and the beast within him was rising. Most warriors could control when they phased, but that control can be difficult to exercise when blinded by rage. When Reijo felt his elongated canines puncture the inside of his lips, he realized that if he didn't get himself under control he would end up frightening Megan, and he didn't want to add to her current distress. *Inhale...exhale....* Reijo forced his body to calm down, concentrating on his breathing until the last of the rage-fueled adrenaline left his system. When he returned to himself, he had to mentally catch up because Megan had continued her tale.

"My father was a police officer, someone who enforces the laws. He heard over the radios that I was found beaten and bloodied. They eventually arrested the guys who had assaulted me, but I knew just like my father did that even if convicted they wouldn't spend forever locked away. Besides the fact that just like there are good people in my world, there are also bad.

"I was scared for a long time. It was difficult for me to walk back and forth to school, and I started shutting myself away. Then my dad introduced me to an old friend of his. They had served together when my dad was in the navy. Mr. Jones was a navy SEAL."

Reijo's eyes widened and his brow furrowed in confusion, "He was a dark blue aquatic mammal?"

Despite how difficult this story was for her to tell, Megan couldn't help but laugh. "Not quite. The navy is our military branch that specializes in water-based warfare. A SEAL is an elite warrior who is trained to be a fearsome fighting force either alone or in small teams. Very few of even the best warriors make it through the training necessary to earn that title. As I was saying, Mr. Jones was a SEAL, and now that he had retired from military service, he ran a dojo: a place to teach martial arts training, self-defense…a warrior's training, to anyone willing to learn. My dad thought that if I knew how to protect myself that perhaps I wouldn't be so afraid anymore—that I could somehow take back part of what those guys had taken from me.

"I was a determined pupil and quickly excelled in aikido, judo, and karate…. In the end Mr. Jones even taught me krav maga. Each of these forms has different specialties and uses. Some teach me how to pin and hold someone larger and stronger than myself; some teach me to use my opponent's own strengths against them or how to disarm someone who has a weapon. I have continued my studies, no matter where I have been, keeping my skills sharp."

Sometime during her recitation of her history, Megan had sat down next to Reijo again. Without thinking he had placed one of his large hands on her thigh, his thumb drawing small comforting circles. Megan laid her hand over Reijo's and squeezed it gently before looking up at him, her eyes locking onto his.

"Reijo, I won't let anyone take that choice from me again. Nor will I let it be taken from my daughter." Fresh tears pooled in Megan's eyes.

"Sshh, *jinaria*. We will figure something out." He reached up and caught her tears in his hand.

"Please promise me that if something happens to me, you won't let them do what they plan to do to Abby."

"Megan, *jinaria mio*." Reijo wanted to take away the pain in Megan's eyes; he wanted her to forget all of her past hurts and future worries. He gently guided her tear-streaked face towards his own as he lowered his head and captured her lips. His kiss was feather light and gentle, almost as if he was afraid she would break.

At first Megan was hesitant, but his tender touch stirred something strong inside her. She reached her hands up and pulled him towards her, demanding that he give more to their kiss. With a deep groan of want, Reijo obliged.

They both lost themselves in the sensation of the other. Soon Megan had crawled into Reijo's lap, wrapping herself around him. Reijo's hands fisted into the silken strands of her hair. He used those fists full of hair to pull him and Megan apart.

Both of them were panting from lack of oxygen and racing heartbeats. Reijo stared down at Megan; his blue eyes had turned almost black with his darkened desire.

"We must stop, Megan." Reijo's face contorted almost as if saying that caused him pain. "I will not be one of the men who takes your choice from you." Reijo dropped his eyes, looking away from Megan in shame.

Megan placed her small hands on either side of his rugged face and coaxed him to look at her once again. She held his gaze for a long time, until he was sure that she was sincere with what she was saying.

"Reijo, this is my choice. I choose to be here with you, in this place. I choose you."

A deep growl rumbled deep within Reijo's chest as his restraint broke. The beast within him roared in triumph because she had chosen him. Reijo knew that after this night he would never let this little earth woman go. She was his and no one else would touch her as long as he still drew breath.

CHAPTER TEN

"Are you sure, *jinaria mio*? Because there will be no going back from this point." Reijo flipped their positions, pinning Megan into the soft mattress. "If you want to stop, we must stop now."

Reijo gazed into Megan's eyes as if looking for his own salvation. Megan paused, gently brushing a lock of his hair away from his eyes. She smiled a soft, sad smile.

"My future is bleak, Reijo. Please." She punctuated her request with nipping kisses along his jaw. "Please give me something beautiful."

His eyes darkened with hunger and something else that Megan dared not hope for. This man, this beautiful alien from another planet, had ensnared her senses and was quickly worming his way into her heart. It was a dangerous game she was playing, but in that moment she didn't care. She needed Reijo to wipe away the memories and hurt that haunted her. She needed him to take away the fear for the future, even if it was just a temporary respite.

Reijo undressed Megan with painstaking slowness. Each button was followed by the nuzzle of his nose and kisses or the laving of his tongue. When he finally reached the last button, he pulled open the shirt and ran his rough hands along her rib cage. His hand teased her nipples through the white lacy material of her bra. He seemed fascinated as it pebbled against his touch.

"So beautiful," he whispered reverently, as if he was worshipping at the feet of a goddess instead of Megan.

In that moment, Megan felt beautiful. No man, not even her beloved Richard, had looked on her with such hunger and desire. The intensity of it frightened her a little. Reijo's hands kneaded their way down to her jean-covered thighs, and he trailed kisses down her body. Megan's entire body flushed, and the heat settled low in her body. She was aching with need, and the man hadn't even finished undressing her.

He laid his head at the apex of her thighs and for a moment paused like a man in prayer. Megan was almost afraid he had decided to stop, but then he inhaled deeply.

"Do you know you have the most intoxicating scent?" He nipped the inside of her thigh through her jeans. "I wonder if you taste as good as you smell?" He smiled up at her and her breath caught when dimples appeared. God, she was a sucker for dimples. Megan's tongue darted out as she wet her lips, causing Reijo to groan with desire.

"Why don't you find out?"

Reijo unbuttoned her jeans and slid them slowly down her legs until he tossed them to the floor. Megan's open shirt soon joined them, leaving her in nothing but her serviceable bra and panties. Reijo's eyes devoured her as if she was posed in her sexiest lingerie. Never before had Megan felt so desired by another man. The feeling was intoxicating. It made her want to be wanton, when normally she was a shy lover.

Reijo pounced, causing a startled gasp from Megan and then a giggle as his breath tickled her most intimate parts. He pulled her underwear off, leaving her neatly trimmed mound bare to his gaze. Her giggle quickly turned into a moan as Reijo's tongue swept her slick folds. He sucked and teased the sensitive bud of her clit, sending electric shocks through her entire body.

It had been so long since someone had touched her intimately that when Reijo entered her with deft fingers, it took no time at all for her body to shatter into a kaleidoscope of colors and sensations, and she cried out.

Coming down from her orgasmic high, she realized that Reijo had left her side and was staring down with her in concern.

"What's wrong?" She didn't want him to stop; she wanted so much more. She hadn't even had the chance to explore him, and that was a journey she really wanted to take.

"Did I hurt you?"

Megan started to laugh until she realized he

was serious. Then it dawned on her, with so few females available Reijo, may not be that experienced in love-making.

"Is this your first time, Reijo?" She reached out to draw him closer, needing to touch him to reassure him that she wanted his touch.

Her strong warrior blushed and stammered. "I've been educated in the ancient texts for this but they did not describe your reaction."

A seductive smiled spread across Megan's face. She was dealing with a virgin. The idea seemed ludicrous. If he had been on Earth, Reijo would have had hundreds of women trailing after him. But here, he was all hers.

"Darling." She pulled him to her and pushed him down onto the mattress, "I assure you my reaction was a good thing, which I hope happens quite frequently tonight." She straddled his hips, her wet heat pressed against his impressive erection. She arched her back to unfasten her bra, and Reijo could only watch in wonder.

As her breasts sprang free, she looked down at Reijo and smiled. Her hair cascaded down around her shoulders in a wave of flames. Megan's hands found the hem of his tunic and she pushed underneath it, her fingers exploring the hard planes of his abdomen.

Reijo practically growled; her touch was exquisite torture. Instincts as old as time rushed into his mind; he wanted to grab her, tame her…. He wanted to claim her. He could feel his muscles contorting as his body attempted to phase. It took every ounce of control he had not to give into the beast within him.

He was brought back to Megan when she said, "You have too many clothes on. I want to feel your skin." She jerked his tunic off and threw it into the tangled pile of her own clothes. She shifted off of him to work his pants down his legs.

Her eyes widened as his cock sprang free from its confines. "Wow, you're a big boy all over aren't you?" She tossed his pants with the rest of the clothes. Her mouth watered. Reijo had to be the most gorgeous man that she had ever seen. He was like a work of art.

Megan leaned over and kissed her way back up his legs, her long red hair caressing his body in the wake of her mouth. Reijo groaned. Part of him wanted to flip her over and bury himself deep within her heated channel, but the other part thought that her kneeling above him with her bright hair spread across his dark skin was the most sensual thing he had ever experienced and he wasn't ready to give that up yet.

Reijo's world narrowed to Megan's mouth as she licked up his shaft and then wrapped her lips around its swollen head. He nearly came up off the bed; as it was, he fisted his hands into her hair. If he had been in his right mind he would have worried that he was being too rough, but he couldn't form a rational thought any longer.

Megan felt his hands pulling at her hair, urging her to increase her pace. She loved that she was cracking his control and she wondered if she could get it to shatter completely. She purred deep in her throat, sending the vibrations throughout his entire body.

Reijo gasped and bucked. He was about to explode, and he couldn't have that. He wanted to be buried deep inside of Megan before that happened. He released her hair and hooked his arms around her and hauled her up to his chest.

Megan was surprised at the sudden manhandling and was even more surprised when he flipped her over and hauled her ass into the air. Megan braced herself for his entrance, knowing that her body would need to adjust to his size.

Reijo leaned across her back, reaching around to fondle her heavy breasts. The fingers of his other hand tickled and teased her wet slit and clit. She arched back into him as she felt another orgasm building.

"Please, Reijo"

"You are so wet, *jinaria*. Are you ready for me?"

"Oh, yes…please…I need you inside me." Her plea was breathless and wanting.

Reijo grabbed her hips and angled himself, rubbing her entrance. Megan tried to push back, wanting him to fill her, but his iron grip wouldn't let her.

"Please, Reijo…."

"What do you need, *jinaria*?"

"Please…."

"Say it," he growled. "I won't give you what you need until you say it."

"Reijo. I need you," she whimpered in want. "Only you."

Her confession broke something within Reijo. She was his and he would claim her for his entire life. Gone was the deliberate tease as Reijo entered her hot channel in one claiming thrust. The gentle lover was gone, replaced by the beast claiming his mate.

The single thrust filled Megan almost to the point of pain. But that discomfort soon faded beneath the colors of heady sensation. Megan felt as if she was on a precipice; she was about to fall and fall hard. Her orgasm started to build, wave after wave cresting higher and higher.

Reijo was riding his own wave of feeling. He never knew it could be like this. He would never give this woman up; he finally felt like he had a reason worth fighting for. His pace increased as his own release began to build. He wanted…no, needed Megan to fall over that edge with him. He braced himself with one arm, but with the other his fingers found the little pleasure button he had discovered earlier. It was an intoxicating sensation to feel his own shaft pistoning in and out of Megan's delectable body.

Closer and closer to the edge they both came, until finally Megan fell first, followed soon by Reijo. They both screamed their release into the world and soon they were flying high on waves of sensation.

Megan felt a sharp bite at her shoulder, but the pain soon turned to pleasure as she rode the last of her orgasm back to earth. She smiled like the cat that ate the canary when she thought about the fact that Reijo had lost his cool and bit her. Maybe she would bite him back next time.

Reijo collapsed on top of Megan. What had he done? He couldn't stop the phase when he had climaxed and had marked Megan, claiming her as his mate. Claiming had been forbidden after the women started moving from household to household.

Reijo rolled over, gathering Megan into his arms. She tucked herself against his chest, and he was amazed at how right she felt there.

"That was amazing." Reijo's dimples appeared as he grinned at Megan's statement.

"Give me a slight rest and we can do it again if you want. You do want, right?"

Megan playfully slapped his chest. "Fishing for compliments?" She giggled and looked up at Reijo's face and saw his uncertainty there. She reached up and smoothed the worry from his face. "I would be here with you always if I could, Reijo." Megan surprised herself with that statement and the fact that she meant it.

Reijo caressed her silky hair but said nothing. He was far away and Megan wanted him back in the here and now. As much as they may want more, the next few nights may be all they would be allowed.

Her hands traveled down his beautiful body and his manhood quickly grew against her touch. Without a word, Megan brought him back to the here and now. She straddled him, lowering herself ever-so slowly down his member. The heat between them flared to life once again, and Megan spent the rest of the night keeping Reijo in the here and now.

They may not have a future, but she was going to brand the present on both of their memories.

CHAPTER ELEVEN

Reijo was startled awake when Megan suddenly bolted upright in the bed.

"Abby!"

Heedless of her glorious nudity, Megan ran out of the bedroom towards her daughter's room. Reijo took a moment to admire how her pale skin glowed in the light of the double moons. Her hair flew behind her like a torch's flame. She was the embodiment of an avenging goddess from the stories of old.

Reijo wondered what had Megan suddenly fleeing, and then he heard it. Abby was crying out in fear. How had Megan heard it before he had? Reijo jumped from the bed and hastily dressed. He rushed into Abby's room half expecting to fight off an attack. What he found instead was a wide-eyed child clinging to her mother. He watched as Megan rocked her daughter back and forth while humming a sweet little tune. Before his eyes he watched the hurt and fear melt away from the little girl's body. It made him think of his own childhood in the dorms of the training schools he grew up in. There had been no one to sooth away his fears and hurts. It made him wonder how much they had denied their precious few children by taking their mothers from them. It had been the practical choice, but was it truly the right one?

The sweet little tune turned into a haunting melody of love and loss, despair and hope as Megan added her voice to the lyrics. It seemed an old song passed down from mother to child because soon Abby was singing it along with her mother.

Reijo felt like an interloper on such an emotion-filled vignette. But even as his rational mind said he should leave because he did not belong there, the beast within roared at the sound of her voice demanding he claim her—demanding its mate.

He had already started the process of the bonding when he bit her shoulder last night. Reijo ran a hand through his hair in frustration. The bonding had been forbidden once it became necessary to pass women around to keep a viable genetic pool going.

The decision had been a practical one. *Practical*—by the two moons how he hated that word. The enzymes in their saliva could create a symbiotic bond between mates. Bonded pairs could not be separated physically for long stretches of time without becoming physically ill. That fact alone had kept many mates from bonding even before it had been outlawed.

But Reijo couldn't stop himself. His instincts

had taken him over and demanded that he mark her, claim her as his own. He had no idea how the enzymes would affect a human woman. It typically took three bites for a Vukasin woman to be fully bonded. It was possible that a single bite could bond Megan or, conversely, the enzyme may not affect humans at all.

On the whole, Reijo secretly hoped that Megan was already bonded to him. He didn't want to ever let her go. His heart had been taken over by two tiny women. For once in his life he felt complete.

The sun rose over the horizon, filling Abby's room with a stream of light. Megan and Abby appeared to be in a halo of light like some magical gift: a miracle from the god and goddess themselves. In that moment, Reijo knew she was his salvation, his future, and he wondered if she perhaps might save the future of his world as well.

*****

It didn't take long for Megan to get her daughter dressed. They still had nothing to pack, though Reijo had assured her that once they arrived at the stronghold new clothing would be a priority for her and Abby.

She was hustling her daughter to the dining room of their suite for breakfast when all conversation stopped dead as she entered the room. Six pairs of eyes stared at her, some with longing, others with a fierce hunger. Megan was about to demand what the hell was wrong when she remembered last night's conversations about being able to smell a mate on a woman. She blushed a deep shade of crimson as she realized that every man in this room knew exactly what she and Reijo had done the night before.

Pulling herself up to as much of her barely over five foot frame would allow, Megan regally entered the dining area. She was an adult capable of making her own choices. *At least for now*, the voice in her head mocked.

Megan filled her plate and ate quickly. She needed to flee the tension-filled table to collect her thoughts. She got up to clear her dishes away when she suddenly found herself pinned against the wall face first by Akia, who was pushing aside the collar of her shirt.

Megan stomped on his instep and elbowed him in the gut. She heard a satisfying grunt as he released her and backed away.

"What the hell is wrong with you?" Megan glared at Akia's pissed-off face. She had no idea why she suddenly upset him and, frankly, she didn't much care at the moment. These stinking entitled males were jumping all over her last nerve. She had to get some space before she went postal on one of them.

Megan grabbed Abby's hand and drug her out of the dining area. She passed by Reijo without even acknowledging him, but he would have none of that. Reijo reached out to embrace Megan with a happy grin on his face that fell only a little when he spied the anger clouding her face. Megan stiff-armed him, preventing him from hugging her and glared up at him.

"You." She poked Reijo in the chest forcefully. "Deal with them." Her finger pointed towards the room she had just left. Without another word, Megan stormed past Reijo, leaving him to figure out what had upset her all on his own.

*****

Reijo walked into the dining area prepared to demand answers, but he found himself punched in the face before he was fully in the room. The unexpected blow staggered Reijo, and he went down on one knee. Looking up he found a furious Akia looming over him.

"How could you? It's forbidden!" Akia shouted at him. "You would give up your honor to rut with some whore?"

Reijo saw red and his beast crept dangerously close to the surface when Akia referred to Megan as a whore.

"Watch your words, Akia," Reijo growled, his body shimmering as he fought the phase.

"She is destined to be passed around from clan to clan. You cannot have her even if you are *Kijani-a*." Akia sneered on Reijo's title.

Reijo slammed his forearm against Akia's throat. "Enough!"

Akia's gasp turned to growls as the angry man phased into his hulking wolf-like form. A lifetime of frustration erupted. Akia, the good twin…the twin, who always followed orders and did what he was told, attacked his commanding officer. He pushed himself away from the wall, allowing the beast to take over.

Fur and claw flashed as Reijo tried to calm Akia, but it was soon apparent that he was on the losing side if he did not phase himself. His bones crackled and reformed. Fur rippled across his body as his face elongated and fangs emerged.

Reijo was fully phased and about to launch a counter attack when an earth shattering scream stopped the battle dead.

*****

Megan was braiding her daughter's hair when the sounds of battle erupted. Her first thought was they were somehow under attack. Her second thought was that she had to protect Abby. She looked around the room wondering where to hide her child, when her eyes landed on a piece of furniture that must be a wardrobe. She opened the doors and sighed with relief as she saw it would be large enough to hide Abby.

She lifted her daughter into the hiding spot and kissed her cheek.

"Baby girl, I need you to be real quiet. Whatever you do, don't come out of there unless Reijo or I come and get you. Can you do that for me, sweetheart?" Megan cupped her daughter's cheek and looked her directly in the eye, trying to convey the importance of this request. Abby was silent, her eyes wide and bright with fright. She nodded once.

"I love you," Megan said softly as she closed the doors to hide her daughter.

Megan walked down the hall quietly. She had no weapon, but she knew from experience that even with these hulking giants around her, if she could catch them by surprise, she could do some damage. She hoped that whoever had attacked them was too occupied with the guards to detect her scent as she crept back into the common area.

What she saw confused her. One of those werewolf-looking things was attacking Reijo. The rest of the guards just stood around doing nothing but trying to stay out of the way of the furious fight.

Reijo was losing ground and Megan was afraid that he would be seriously injured or worse. The creature pushed Reijo into a corner and Megan was about to launch an attack against the creature of her own in a desperate bid to save Reijo.

She shifted her weight, gathering her courage to jump into the fray. Her muscles were taunt and then she hurled herself into a run at the creature's turned back. She tried to catch Reijo's eyes to let him know she was coming to help him, but his concentration was solely on the attack in front of him. She brushed off the hands of the other soldiers as they tried to stop her as she passed them.

Her eyes never left Reijo's beloved face, which is why she came to a screeching halt mid run. Reijo's face contorted and changed. Megan watched in horror as fur appeared in a wave across his body. *Oh my god! He is one of those creatures.* Her mind screamed in denial until she realized it wasn't her mind screaming; it was her.

*****

Akia and Reijo stopped mid swing at the sound of a woman screaming. Reijo shoved the distracted Akia away and ran to Megan only to have her recoil in fear. By the moons, all he did was phase. He was highly confused by her reaction. She had seen phased soldiers at the palace and hadn't reacted with this much fear. He forced the beast to subside, returning to the man she was used to seeing. He needed to understand what was going on, and it was easier to speak in this form.

He watched the emotions play across Megan's expressive face. Her initial shock and fear gave way to anger and distrust. Reijo reached out his hand to cup her cheek but she knocked it away, her eyes like daggers straight to his heart.

With one last shot of betrayed eyes, Megan turned on her heel and stalked back to her bedroom. Reijo made to follow when a weathered old hand clamped down on his shoulder with surprising strength.

"Let her go, boy." Kavi's tone reminded Reijo of his time in the school room many years ago. "She obviously has a lot to process."

Reijo's shoulders slumped. Megan's rejection of his touch hurt more than any of the blows landed by Akia. Speaking of Akia....

"Akia!" Reijo growled, "You will be punished for your attack on your superior officer. Now speak your grievance, so I may judge fairly."

Akia glared defiantly at his commander. "You may have the *Khalon*'s ear; but you have no right to deny the other clans or men a chance to continue their line."

"I have no intention of denying anything to the other clans."

"You began the bonding," Akia accused. "You know what will happen if the two of you bond."

"I know." Suddenly Reijo was very tired. The weight of his world's predicament had never weighed on him as much as it did in this moment.

"Then why?"

"Why? If I could answer why, I wouldn't be torn apart inside." Reijo collapsed into a nearby chair. Akia had never seen his *Kijani-a* in any other state besides absolute confidence; but he was noticeably shaken.

Akia was trying to process what this might mean when Reijo spoke to him again.

"Akia, would you doom Megan to a life of slavery? Would you watch her laughter fade, the fire of her passion dim, the fight of her spirit give up, as year after year she is used as no more than a brood mare, with no mind of her own, no thought given to her emotions?"

Akia shifted uncomfortably because he had never allowed himself to think of the breeding program in those terms.

"Would you want to see little Abby grow up fated for the same? But even more than that, Akia," Reijo's bright blue eyes seemed to flare with an inner fire as his gazed pinned Akia where he stood, "would you be happy living with a woman, loving her body, learning her heart and mind only to have her taken away after a couple of years or once her belly swells with a child created of you and her? What if that child was a daughter? Would you hand her off to be passed around like a whore you accused Megan of being?"

Akia deflated, slumping to the floor. "But what else is there?"

Kavi interrupted. "Many generations ago, before women were no longer being born to our people…a man and a woman bonded for life. They fought side by side to bring honor to their families. Even though much of the ancient times were filled with turmoil and conflict, their writings…the stories and the poetry…made it seem as if that bond was worth fighting for."

Reijo smiled at the old man and looked to Akia, "Akia, I do not know what is in store for the future. But I do know two things: one, I have a battle on the horizon, and two, I would fight anything if it meant Megan stayed by my side. I need to know not just as your commander," Reijo looked at all of the men in the room, "but also as my friends…. Where do you stand?"

*****

"A fucking werewolf!" Megan paced frantically. She had retrieved her frightened daughter and took a moment to sooth her before excusing herself to her own room to think. "I had sex with a damn werewolf. And not just any werewolf," Megan gave a mirthless laugh as she continued her verbal rant to herself, "but an alien werewolf."

It didn't matter that the sex had been fantastic. It didn't matter that a small hope had bloomed in her heart that perhaps they could find a way to be together. The fact that they were entirely different species was made painfully clear just a few minutes ago.

A soft knock on her door halted Megan's monologue. Reijo poked his head around the door.

"Megan can we talk?"

"What the hell does your furry little butt want now?" Arms crossed, Megan glared at Reijo.

Reijo took a steadying breath. At least she hadn't told him to get out or go to hell. "I'm sorry...."

"For what, Reijo? What exactly are you sorry for?"

"I thought you knew about the phase. You didn't flinch away from the guards at the palace, so I had assumed you knew." Reijo sat down on the bed. His shoulders were hunched and his hands clasped in front of him. He looked almost defeated and Megan's heart softened a little.

"I'm on a different planet with no idea how things work here. I had never seen anyone shift before. I had just assumed that the guards were another species found here. I didn't know Vukasins could change like that."

"Only the males phase. Our women have never been able to phase as far as I know."

"Of course only the males do it. What else would I expect from such a chauvinistic planet?" A hint of a smile lifted the corner of Megan's lips and Reijo found himself trying to repress his own answering grin.

"Maybe we just need a few good women to keep us in line."

Megan snorted, "It would take a whole blasted army of women."

"This is probably true" Reijo's lips quirked up at the corner.

"Why did Akia attack you? Was it because of me? Because we had sex?"

Reijo wrapped an arm around Megan's shoulder and squeezed. "It was nothing that you did, *jinaria*. The fault was all mine."

"*Jinaria*...you have called me that before. What does it mean?"

"It means that you are my treasure...something precious to me." Megan's body flushed at those words and hope flared to life in her heart that perhaps Reijo cared for her as much as she did him, even if he was furry sometimes.

Reijo stood holding out his hand. "Megan, let's go home."

Megan's heart stuttered. Reijo had no idea how his simple words affected her. She no longer had a home, and a home was the thing she wanted most desperately. She tried to douse the small flame of hope, but she couldn't completely. Home...what a concept.

CHAPTER TWELVE

They had traveled most of the day. The journey from the village which contained the transport station to the village surrounding the stronghold took almost all day. Everyone was looking a little weary and, frankly, bored.

"Momma! Look at the kitty! Big kitty." Abby was pointing to something outside of the carriage window. Megan and Reijo both stuck their heads out of the windows. A man was facing off across from a giant cat-like creature. It looked like a two-tailed black panther with bony armor plates in strategic areas. Megan recognized it as the ghost lion from the inn's sculptures.

"Damn the moons," Reijo grumbled before hitting the roof of the carriage to alert the driver to come to a stop.

"What's wrong?" Megan asked, concerned.

"Ghost cats are protected in this area as the clan totem. Every once in a while we have to put one down because it has gone rabid and starts attacking the population." Reijo alighted from the carriage, drawing the blade that was ever present at his side.

Megan watched despite the fact she really didn't want to see the death of such a majestic creature. But something didn't add up. The ghost lion didn't look like it was trying to attack the man; it looked like it was trying to get around him and into the house. She wasn't sure about what constituted rabid on this planet, but on earth the creature would have been attacking whatever was in front of it. Something about this situation felt wrong and Megan wasn't sure why. So against her better judgment, Megan left the relative safety of the carriage while telling Abby to stay put.

Reijo was instructing the guards to circle around the ghost lion to prevent its escape when Megan touched his arm to get his attention.

"I don't think that ghost lion is rabid, Reijo," Megan whispered.

"Of course it is. Why else would it walk right into the village?"

"I don't know, but really watch it. It's not trying to attack…. It's almost as if it is trying to get around the man."

Reijo turned and watched the scene between the villager and the ghost lion. Megan was right. The cat was trying to maneuver around the man; it was the man blocking its path. But he still didn't understand why the creature seemed so intent on getting to the house. It made no sense. The ghost lion should either be attacking or escaping.

While Reijo was lost in the implications, Megan advanced towards the big cat. Her voice was pitched low and soothing. Reijo swallowed the curse that wanted to burst forth at her recklessness. The woman was going to get herself killed. But he didn't dare make an aggressive move at the moment for fear that it would cause the ghost lion to attack.

*****

The ghost lion was lethally beautiful. Even in its tensed state it was graceful in its movements. Megan had no idea why she was attempting to sooth the beast. Back home she had tamed the odd feral cat or dog in the neighborhood; but this was no house pet. Yet somehow, Megan sensed a kinship to the creature.

Megan hoped that the body language of this creature held similar meaning to the body language of animals back home. She reasoned, more to steady her own nerves than anything else, that if the Vukasins and humans reacted similarly…then a cat was a cat no matter what planet it was from.

The cat was tensed and frightened, though it didn't seem to be frightened for itself. The villager facing it, on the other hand, was angry when he should have been terrified if the creature was attacking him. He was yelling at Reijo to kill the beast and even attempted to shove Megan out of the way when she wedged herself between him and the giant cat.

Megan regained her balance and ignored the villager, keeping her entire focus on the ghost lion. The creature studied Megan, its bright golden eyes a sharp contrast to its midnight fur. Megan crooned softly to the cat, but her own heart was racing. Megan knew that the creature would never relax if

Megan couldn't relax herself. So she did the only thing she could think of to calm herself and the creature; she sang.

She chose a gentle lullaby that had never failed to relax Abby into blissful sleep. The melody was old, passed down from mother to child to countless generations. As she let the melody wash through her soul, Megan began to relax. Her eyes never left the ghost lion. The creature sniffed the air but lay down, its eyes mesmerized by Megan. There was intelligence there beyond beastly instinct.

Finally the tension left the body of the cat and its ears perked forward. Tentatively, Megan approached the large creature, holding out a hand so it might know her scent. The gathered men gasped as she lowered herself to sit barely a foot away from the dangerous animal. They were even more surprised when the great cat approached Megan and head butted her shoulder.

The cat lay down in front of Megan and she reached out to run her hands through the thick fur. *This must be what petting a tiger feels like*, she thought. No sooner had the thought left her head when she and the ghost lion locked eyes and the strangest thing happened.

Images slammed into Megan's mind. It was a cacophony of light and sound. It was difficult to make out anything specific, but she was able to register the image of a pair of cubs in a cage. Slowly her vision returned to normal and she petted the giant cat, trying to convey that she saw it. She knew instinctively that those images had come from the ghost lion, whom she now was certain was the mother of those cubs. She knew it with the same certainty that the villager was the one who caged her offspring.

Reijo turned from questioning the villager when Megan called out to him.

"Reijo, is there a black market for protected creatures on this planet?"

"Yes. Collectors and hunters prize the ghost lion pelt." He frowned at her question, but honestly this whole encounter left him off kilter. "Why do you ask?"

"I believe this man has two cubs that belong to this creature. Would you please check for me?"

The villager turned a deep shade of red. He yelled obscenities and charged towards Megan in a rage. He was faster than Reijo thought and would reach Megan before he could be stopped. Reijo's only hope was that the first blow of the villager's tool didn't do too much damage to Megan. But Reijo needn't have worried because the man was pinned to the ground by the snarling ghost lion, leaving Megan unharmed.

Reijo motioned for his guards to search the premises and he approached Megan and the cat slowly.

"Can you keep it from killing him?" Reijo asked Megan.

"I have no control over her."

"Could have fooled me," Reijo muttered.

It didn't take long for the guards to return with a mewling cage. Inside was a pair of cubs. With a final saliva-dripping snarl, the ghost lion moved away from the villager and stalked towards the cage. Reijo's guards nervously brandished their weapons as the cat growled at them as she approached.

"Open the cage and step away," Megan advised.

The men did as they were told. The little cubs clamored all over themselves to get out of the cage, their tiny roars calling for their mother. The large ghost lion called to them in a low rumble and the cubs fell in line behind her. She roared and flashed her vicious teeth at the villager before disappearing into the mountain forest.

The whole group watched the large cat disappear with stunned expressions on their faces. The villager tried to slip away while the rest were distracted with their wonderment, but Akia caught him.

"What in the two moons just happened?" Reijo barked.

"Something that hasn't been seen in a millennium, my boy." Kavi stood next to the carriage holding Abby's hand. Reijo couldn't miss the impish grin he had on his face. "Megan, how did you know there were two cubs being held?"

Megan frowned in thought, not sure how to explain what had happened. "I saw them…. I think Kilala showed me somehow."

"Kilala? Who's that?" Reijo demanded.

"That is the name of Megan's ghost lion," Kavi explained. "She's forged a connection, a phenomenon that hasn't occurred for generations, and by default she is now a member of Clan Tiaret."

"I don't understand." Megan was confused by what Kavi was saying.

"Most people dismiss it as legend, but the stories of our clans state that our totem animals chose us. In fact, legend says that in the beginning of the clans, only those warriors who forged a connection with the totem animal were given full rights within the clans. Of course this was when the clans were individual nations rather than a single government."

"So how does that make me a member of the Tiaret Clan?"

"You have forged a connection; this is proven by the images that ghost cat shared. What's more, I suspect that particular cat will always be near should you need her. After all, she did give you her name." Kavi smiled at Megan as her brow furrowed while she processed what he had just told her. Over her head, Kavi gave a pointed look to Reijo, silently communicating that he needed to speak with him privately.

CHAPTER THIRTEEN

The mountains were beautiful. It reminded Megan, in many ways, of the vacation she had taken to the Rockies. The high peaks were laced with snow even though the weather lower down was temperate. A thick forest of trees surrounded them. Reijo and Kavi had explained that the village had been carved out of the virgin forest generations ago. One thing the Vukasins seemed to do better than Earth was the conservation of the environment. The communities seemed to be created with the idea of harmonizing with the wilds surrounding them in mind.

The village had been the halfway point in their journey that day. A straight line from the village to the Tiaret stronghold was a relatively short distance, but the winding mountain path the carriages were forced to make made the trip seem much longer.

Abby was beginning to fuss and fidget from being cooped up so long, and Megan's patience with her daughter's foul mood was wearing thin. Out the window of the carriage, Megan saw nothing but forest and rock. She was about to ask Reijo if they could stop and stretch their legs, hoping that some activity might improve Abby's mood, when the carriages rounded a sharp curve that had hidden their destination.

Out of the mountain mists rose an indomitable stone structure. This was not the smooth, shining white stone of the palace. No, this stone was dark and variegated; giving it a wild appearance like its surroundings. There was a feeling of order derived from chaos. It certainly fit Reijo's personality. Megan mused that outwardly he was tightly controlled, but their shared night of passion had proven that underneath all of that control was a wild passion just waiting for an outlet. Megan sighed, trying to force her mind from her wish to be that outlet.

Abby watched in awe as the shadow of the portico crossed above them. The walls of the stronghold were tick and high. It reminded Megan of old European castles. Evidently it reminded Abby of the same thing.

"You have a castle!" Abby bounced up and down in her seat, clapping her hands. "Does that mean you are a prince? Or are you a knight?"

"Knight?" Reijo looked to Megan for clarification.

"Ideally, a knight was a warrior who pledged to follow the code of chivalry, to defend the weak and be a voice of grace and justice. In reality they were warriors who pledged themselves to lords and kingdoms in exchange for power or wealth. The truly chivalrous knights have had their stories passed down through the generations."

Reijo nodded and turned to Abby, smiling. "I suppose you could call me a knight then."

Megan crossed her arms while she regarded Reijo, her fingers playing a nervous tattoo on her forearm. Reijo noticed her staring at him with a slight frown on her face. He gazed directly into her eyes and raised an eyebrow in question.

She shrugged and answered his unspoken question, "I was just trying to figure out if you are a chivalrous knight or not."

*****

It had been an eventful day. Reijo took Megan and Abby on a tour of his home. He loved the fact that the flower garden had made Megan smile. Both of his women decided to turn in early. His women…he really liked the sound of that. After seeing to their care and arranging for new clothing to be brought to the stronghold tomorrow, Reijo made his way to the study, where he found Kavi waiting for him.

Reijo watched as Kavi circled the room with a device in his hand. Being the head of Vukas's military, Reijo recognized it as anti-intelligence equipment. Its specific function was to alert the user to any monitoring devices in the area.

"Getting paranoid in your old age, Kavi?" Reijo walked across the study and opened a cabinet on the far wall. He removed a decanter of his favorite wine and poured himself a glass. He in turn poured a stronger spirit for Kavi, having remembered his preference from long ago.

"We need to talk, Reijo, and it would be best if our conversation remained between us." Satisfied that they were free to talk in this room, Kavi took the offered drink and sat in one of a pair of chairs near the fireplace. A fire had been laid earlier, since even in the summertime the mountain nights can be cold.

Kavi took a swallow of the fiery liquid, wincing as it made its way down his throat. He concentrated on the bluish liquid as he swirled it around his glass, before setting it aside on the small table near his seat. He fixed his gaze on Reijo and sighed.

"You know there is much unrest between Ghaleb and the council," Kavi stated.

"I had heard that, yes."

"Did you know that Ghaleb had opposed the breeding program?"

"He told me as much, though I don't understand why he didn't just overrule the council. He is, after all, *Khalon*; the council is there only as long as the royal family wishes it."

Kavi gave a mirthless laugh, "Leave it to a soldier to think in terms of black and white. It's not that easy, Reijo. Ghaleb is the end of his line. Without an heir, the Ivailo Clan will disappear, which means another clan will take its place. The Ivailo knew they were declining just as the rest of the planet was and as such created laws giving much of their power to the council. Their thought had been to give Vukas stability even if the royal family should fall."

"So now Ghaleb is caught in that safety net like a bug in a dragon-spider's web," Reijo concluded.

"Not just that, but there is a hidden faction that is trying to forcibly take the throne. It is one of the reasons Ghaleb needs the support of the council now more than ever. So he conceded to the breeding program." Kavi picked up his glass and took another swallow. He seemed to be trying to gather courage for what he was about to say.

"I get the feeling you aren't telling me everything. I doubt Ghaleb wanted you to tag along on this trip for just your health."

Kavi gave a dark grin. "I may be old, boy, but I'm still useful."

"So spit it out….why are you here?"

"I was here to figure out if young Megan had enough fortitude to perform the *Mate Avi Keiger*."

Reijo leapt to his feet, "Are you insane? That ritual hasn't been performed for generations because it is so deadly. Not to mention I don't recall a woman ever performing it."

Kavi waited for the rush of anger to leave Reijo. When he finally quit pacing and sat down again, Kavi continued, "You are correct that it can be deadly; but it may offer a way for you and her to be together."

"I won't sacrifice her life, Kavi. I can't."

"Not even for her freedom?"

"I don't see how this would win her freedom."

"That is because you refused to study the laws, boy. But it is a good thing that Ghaleb did. These are ancient laws that haven't been called into use for generations. They are forgotten by most but still valid and iron clad. Not even the council could go against them without starting a civil war."

"So why didn't Ghaleb offer up these laws as challenge in the first place?"

"And give the council the opportunity to make legal inroads with them? Not to mention that this will be seen as a rebellion to most members of the council. Ghaleb needs their support to keep his throne. We need him to keep his throne because if the whispers are true the family wanting to take it from him would destroy Vukas in a bloody way. That was why this had to appear to come outside of the royal family. The population and even the council would understand an outsider fighting for their freedom and right to choose."

"Why Megan?"

"Megan may be a woman, but she is a warrior all the way through to her soul. It will take all of that warrior spirit to survive the *Mate Avi Keiger*."

"Why are you telling me this instead of speaking with Megan herself?"

"Because you love her." Kavi sat back in his seat, steepling his fingers under his chin. "That love can be a source of strength for both of you or it could be your downfall. Besides the fact that her connection to Kilala complicates things."

"How so?"

"We would be evoking ancient law. That law, if she was successful, would have allowed her the right to form her own clan, have a seat on the council itself. But ancient law now dictates that her connection to the ghost lion makes her noble of the Tiaret Clan. This leaves her with no seat on the council, though she can still gain the rights of a warrior. It is now up to you, whether the clan stands with Megan or with the council."

Reijo sat thoughtfully. By all rights, as the head of the Tiaret Clan, he should have held the council seat. But politics bored him and he had allowed his cousin to take the seat in his stead. Now it looked like he would have to be involved in politics whether he liked it or not.

"By the moons, Ghaleb maneuvered me good. The bastard has wanted me on the council for ages."

Kavi laughed and then finished his drink, "Well, he was taught by the best. You have much to consider, Reijo. I need to discuss this with Megan soon, as she would need to prepare, but I need to know where you stand before I do. Without your support and the support of the clan all of this is for naught."

Reijo stood up with Kavi, clasping the old man's hand. "I must discuss this with the clan. It is not a decision I can make on my own when it puts the entire clan in danger."

"I understand, but the time set aside for the ritual fast approaches. So do not dawdle over your considerations."

"I will call a clan gathering tomorrow. Most of the families within the clan have someone near that can represent them. Besides, I think it would be nice to give Megan and Abby a couple of days just to enjoy themselves before we drop this into their laps."

Kavi walked to the door. As he left, he turned back to Reijo with a level look, "She's stronger than she looks." With those words he left.

Reijo threw back the last of his wine and stared at the flames. He knew how strong Megan was. She never ceased to amaze him; but they weren't asking for a simple demonstration of fighting. She was not familiar with the dangers of this world. Could he really ask her to face the unknown, which could kill her, for his cousin's political plans?

If it was just about the politics, Reijo would have told Kavi no hands down. Yet Kavi said this was a chance to gain Megan her freedom, and Reijo knew that without that freedom for her and Abby, Megan would never truly be happy. Reijo wondered what Megan's possible success would mean to the other Earth women. Would Abby have to go through the same ritual when she came of age? The thought of that child facing death twisted a knot in Reijo's stomach. Somewhere along the way that little girl came to mean as much to him as her mother did. He would protect her like his own daughter.

The thoughts just kept swirling around in Reijo's head until he hurled his wine glass into the fireplace in frustration. The fact of the matter was he didn't have enough information. He knew of the

Mate Avi Keiger mostly from old stories and history lessons. He needed to know the laws surrounding it; he wouldn't be able to strategize without all of the facts. A commander knows that the more information you have about a battle the better your odds of winning are.

With those thoughts, Reijo left his study to contact important members of the clan to call a gathering. It should take no more than two days for all of them to get to the clan stronghold. While he waited for those people to arrive, he decided it would behoove him to spend some time with an expert in the law; and thanks to Ghaleb's interference he had the best expert living under his roof. It was about time the old buzzard raptor started earning his keep.

CHAPTER FOURTEEN

It had been a blissfully quiet couple of days. True to his word, Reijo had arranged for Megan and Abby to get new clothes. For the time being, the tailor had quickly altered tunics, pants and even a dress or two. He was quite surprised that Megan had insisted on a few of the more masculine outfits. He also sat with her to design a few things based on her taste, which he promised to have delivered within the week.

Megan walked through the walled garden off of the family quarters and thought how simply having access to a new outfit and clean clothes can change the way you view the world. Reijo had been especially attentive to her and Abby when not in meetings with the clan leaders.

Megan knew that something was going on. She would have pinned Kavi down to demand an explanation if she wasn't afraid of ruining the illusion of contentment by forcing reality into it. But she knew that it would be foolish for her to remain ignorant of what was occurring for much longer.

Megan was alone as she wandered. Kavi had taken it upon himself to act as Abby's tutor. Megan's daughter was sequestered with the older man having her lessons this morning, and Megan wouldn't see her again until lunch time.

It felt strange to have nothing to do. Megan had always worked, and this forced relaxation was stressing her out. It was one of the reasons her mind kept wandering and wondering distractedly.

In her distraction, Megan meandered to the far edge of the garden. While still within the walls of the stronghold, it was a good distance from the living quarters, and Megan knew that just on the other side of the wall the wild forests of the mountains butted right up.

These far reaches of the garden were left a little wilder than the well-manicured flower and herb plots near the house. But there was a wild beauty to the untamed bushes and wild flowers. Megan leaned down to pluck a particularly pretty blossom that caught her eye, when pair of intense golden eyes startled her.

She had seen eyes like that before on the ghost lion called Kilala. Megan slowly backed away, knowing that if she ran she would trigger the great predator's prey drive. The black shadow of a great cat stalked out of the tangle of bushes. Deep inside Megan knew that this was not the mother cat whose cubs she helped rescue.

The beast crouched low and growled, never taking its eyes off of Megan. She knew that she would never make it back to the house in time. Megan had never been much of a hunter, but her father being a cop had made sure she knew how to handle a firearm. She wished she had one now.

She watched as the body language of the cat changed. Her martial arts training served her well because she was able to anticipate the creature's attack. The ghost lion launched itself at Megan and she just barely dodged the massive weight of the cat landing on her. As it was, the cat struck out with one of its massive paws, clawing a series of gouges on Megan's arm as she blocked the blow meant for her vitals.

Megan couldn't help the scream that erupted from her throat as the claws raked her flesh. A couple more blows like that and she would be finished. *I survived being kidnapped by aliens only to end up dying as a kitty snack,* Megan thought.
*****

Reijo and several other clan members emerged from their conference. He was frustrated at the lack of progress they had made. The clan would band together to protect one of their own, but many of the more cautious members questioned the validity of Megan's connection to their totem animal. Unfortunately, Reijo had no idea where Kilala was. Even if by some miracle they found the cat, how were they going to prove a psychic connection between her and Megan?

The clan members prattled about mundane topics while Reijo stewed in his own issues. The group had entered the gardens to just get outside for a few moments before heading back into the conference room to continue the debate over Megan and Abby's future.

A decidedly feminine scream of pain echoed from the far reaches of the garden. A chill went down Reijo's spine; Megan was in danger. Without so much as a word to the men walking with him, Reijo launched himself over a hedge, drawing the energy blade he always carried with him.

Reijo could hear the confusion behind him and noted that a few of his kinsmen followed on his heels, but he didn't care. His only thought was to get to Megan. He rounded the last turn in the path and froze.

There was Megan clutching an injured arm dripping with blood circling a stalking ghost lion. Reijo was afraid to make any noise for fear that the huge cat would pounce. Behind him a few of his kinsmen gasped as they rounded the corner to see the standoff between the ghost lion and Megan.

The cat's muscles bunched as it prepared to pounce. Reijo knew that if the full weight of that cat hit his Megan she was done for. So he did what any foolishly in love man would do when the one most dear to him was in danger; he phased and roared a challenge to the great cat.

The ghost lion turned at Reijo's outburst and bared its fangs menacingly at the warrior, but then it turned back to what it considered easy prey. Reijo was running full tilt towards the creature as it sprung its attack. Reijo screamed his denial as he realized he would never make it in time to save Megan.

Suddenly a blur of black streaked across Reijo's vision as a second ghost lion entered the fray. It ferociously attacked the other cat who had threatened Megan. Reijo stopped and phased back into his typical shape, watching the battling cats closely as he skirted around them to get to Megan.

Two young cubs protectively flanking Megan's legs confirmed that the second ghost lion was Kilala. The mother cat had saved Megan's life.

The inhuman screams of the battling cats along with the sounds of ripping flesh told Reijo that Kilala's heroics may cost her dearly. He turned towards the raging battle, unable to tell which cat was which. They twisted and turned in impossible positions, each trying to attack the soft underbelly of the other while protecting their own. The skill and ferocity of the ghost lion was awe inspiring. It was this prowess in battle that made it a proud totem for the clan.

Reijo wrapped his arms around Megan, holding her close, the fear of losing her still coursing through his body. He had to touch her to make certain she was in fact alive. With his arms wrapped around Megan he saw his kinsmen gawking at the battling ghost lions, with a few of them pointing towards the cubs at Megan's feet, whispering. While this was not how he would have preferred convincing them of her connection to the clan, perhaps he would be able to use it as such.

Finally one of the cats was able to wear down the other, causing it to make a mistake. The ghost lion took advantage and quickly clamped its powerful jaws around the throat of its opponent, squeezing the life out of it. With a final sickening crunch, the crushing jaws ripped through flesh and tendon to pulverize the bone, leaving one of the cats limp and lifeless. The question was, which one? Reijo promised himself that if it was Kilala that had fallen he would make sure her cubs survived in repayment for saving Megan.

The victorious cat turned from its victim and headed towards Megan. Reijo tensed, gripping the hilt of his blade in case he should need to plunge it into the heart of this cat. The poor creature collapsed at Megan's feet, its sides heaving from the exertion. The cubs whined and nosed the injured cat, licking at its wounds. Thank the moon goddess, it was Kilala.

Megan rushed to Kilala's side, heedless of the danger an injured wild creature could possess. Reijo noticed tears streaming down Megan's face as she gingerly touched her savior. Kilala tried to lift her head to lick Megan's hand, but the effort proved too much.

"We have to help her, Reijo." Megan choked on the words. "She saved me."

Reijo knelt down, wrapping his arms around the trembling Megan. "We will, *jinaria.* I promise."

They stayed like that for a moment until Reijo had to take command and organize his kinsmen. Megan kept the cats calm as men with a healthy respect for the damage such creatures could inflict carefully lifted the injured cat to carry her back to the strong hold.

CHAPTER FIFTEEN

The rambunctious cubs frolicked around Megan's legs as Abby squealed and chased the young cats. Kilala was bandaged and resting in the corner of the sunroom, her golden eyes keeping watch over her children. Every once in a while she would let out a growl to reprimand the cubs if they started getting too rowdy.

It took some convincing to get the household staff and other guests to agree to allow the ghost lion to recuperate in the stronghold. If Megan hadn't charmed or brow-beaten everyone involved it probably would have never happened. She would make an amazing general, Reijo thought.

The clan representatives were still reluctant to get involved with opposing the council even after witnessing Megan's connection to Kilala. But Megan's steadfast resolve and leadership abilities had won the majority of them over. So last night they voted to formally recognize her as a noble of the Tiaret Clan.

Unfortunately, that only afforded her the rights of any other Vukasin woman, which were not many. While it would allow her a choice of who she was with, she would still have to leave them and her children would be taken from her to be taken care of by their fathers in the government schools. Reijo knew that Megan would never leave a child of hers. Something more had to be done.

It was for this reason that Reijo found himself watching Megan as she laughed with her daughter. Megan would have to battle for her own happiness. Reijo knew the risks, and it made his heart stop when he thought about Megan taking those risks, but she had a right to know. She had a right to choose.

Abby's laughter tinkled like shining stars and Reijo sighed. He wanted this. He wanted to keep them there with him, to have this happy home always. Megan wouldn't be battling for her own happiness, but his as well. It was a revelation that his future depended on this one small but capable woman.

Reijo pushed away from the door jam and made his presence known. Megan's eyes met his and her whole face lit up with pleasure. Reijo couldn't help but return the smile. Soon he sobered; time was running out and Megan needed to know.

"What's wrong, Reijo?" Megan's smile vanished from her face as she sensed the tension in Reijo. She knew that he was having some very heated meetings with the other members of his clan. The strain the last few days was palatable. She also guessed that the discussions involved her, at least in part. Many of the recent visitors had watched her with speculative eyes.

Megan was almost afraid to hear Reijo's answer. She worried that he had come to tell her that she was to be shipped off to begin her duties as a breeder and she didn't want to leave Reijo. The large man had wormed his way into her heart.

"There is something important I need to discuss with you Megan. Something that will greatly affect your future. Can we go to my study?"

*****

When Megan walked into Reijo's study she found Kavi sitting by the fire place. When he saw her he smiled and rose from his seat, giving her a small bow of respect.

Halfway across the room, Megan whirled around, causing Reijo to run her over, knocking her off balance. His strong arms wrapped around her, keeping her from falling into a heap on the floor. His arms lingered a little longer than necessary. The feeling of him wrapped around her sent heat rushing through Megan's blood. Her womb clenched with want.

She pushed aside her emotions and used both hands to push Reijo away from her. If they were going to tell her what she thought they were, her world would shatter because she would never allow her daughter to be used as some breeder. She would find a way to escape and hopefully get home. But escape would mean never seeing Reijo, the only man to stir her blood since Richard, again.

Megan was lost in her own thoughts when she belatedly realized that Kavi had been speaking to her.

"I'm sorry…could you repeat that?"

"We may have found a way for you to be free to choose," Kavi repeated.

Megan slipped out of Reijo's arms and sank down into a chair near Kavi. The enormity of his statement hit her hard. If she was free to choose, did that mean she could choose to stay with Reijo?

Reijo growled at Kavi, "You should tell her how before you get her hopes up too high."

"What do you mean?" Megan's head shot up and her eyes locked onto Reijo. Was it possible that he didn't want her here? Is that why he didn't want her to hope?

The *Kijani-a* ran a hand through his hair, a habit that Megan had noticed he did when he became agitated. She looked at him, really looked at him. There were circles under his eyes and he flexed his neck and shoulders as if trying to work out a thousand knots. She knew he had been closed away with various meetings involving his clan members. From the looks of it, whatever business he had to deal with did not seem to be going well.

"What you would have to go through could kill you, Megan." Reijo stomped over to the fireplace, resting his head on the mantle. He couldn't look at Megan as he spoke. "Even if you survive the trial, there is no guarantee that we will be successful with the political maneuverings afterwards. So you may risk your life for naught."

Megan looked at Kavi and he nodded in confirmation. "Will I ever be free if I don't face this trial?"

Kavi sighed. "Eventually, the families that oppose what is going on may change the circumstances of the women that the council is bringing from your world, but politics move slow and I doubt they would change in your lifetime, maybe not in Abby's either."

"What happens to the other women if I can pass this test?"

Kavi looked over to Reijo, unsure of how to proceed.

"She has the right to know the truth, Kavi."

"If you survive the trial, Ghaleb can insure your rights to choose—possibly even extend it to your daughter—but the truth of the matter is we would still need some powerful politics to give a choice to the rest of the women."

Megan leaned back in her chair and crossed her arms. A frown marred her face but she remained silent. Megan wasn't a stupid woman. Years of being a military wife made her very conscious of politics and shady political chess games. Nothing was ever as straightforward as it seemed.

"I assume that Ghaleb has a plan?" Megan cast her steely gaze on Kavi. She had to know what she was getting into before making any decisions. She could handle being a pawn on the chess board out of necessity, but she preferred to be the queen.

Kavi smiled. He had hoped that Megan would step up to the challenge and he wasn't disappointed. His former student had chosen his game piece well.

"I want the details…all the details—including as much as you know about each party's particular political game. I also want to get in touch with one of the Earth women. Her name is Himeko. If I don't get to speak with her, then I won't play this game the *Khalon* has created. Because frankly, no one on this planet truly has our interest at heart."

"Fair enough." Kavi looked over by the fireplace at Reijo. "Do you have something we can make notes on?"

Reijo retrieved an empty journal and a writing utensil.

"I will tell you what I know from my time at the palace as well," he stated as he sat next to Megan. He didn't like what they were asking her to do, but Reijo would make sure he would provide Megan with as much help and preparation as he could.

*****

The image projected on the wall wavered; it was a little disconcerting to Megan to see Himeko's doll-like face distorted by the artwork and book shelves. The connection with the Nardo Clan stronghold was spotty thanks to a hurricane-force storm assaulting the coast where they were located.

"I've looked over the laws and text that Kavi sent me as well as read what I could find here in Daray's home. As far as I can tell, if you succeeded then you would have all the rights given to the men of this planet as a recognized warrior, but it would only be for you. Each woman would need to survive the trial themselves." Himeko confirmed what Kavi and Reijo had told Megan.

"That's what I thought, but I'm not sure every woman could survive what they are describing to me. With training perhaps…."

"Even with training some of us just wouldn't be physically able to conquer such wild conditions without help, and since a central part of the ritual is this is to be done as a solitary warrior, it is highly unlikely they would recognize even a small group or pairs." Himeko's face blinked on and off, causing Megan to miss the last part of her train of thought.

"Can you repeat that? The storm has you breaking up pretty bad."

"I said changing the laws is our best bet, but you are going to need to get some assurances from Ghaleb laid down in writing that the breeding program would be put on hold until after your trial."

"Kavi is already working on that angle for us."

"Good. Make sure you press your political agenda as soon as you are recognized by the council. Don't let them dicker back and forth. I'll try to convince the Nardo Clan to let me come to the proceedings; in fact, if we could get all of the women it would be best. Hopefully putting faces and names to individuals will make them seem more like people instead of a program."

"I'll see what I can do. I have locations on all of the women in our group, but I can't find the original woman who came here. It's like she just disappeared."

"I'll try to see if I can dig up any clues on my

end. Send word to the other women to do the same. I'd hate to think what could be happening to her if she is just being viewed as a successful experiment." Himeko heaved a huge sigh and refused to look Megan in the eyes.

"Something's bothering you…."

"Megan, if this doesn't work…if our choices are taken away from us, I can't live like that. My family honor…my personal honor would demand seppuku."

Megan gasped. She knew that a few women would rather commit suicide than deal with being forced to have sex against their will, but the traditional "honorable death" by disembowelment was a horrible way to die.

"Himeko, give this a chance to work before you do anything drastic. We may not ever get to go back to Earth, but there are some good men here and the planet is beautiful. I think most of us could be happy, if we had the right to choose."

"I understand and I promise, on my honor, that I will support you as best I can through these trials. I just thought you should know my price if we fail."

The projection turned mostly to static as the storm raged near Himeko.

"The Nardo are telling me we need to take shelter. I will contact you again as soon as I can." With that last statement, Himeko's imaged blinked out.

Megan turned to find Reijo leaning against the door frame of the study. "They will be alright won't they?"

Reijo shrugged. "The Nardo stronghold has seen numerous storms and is still standing. I'm sure Daray will do what he can to keep your friend safe." Reijo crossed the room and wrapped his arms around Megan, giving her a small squeeze. Megan melted into the comfort of his body, letting the heat of him warm the cold worry in her stomach.

"I have a question," Reijo murmured into Megan's hair as he held her.

Megan looked up to meet Reijo's eyes. Damn, he was a truly beautiful man. "Yes?"

"Sep-oo-koo…this is a word my race has no translation for. I overheard the woman use this and I don't understand."

"First, the woman's name is Himeko. Second, to understand seppuku you have to understand the culture Himeko comes from. She is Japanese. Traditionally Japan has been a highly formal society with very strict codes of conduct. In that society, personal and family honor are given the highest importance."

"And this sep-oo-koo deals with honor?"

"In a way. It is a ritual suicide, where they use a blade to disembowel themselves. This is performed as a last honorable act to either erase the stain of a dishonorable act or to preserve honor when they would be forced to perform a dishonorable act should they live."

Reijo pushed Megan out of his embrace and held her at arm's length. He stared intently into her face to read if what she was telling him was the truth. He scowled when he could find no guile in her face.

"Why would she do such a thing?"

Megan shrugged away from his hands and turned her back on Reijo. She walked over to the study's window looking towards the twin moons shining in the night sky. She wasn't sure how to answer him, even though she knew she needed to, so she remained silent as she collected her thoughts.

"Megan, answer me!" Reijo growled.

"It's not a simple answer, Reijo." Megan turned back to face him, leaning against the cool glass of the window. "You have to understand, you are dealing with many woman from very different cultural backgrounds. But to be honest, in most of the cultures of Earth, forcing a woman to have sex with numerous men against her will is a highly dishonorable act. None of the woman you have brought here would accept that willingly. A few might be willing to have multiple sexual partners and even have children by more than one man, but only if it is their choice and they get to choose who they are with and for how long. Yet, you must understand that for the majority of us sex and family should be tied to marriage."

"Marriage? I am not familiar with this idea." Reijo sank into a chair. He was beginning to realize that the council knew nothing of these women and hadn't considered that their way of life was so vastly different from that of a Vukasin woman.

"Marriage is both a spiritual ritual as well as a secular contract where two people promise to love, honor, and cherish each other until death. Ideally, we choose one mate to be in our life."

"We call that the bonding though it has been outlawed for many years now. And you had this marriage with your dead mate?"

"Yes, Richard and I were married."

"And that was why you did not seek another when he was gone for so long?"

"I promised to be with Richard and only Richard until 'death do us part.'" Tears shimmered in Megan's eyes. "I fulfilled my promise."

"But you have mated with me and I do not think you wish to commit suicide."

"I chose to be with you, Reijo." Megan's eyes flashed and her fist thumped her chest, "My choice. Himeko doesn't have a choice right now and in her culture the sexual status of an unmarried woman is a major point of honor to a traditional family. In her culture and in her own mind she would dishonor her family if she allowed them to rape her." Megan held up a hand to stop the explanations she had already heard. "You can dress it up however you want; but bottom line is if you force a woman to have sex with someone then it is rape. Himeko would rather die an honorable death than allow that to happen."

"I didn't know…."

"I know," Megan rubbed the bridge of her nose," but you need to understand something and you need to make sure that Ghaleb and the council understand it as well, Reijo. Most women from Earth would rather die than be repeatedly raped. If your breeding program goes through, you better be prepared that most of us will not go meekly along with those plans. We will fight; we will manipulate and kill if necessary. Some of those deaths will be our own, but I can guarantee that some of them will be Vukasins."

"Your species is truly formidable."

"Especially the women. One of our famous writers, a Mr. Rudyard Kipling...a man by the way...wrote a famous poem called 'The Female of the Species' and the chorus states 'the female of the species is more deadly than the male.' It talks about how for all of the species of Earth the female is more dangerous, even when it comes to the human species. If we can't knock some sense into your council, then this planet will see firsthand just how deadly a human female can be."

CHAPTER SIXTEEN

Ghaleb sat in his private quarters, having swept the area for listening devices first. Both Kavi and Reijo had reported that these tiny Earth women were not going to docilely follow the dictates of the council. The households within the other clans housing the women until concrete decisions were made were sending him similar reports. These females may be small physically but their spirit more than made up for it.

He took a drink of wine, wishing it was a stronger spirit. Ghaleb hated using women as chess pieces in this stupid political game with the council. He had been against the breeding program from the beginning. It went against his moral sensibilities to force any sentient being into a life of slavery, which is what this amounted to no matter what pretty words you used to dress it up. He had already seen firsthand what reducing someone to a second-class citizen would do to them.

Ghaleb stared out the window to the twin moons. It was easy to make out the details of the lush landscape from their light. It only darkened when one moon hid the other. Male and female, god and goddess; when they both shined down the path was easy to see. When one hid the other the way became obscured. He felt like it was a fitting analogy for his planet.

Ghaleb turned from the window, but he couldn't shake the memories that crept up on him. Growing up he had been without a feminine influence like most of the population until his cousin Aliah arrived. She had been as bright as the sun and filled with laughter—until her menses had started and then she had been forced to choose a male to mate with. For the next couple of years she seemed resigned to her life, until she bore a son. The council forcibly removed her from the family she and her mate created, and when she refused to choose another household to join they choose for her. With each child taken from her, she became more of a shadow of herself until there was nothing of the bright vibrant young girl Ghaleb had remembered from childhood. It hadn't surprised him when she died during the birth of her last child. Ghaleb honestly believed that she had just given up the will to live. The needs and desires of the men of their world had overshadowed the female, and his dear Aliah had lost her life because of it.

When the throne had passed to him upon the death of his father, Ghaleb had already decided he would try to preserve families and raise the station of the women of his world. Unfortunately, it had proven to be much harder than he had anticipated. The regime was too entrenched. He knew he needed a woman to fight for her own cause because the men in charge needed to be shaken from their chauvinistic beliefs that they knew what was best; the women needed a leader to rally around.

He hoped that he had found the woman he was looking for in Reijo's Megan. She had already turned the cowed woman from Earth into fighters in such a short time. Ghaleb desperately hoped that fire would spread and flush out the treachery within his own court in the process.

He swallowed the last of the wine in his glass and threw his cup in the fireplace, where the flames flashed when the remnants of alcohol on the shattered glass burned away. He was the ruler of an entire planet but he had to rely on the actions of one tiny off-worlder.

A quiet knock on the door brought Ghaleb back from his musings.

"*Khalon*, the council representatives from the Tanis Clan have requested an audience." The servant bowed low, avoiding any eye contact.

Ghaleb growled, causing the servant to flinch, before he composed himself into the calm façade he tried to show the rest of the palace population.

"I will see them in the council chamber in half an hour."

"Begging your pardon, *Khalon*, but they are insisting on a private audience."

"They can insist all they want; they will either see me in the council chamber or not at all. Now go!" The servant scurried out of the room, closing the door behind him.

Ghaleb sank into his chair. Damn Bel of Clan Tanis! He had been scheming to destroy the Ivailo royal line for years. When the Ivailo conquered the other clans, bringing them under a single ruling house, the Tanis had been the second strongest clan and part of the agreement to bring them under Ivailo rule was that should the Ivailo ever fall, then Clan Tanis would be next in line for the royal house.

Few of the other clans remember the particulars of the unification, but Ghaleb was certain that the house of Tanis never forgot that one stipulation. Before the loss of their women, Clan Tanis had never moved against the royal house because the Ivailo Clan greatly outnumbered them and had many alliances to the other clans due to multiple marriages through the years. It was joked that the Ivailo always had an abundance of children. But all of the clans' numbers had dwindled as fewer and fewer women were being born. Somehow the Tanis had not declined as quickly as the other clans, and now they were trying to set themselves up as saviors of the planet with this breeding program after the genetic compatibility was discovered with the first human woman.

A woman who disappeared shortly after her pregnancy was discovered. Ghaleb had no proof, but he was fairly certain that she was being held by the Tanis Clan. His gut was also telling him that the decline in female births also had something to do with the Tanis. Yet, without proof, he could not accuse the clan of any wrongdoing.

Unfortunately, the planet's scientists had not been able to ascertain a cause for the declining female population. Since the majority of the science and medical professionals came from the Tanis Clan, it was difficult to separate truth from lies when it came to those research reports.

Well, it was time to tweak the ghost lion's tail. Ghaleb had his advisor call an informal council meeting to deal with the Tanis issue. He knew that once this game of chess began, Ivailo would either conquer once again or fall for good. He hoped that his pieces could successfully take the board.

*****

"I wouldn't think you would want your troubles aired before everyone, *Khalon*." Bel of the Tanis Clan sneered the royal title as he made his way through the ornate carved doors of the council chamber. Like many of the Tanis Clan, Bel was a man softened by overindulgence. He still carried the impressive height of most Vukasins, but he lacked the hard planes of muscle that the warrior and agricultural clans tended to carry. He was ten years Ghaleb's senior and always seemed to resent having to show respect to one much younger than he. He displayed his wealth in the most ostentatious ways, with more fine fabric and jewels than the vainest woman would wear.

Ghaleb relaxed into his throne at the head of the council table. His ornate throne, like the carved doors, seemed out of place in this orderly chamber. Despite this being an informally called meeting, the majority of the council representatives were in their seats on either side of the long, polished, black stone table. Many had arrived early to await the showdown between Ghaleb and Bel. Ghaleb knew that the Tanis Clan had been quietly collecting support from the other clans, and as best as his spies could tell, the representatives were fairly evenly split between the current royal house and the upstart. A few of the representatives were on the fence, and a few others could be persuaded to change allegiances with the right incentives.

Sighing, Ghaleb sincerely hoped this gambit would work. But it was too late to turn back because of doubts now. Bel was about to send the opening sally.

"Whatever grievance you wish to speak with me about, you may do so in front of the council. My reign shall be marked by open transparency within the political realm." Ghaleb raised his voice just enough so that every council member was sure to hear him, without seeming to raise his voice at all. Many councilors nodded their agreement. It was this appearance of fair and open dealings that had kept much of his support viable within the council.

"Very well. Why have you willfully disregarded the dictates of this council, *Khalon*?" A gasp went up across the council chamber. Everyone knew that while the royal house had certain veto powers, the council could overrule them, and if they did overrule them, the council's decision was final.

"And which dictate would that be, Council Representative Bel?"

Bel slammed his fist on the table, his great

girth vibrating with the impact. "You know very well which dictate I am referring to!"

A cough down the council table drew everyone's attention. "For the clarification of the rest of the council, please specify." A well-honored and aged representative from the Dyami Clan spoke. While Ghaleb respected the man personally, he knew that the majority of the Dyami were pushing to side with the Tanis.

"Why have you not turned the women from Earth over to the breeding program?" Bel demanded.

This was the opening move that Ghaleb had been expecting. He knew that delaying the handover of the women would push the Tanis into making a claim that he was defying the council, and while that may be the unvarnished truth, any decent politico knew that you could spin anything to your advantage, which is what Ghaleb planned on doing.

"The women themselves have put a wrench into your plans, Bel. They organized and rose in defiance against the council's dictates. I felt it was best to divide them as well as give them an opportunity to understand the position they are in."

Bel waved a dismissive hand. "Bah! They are only women, and weak little things at that. Hand them over and we will force them to follow the council's dictates."

Ghaleb burst out laughing, causing Bel to turn almost purple with pent-up rage. "You underestimate these Earth women greatly if you truly believe that." Ghaleb scanned the council chamber, meeting the eyes of every member there. "By now most of you have probably heard rumors of the ruckus one of these Earth women caused here at the palace." A few murmurs and head nods filtered through the crowd.

"Stupid rumors," Bel dismissed. "Who would believe that such tiny creatures could take on a fully phased Vukasin soldier."

"You are right, Bel...especially since the accurate account is she took on a half dozen fully phased soldiers and defeated them. I can vouch for this tale since I witnessed it personally."

Whispers among the crowd increased. Ghaleb had gotten their attention; it was now to put his real plan into motion.

"So one woman is strong; get rid of her and the rest will toe the line," Bel growled in frustration.

"How dare you even suggest that this council commit cold-blooded murder against one of our own?!" Ghaleb stood to his full height, slamming his hands down on the table, glaring at Bel.

Bel refused to be intimidated and jumped to his own feet to stare down Ghaleb. "She is not one of our own; she is a breeder...a woman brought here for a single purpose. If she gets in the way of that purpose then I say dispose of her and find another."

Bel's cold-blooded statements confirmed everything that Ghaleb had heard about the man, but what dismayed him more were the other council members that nodded their heads in agreement to his statements.

"That is where you are wrong, Council member Bel. I received word from the Tiaret Clan recently that this woman, Megan O'Connor by name, has forged a psychic connection to a ghost lion, the totem animal of the Tiaret Clan. So by ancient, irrevocable laws, she is now a noble of the Tiaret and afforded all rights thereof." Ghaleb sat back down and watched the crowd as they digested this new piece of information. Many remarked how such a connection hadn't been heard of in generations, calling it a miracle and an omen from the god and goddess that their blessings will be bestowed once more. Others were more cynical, questioning how such a claim could be verified.

It was the representative from the Nardo Clan that brought the council back to order. "Even if what the *Khalon* says is true, then she will be afforded the rights of a Vukasin woman and be able to choose whom she resides with for two years or when a child is born, whichever comes first. However, it does not change the circumstances of the other women unless they too have formed such connections." The council all turned to Ghaleb in question.

"I have not received any other reports of such occurring."

"Then the point is moot and I demand that the rest of the women be delivered for their role in the breeding program," Bel bellowed.

Ghaleb's mouth quirked up at one corner, "I'm afraid you are wrong yet again, Bel. The point is not moot, since Megan O'Connor has demanded two things from this council as a lawful noble of the Clan Tiaret."

"And what is that?" Bel asked through

clenched teeth.

"She has demanded the right of *Mate Avi Keiger*."

"Preposterous! That trial hasn't been performed for generations, let alone by a woman. She would never survive!" the Dyami representative proclaimed.

Ghaleb shrugged. "If she does not survive then your troublesome female solves the problem of her existence for you. It really doesn't matter what you think anyway." Ghaleb waved a page over, carrying a heavy tome that the rest of the council recognized as the book of clan laws that existed in every clan even before unification. It was said that these laws were handed down by the very gods themselves. While few might still believe in the divine origin of the laws, no one would dispute their immutability; these were the foundation of their culture and society.

Ghaleb opened the tome and began reading: "…any person many challenge the *Mate Avi Keiger* at the joining of the god and goddess moon by the power of their own person, starting with only the clothes on their back. Should such a person survive until the moons are once again two and return to the designated place with their life still intact, they shall from that day forth be called a warrior of Vukas with all of the rights afforded with such a title, equal to any man."

"Since the law clearly states that she cannot be denied the opportunity to attempt that trial, then the council is not needed to rule on that request," the

Torolf representative said.

"Quite so," Ghaleb responded.

"I am assuming that is not the case with the second request."

"It has been requested, by all of the Earth women, that any decisions regarding their future be delayed until the success or failure of Megan's trial is determined for there may be others who wish to challenge the trial. Not to mention, it is my personal belief that should she be successful it would demonstrate that these women have much to contribute to our society and should be included in the decisions regarding them."

The aged Dyami representative rose from his seat. "You have given us much to consider, *Khalon*, and I suggest that we adjourn and deliberate before making a decision."

Bel interrupted. "I would beg to differ. I think that the issue of the *Mate Avi Keiger* be decided now since one of the two joining of the moons occurs within a fortnight. If she is to challenge I believe it is best for all that she do so at the quickest opportunity."

"You would have her attempt this trial during the storm season?"

"If she is truly capable it should not matter."

The council took some time to debate the matter, but in the end Bel won the vote but agreed that any action towards the breeding program would be shelved until after the *Mate Avi Keiger*. They would reconvene afterwards to make formal decisions regarding the women's fates. Ghaleb just hoped it would be enough time to get all of his game pieces in place.

CHAPTER SEVENTEEN

"Two weeks! How can we prepare her to survive alone in that jungle in two weeks?" Reijo had been ranting since he received word from Ghaleb of the council's decision. Kavi was just as worried as Reijo was, but he had a little more faith in Megan's ability to overcome this ordeal.

Of course it wasn't Megan that Reijo really doubted, but this whole scenario. His contacts at court had informed him that the Tanis Clan was stirring up the population against not only Ghaleb and the royal house but Megan as well. They painted her as a viper that was set against denying the Vukasins the right to procreate. They had also made it very clear that if she didn't survive the trial that more women would be brought to the planet for the various households.

Kavi settled himself into a comfortable chair, his old bones creaking. He watched as his former student tried to pace away his troubles. The old man sighed. He now knew what Megan had meant when she said that one of the curses people intoned on her planet was "May you live in interesting times." He was getting too old for the political games and longed for the days when he could properly scold an errant student.

"You can't interfere, my boy."

"Don't you think I know that? If I help her then the challenge is invalid, but I wouldn't send one of my soldiers out into the wilds with a measly two weeks of training."

"Your woman is smart, Reijo. She asked me to help her learn just the basics of plants to forage for. She concentrated on memorizing those that would be in season and most likely to be abundant. She asked if there is any animal life that would be inedible. Right now the biggest worry is her falling into a trap set by some of the carnivorous plants found in the jungle, and at this moment she is studying the images of those and how to extract herself should she stumble on to one anyway."

Reijo ran a hand through his hair, pulling on his locks. With a groan he slumped into a chair. "If it were just the wilds I wouldn't be this worried, Kavi. But the Tanis are dead set against her succeeding. There have been rumbles in the court about a coup against the royal house, and you know as well as I that the Tanis have wanted that throne since its creation."

Kavi steepled his fingers and rested his chin on their tips. He was silent for a moment, trying to absorb what Reijo wasn't saying.

"You suspect them of something, don't you?"

166

"I do. And I am afraid that Megan is in the middle of whatever plot they are planning."

*****

Megan hadn't been able to reach Himeko since their last conversation. Reijo had told her that it wasn't unusual for communication to be knocked out during a hurricane and she shouldn't worry, but she was worried. After being told that she would have to survive on her own for approximately six weeks, without bringing any supplies or tools with her, she was glad her dad had insisted on the family taking a survival course one summer. But she still needed to get word to the other women that this was going down in just a couple of weeks; Himeko was the last of her group, and she couldn't reach her. They were still looking for the original woman who started all of this, though one of the other women thought she was making headway with that. Someone needed to care for Abby if anything happened to Megan. There was just too much swirling around in Megan's head for her to concentrate on anything productive.

She needed a break, which was why she headed out to the garden. Normally Megan would have Abby in tow, but the young girl had gone off with the stronghold's school class. Being the only girl made her a bit of an oddity, but Megan still thought that it was good for Abby to have children to play with and not just adults, even though children were in short supply. Her class for the entire clan consisted of only three boys of various ages.

Kilala and her cubs followed Megan

outdoors, so Megan felt safe enough to let her mind meander. Megan wandered down the path, heedless of destination. Before she realized just how far she had come, Megan found herself on the path headed towards the village that surrounded the stronghold. She decided to continue on and do some exploring.

It took her about half an hour to reach the edge of the village. The reactions from the populace would have been comical if she thought about it. Most were openly curious; a few seemed to almost be afraid of her, but a few were openly hostile. She couldn't understand the ire of some, seeing as how she hadn't set foot in the village other than her brief stop with Reijo, unless of course the man they rescued the cubs from had spread his vitriol against her.

Megan was never one to back down from a challenge, so she walked into the village square-flanked by the family of ghost lions. An outsider might have mistaken her for a queen with her head held high and shoulders squared regally.

Kilala cut in front of Megan and growled low in her throat. In the weeks since the cat had saved Megan, most of her wounds had healed and her cubs had grown considerably. Now all three made a protective circle around Megan, causing her to study her surroundings with a critical eye. She couldn't spot where the threat was coming from, but she trusted the instincts of her animal companions to know that there was a threat somewhere. Her eyes surveyed the immediate area. Most of the people seemed to be going about their daily business; a few gawked in curiosity, but none seemed to pose any threat.

Megan turned to head back to the stronghold, thinking that perhaps just being in a crowd of people had set the big cats on edge. Somewhere along the roofline across the square, a pop of displaced air was heard. Before Megan could register the familiar sound of a gunshot, a burning pain slammed into her left shoulder, knocking her to her knees. Another pop and a tuft of dirt erupted next to her head. Thankfully whoever the shooter was, he wasn't a sniper-level marksman.

By this time, the people realized that someone was firing a gun and began to panic. The ghost lions kept Megan from getting trampled, and the confusion allowed her a bit of cover as she used her good arm to maneuver herself into a safer position. She knew this wasn't some random attack. Whoever had been firing was aiming specifically for her. The question she needed to find out now was why.

Once she had herself positioned in relative safety, she pulled the communicator that Reijo had insisted she start to carry after the ghost lion incident. She had never been more happy than right at that moment that Reijo had an overprotective streak a mile wide. She pushed the button and heard Reijo's voice on the other end.

"Megan?"

"I'm shot, Reijo, and I need help." Megan moved the communicator away from her ear as Reijo exploded into a loud expletive-laced tirade. She didn't have time to sooth his worries. "Just get your happy ass to the village square and come get me!"

She disconnected the communicator and peeked around the wall that sheltered her. Kilala was pressed against her body with her hackles raised, growling low. Whatever the danger was, the cat was pretty sure it was still out there.

Megan felt the rough tongue of one of the cats as it licked her wound to staunch the flow of blood. It didn't seem to be working so well. Her blouse was plastered against her back and arm. It stained her blouse a dark red. Megan was having difficulty lifting her left arm, and she was beginning to feel lightheaded from the blood loss. Megan's limbs were numb and aching from sitting in one position for too long. If Reijo didn't get here soon she didn't know what would happen.

*****

'Shot! Damn that infuriating woman. Could she not keep her ass out of trouble?' Reijo ran down the hall of the stronghold, barking orders as he went. He snagged Akia as he rushed out the door, heading for the stable. In the short time since he had received Megan's distress call, his staff had his mounts saddled and ready. Reijo and Akia quickly settled themselves in the saddle and burst out of the stable at breakneck speed, heading for the village.

It didn't take long for the pair to get to the village. But even in that short amount of time, Reijo knew that many things could have happened. As they entered the village square, Reijo sent Akia off to organize the guard for a thorough search for the shooter. The people of the village had recovered from their shock, and a throng of them congregated outside of one of the shops directly on the square.

Reijo was franticly searching for Megan when he heard the warning growl of a pissed-off lion on the other side of the crowd. Reijo pushed his way through the mass of people, when an older gentleman stopped him.

"The lady is hurt, but those damn cats won't let anyone near her." He grabbed Reijo's arm. "She was talking to us, but she got awfully quiet a few minutes ago."

Reijo's heart sputtered and he forced his way through, regardless of niceties. When the crowd parted to let him pass, he quit breathing. There was Megan, the color of ash with her eyes closed and an angry Kilala standing over her.

Reijo didn't have Megan's connection to the large cat, but he still had to get to her.

"Sshh, Kilala." Reijo held a hand out palm open, hoping to reassure the beast. "It's all right. I'm here now." He pitched his voice low and soothing. He took a couple of steps closer. The cat sneered at him but didn't strike. "I need to help your mistress, Kilala. Will you let me help her?" He took a few more steps closer until he could lay a hand on the warm fur of the ghost lion. At his touch, the cat let the tension melt from its body and gave a pitiful cry. All three cats nosed the still form of Megan as if to beg her to wake up. Reijo was relieved to see the rise and fall of Megan's breast. At least she was breathing, though from the large puddle of blood surrounding her it was clear she had lost a lot of blood.

Reijo took off his tunic and wadded it up, pressing it against the wound at her shoulder, slowly the bleeding down. With one hand occupied with the wound, Reijo scooped Megan up with one strong arm and carried her to the office of the local physician.

He was so focused on getting help for Megan that he didn't register the whispers of the people around him speculating about why someone would shoot a woman and what it meant that she had tamed not one but three ghost lions.

It didn't take long for the doctor to forcibly remove Reijo and the cats so he could tend to his patient. Akia found his commander pacing in front of the physician's office with the ghost lions, all four of them looking like caged beasts just waiting for an opportunity to rip your throat out.

In that moment, it hit Akia just how deep his commander's emotions were for the tiny little virago that lay in the clinic beyond. He knew that if Reijo ever found out who had done this that man would not live through the night. But right now he just hoped Reijo wouldn't kill him for being the one to have to tell him that the shooter had escaped.

CHAPTER EIGHTEEN

Megan was propped up on a mountain of pillows. She was seriously beginning to chafe at this forced convalesce. It was the third day since she had been shot in the square, and despite the fact that her legs worked just fine, Reijo hadn't allowed her to move from the bed. If that man tried to put her back to bed one more time, she was going to beat the crap out of him.

Finally, Megan's watch dog servant left her bedroom after she informed him that she was tired. Almost as soon as the door clicked shut, Megan was up and putting on real clothes. The wound on her shoulder was sore and pulled a little as she leaned down to lace up the boots she was putting on, but it wasn't so bad as to hinder her. The medical technology of this planet was remarkable. What would have taken weeks if not a couple of months of healing on Earth had only taken a little over a day of treatments here.

Once dressed, Megan slipped out of her

bedroom and away from the guard dogs stationed in the hallway; being tiny compared to these Vukasins had its advantages.

As she neared Reijo's study, she could hear raised voices. She heard her name in the conversation and Megan saw red. She was so tired of these arrogant males thinking that they could dictate her life.

The doors of the study crashed open as Megan stalked through. Reijo turned, scowling at the interruption until he saw it was Megan. His gaze softened and he opened his mouth to speak, most likely to spout some nonsense about how her fragile little self needed to be wrapped up like a porcelain doll.

Megan raised her hand. "Stuff it, Reijo."

The projected image of Ghaleb smiled. "It seems reports of your near-death experience were greatly exaggerated."

Megan propped a hand on her hip and glared. "I got shot, Ghaleb. And considering that I have spent most of my time confined to various houses, I'm willing to bet it wasn't because someone had a personal beef with me. So tell me, *your majesty*, what shit have you plopped me in the middle of?"

*****

Reijo's heart had stopped when Megan came bursting into the room. He was fairly certain that he left strict instructions that she was supposed to be resting. Why couldn't the woman do what she was told for once? But he soon realized that if she was a docile, compliant woman then she wouldn't be the

Megan he loved. He was becoming more and more comfortable with the knowledge that he loved her.

Megan showed her intelligence when she discerned that the reason someone was shooting at her had something to do with the royal house. Reijo knew that Ghaleb's game plan had put her in more danger than either man originally thought. In the beginning they had thought the warrior's trial would be their biggest worry, but now it seemed someone was trying to cheat at the game. Reijo had been arguing with Ghaleb when Megan came in about that very thing. Ghaleb was remaining closed mouth about the whole thing but told Reijo to keep a lookout.

Reijo sat back and watched as his woman manipulated Ghaleb into visiting the stronghold to discuss the situation, since he wouldn't speak about it over the communicators. She easily shot down each of the monarch's excuses until a grand tour had been planned to throw off suspicion. Ghaleb would travel to all the clan strongholds and specifically visit the households that housed the Earth women. On the surface it was to appear that he was checking their wellbeing as well as attempting to draw more support away from his political opposition.

Over all it was a smart plan. It allowed those loyal to the royal house to gauge first hand who was friend and who was foe, while also allowing Ghaleb to meet with his support network. Reijo doubted that he and Megan were the only game pieces Ghaleb had in play.

"I do suggest that you keep a set of loyal

body guards with you at all times, Ghaleb," Reijo cut into the conversation. "You will be more vulnerable outside of the palace walls. If I was your enemy, that would be when I would strike, and while you may be able to surprise your first stop on the itinerary, you know as well as I do that the rest of them will be ready for you even if they do not know your exact timing."

Satisfied that she would get the answers she wanted, Megan informed Reijo that she was going to the kitchen to get some 'real' food, giving him a colorful description of what she thought of his 'healing' foods. His eyes followed her as she walked out of the study.

"You have one hell of a woman there, Cousin."

Reijo turned his eyes back to the projection of Ghaleb, "Yes, I do. And I plan on keeping her alive, happy and with me for the rest of her life. Know this, Ghaleb, if I lose her there is not a force in this universe that will be able to stop my vengeance. Not even the friendship of a beloved cousin."

All of the childhood softness had left Reijo. He had made his choice to sever old ties if necessary to forge new ones with Megan. On one hand Ghaleb was glad that his cousin had found someone to love; on the other he knew that he had to tread carefully or risk losing one of his strongest allies.

"Your enemies are my enemies, Reijo. The vipers have come to nest within the walls of my own house. I am sorry that this has put Megan in danger. The game has progressed much more rapidly than I had anticipated." Ghaleb held up a hand to stop Reijo's interruption. "I will give you everything I know once I arrive, as it is no longer safe to speak of such things here."

Reijo nodded. "Then we expect you to arrive within a few days. I am assuming that certain factions are still pushing for Megan to participate in the *Mate Avi Keiger* in eleven days, despite the fact that she was shot?"

Ghaleb rubbed the bridge of his nose. Reijo noticed the dark circles under his cousin's eyes. Things were obviously not going well at the palace.

"Yes, Bel has been very vocal, calling the injury a ploy to delay even further. Unfortunately, his popularity grows within the council. If things continue as they are it will not be much longer before the royal house of Ivailo will have more power within the government than the Tanis."

"Let's hope you are as good a political strategist as you think you are then."

Reijo said his farewells, switched off the communicator and walked to the window that overlooked the gardens. From the outside, everything seemed peaceful, but Reijo knew that even in that manicured space, dragon spiders devoured other insects and the struggle for dominance and power continued even in the tiniest creature. He just needed to make sure that those he cared for were the ones who survived the struggle.

"Come out, Kavi. I know you are hiding here somewhere."

"You were always one of my more

perceptive students, Reijo, despite your unwillingness to apply yourself."

"I have known for years that the persona of harmless historian and teacher has served you well. It allowed you access to all of the most powerful houses for extended periods of time. I'm sure you garnered much information for the royal house as their eyes and ears. Now tell me what Ghaleb isn't willing to." Reijo turned his dark blue gaze on Kavi. Gone was the by-the-book commanding officer. In his place was left a man willing to not only die to protect the woman he loved, but willing to kill.

"You do realize that all I have is speculation. There is no hard evidence of treason. If there had been, those involved would have already been dealt with."

"I'm not the crown, Kavi. I am a man trying to protect his family."

Kavi took a seat in front of the fire and waved to the chair opposite him. "Take a seat; this will take quite a while."

*****

It took two more days for Ghaleb to arrive at the Tiaret stronghold. Megan completely ignored Reijo's orders to rest. Instead, she had been spending most of her days with some of his best warriors and trackers; learning things that she would need to survive the coming trial. She also had the tailors working on a few things that were her own ideas. She spent her nights enticing a reluctant Reijo into her arms and her body. She knew he desired her, and she also knew that he was afraid of hurting her. But, damn it, if he didn't start initiating some of their lovemaking, she was going to give up on the whole thing.

Reijo interrupted a botany lesson to announce that the *Khalon* would be arriving momentarily. To keep up the appearance of this being a state visit, the stronghold had been polished to gleaming and the household staff was wearing starchy new uniforms. Reijo was looking dashing in his formal military uniform.

For not the first time the last few days, Megan wished she could get the man alone and stripped naked. It frustrated her to no end that he kept finding reasons not to be intimate with her. Megan sometimes wondered if he had grown tired of her or decided that being together wasn't worth the fight, especially after seeing the opposition he had faced from his own clan. She could imagine that it would be even more difficult for him with everyone else. But, she would catch him watching her, and his heated gaze said everything but indifference.

Megan ran upstairs and changed into her own finery. It didn't take long to don the sapphire blue gown she had created. Reijo had no idea that this particular creation was something he had paid for. *If this doesn't get his attention, then he is probably a lost cause.* She twisted her long red hair into a loose chignon, leaving some tendrils free to frame her face. She used some jeweled pins that Kavi had rounded up somewhere to add some sparkle to her hair. She wished she had access to cosmetics, but it had been a long time since a woman had been part of the stronghold. So instead, she pinched her cheeks and bit her lip to bring color to her face.

She exited her bedroom. Her ever-present phased bodyguard's eyes widened when he saw her, and he started panting like a dog in the summer sun. That reminded her of the old cartoon wolf and made her laugh. The sound carried down the stairs.

*****

Ghaleb's carriage just rounded the turn at the pass. Reijo knew that it wouldn't take long for the carriage to pull into the courtyard. He called his commander to double check that the added security was in place.

It was the wide-eyed stare at the top of the stairs that had Reijo turning to see what had captured his commander's attention. Reijo turned to hear Megan's musical laugh as she descended the stairs. The vision before him hit Reijo like a physical blow. He had always thought that Megan was beautiful, but seeing her at the top of the stairs was like watching a fantasy come to life.

She wore a gown of a deep blue, which made her blue eyes even brighter. The dress had a fitted bodice with a halter top that dipped low in the front, showing her ample curves off to perfection. Reijo could feel saliva start to fill his mouth, and he had to swallow and actively keep his tongue from hanging out of his mouth. His eyes traveled up and down her body. Her hair framed her face and glowed like a halo from the light behind her. The dress was floor length, but as she walked down the stairs, Reijo could see flashes of shapely leg from a slit in the skirt up one side. When she reached his level, Megan looked up and smiled at Reijo and his heart stuttered.

"Well, let's go make nice with the politicians," Megan said before walking away.

Megan walked in front of Reijo, and his cock demanded freedom. By the god and goddess! The woman was going to kill him. While her dress was beautiful from the front, but still respectable, the back…oh the back was something else entirely. Her back was completely bare. It carried down to the curve of her enticing backside; any lower and it would be indecent. As it was, Reijo still had visions of his hand slipping into that dress and caressing that curve. He wondered if she wore anything beneath and, looking at the gazes of the men as she walked past, he wasn't the only one wondering.

"Are you coming, Reijo?" Megan turned back and held out a hand.

Such an innocent question had sent his mind straight into the bedroom and heated nights entangled in her arms. He took her hand as he came closer. He looked over her shoulder where she had been shot. Their medic had done a fine job regenerating the cells of the wound to speed recovery; all that remained was a small puckered scar. He hoped that it was healed enough because once he had discharged his duties with this state dinner, he was going to find out just what she had under that dress.

CHAPTER NINETEEN

Megan leaned into Reijo as they stood together as the royal procession arrived. It disappointed Megan to learn that some of the council had insisted on coming with Ghaleb to see the welfare of the women for themselves. She already knew that Bel of Clan Tanis was among those who decided to tag along, something that none of the men were happy about. Bel seemed to be the greatest obstacle to any plans they were trying to implement.

The carriage opened and Ghaleb stepped out. Reijo stepped away from and formally greeted his cousin, but Ghaleb embraced him like the old friend he was. Megan didn't miss the fact that Ghaleb's hug declared to all present that Clan Tiaret and Ivailo were allies.

A man exited the second carriage, and Megan knew without a doubt that this must be Bel. He reminded her of a younger version of Hikmat. He carried himself as if the rest of the world was beneath him. If the entire clan was like this, no wonder Kavi was so desperate to keep Ghaleb in power, if this was waiting in the wings.

Bel's eyes fell on Megan, and she had to keep herself from cringing in disgust. He examined her like she was a bug under a microscope. He walked over to her. When he neared, his nose wrinkled and a sneer crossed his face.

"*Khalon*, is this how the women are to be cared for? Or have you given them to your favorites so they may rut with them first?" Bel's voice carried in the sudden silence as all eyes focused on him and by default Megan. Megan was suddenly glad she had not allowed Abby to come meet their visitors. She wouldn't allow her daughter to be subject to the treatment she was now receiving.

Megan's anger blinded her, and without thinking, she hauled back and slapped Bel across the face. He seemed surprised, not only that she had struck him, but at the strength behind the blow. A clearly defined red imprint bloomed across the odious man's face.

Megan straightened, making the most of her diminutive height. Despite the fact that these men towered over her, she still gave off the aura of regal distain.

"You have not enslaved me yet, Bel. My life and my choices will remain mine to do with as I please."

"As a woman you will do as you're told," Bel bellowed.

Megan shifted her stance slightly; most wouldn't notice, but Reijo was a seasoned warrior, and he could see someone preparing to defend themselves if necessary.

She snorted. "You obviously don't know the women of my planet. We rarely do as we are told."

Bel reached up to backhand Megan. Reijo was about to intervene but he needn't have worried. Megan grabbed Bel's wrist, deflected the blow, and elbowed him in the solar plexus all in one smooth combination, leaving the council member doubled over trying to catch his breath.

"No man touches me unless I allow it. You would do well to remember that." Megan straightened her dress and hair, once again the elegant and composed hostess. "Gentlemen, if you would follow me. We have dinner prepared and waiting." Megan led the group into the stronghold, ignoring the men who tried to help Bel to stand once again.

The ancient representative of the Dyami Clan chuckled. "That is an interesting woman you have there, *Kijani-a*. Are you sure you want to deal with a ghost lioness like that"

"You have no idea, and more than anything." The representative couldn't help but hear the wistfulness in Reijo's voice.

The entire company moved indoors and headed towards the dining room. No one saw one of the extra servants break off from the group and head towards the living quarters, except for a pair of golden eyes hidden in the shadows.

*****

The dinner was a roaring success. Megan had

charmed everyone with the possible exception of Bel. On the whole, she wouldn't even spare a thought for the odious man if he didn't have such a say in her and her daughter's future.

Megan made sure each guest had everything they needed before she headed to Reijo's study. They had one more piece of business to attend to before she could seek her own bed.

She entered the room to find Ghaleb enjoying a glass of liquor that tasted similar to Earth's cognac but was blue in color. Reijo paced near the fireplace, and Kavi had situated himself across from Ghaleb.

"Ah, Megan...glad you could join us." Kavi smiled.

Megan took a seat and accepted a glass of water. Kavi had figured out rather quickly that Megan preferred not to drink alcohol, so he always made sure to have fruit juice or water available instead.

"Alright, boys...let's get to it."

For the next hour the four of them discussed the shadow politics taking place in the capital and how they affected the women from Earth. Megan learned that not only was Ghaleb's reign being threatened but that the house positioned to take control, should it fall, already had a detailed plan to enslave not only the women already here, but thousands they would raid from her home planet. Their control of fertile females would keep them in power for many years without opposition, but the women would be nothing but property. It was obviously in her best interest to keep Ghaleb in power.

"So we need to figure out a way to chip away at the Tanis power base is my understanding." Megan summed up what she had taken from their conversation. "I'm assuming that my successful completion of the *Mate Avi Keiger* is your opening gambit?"

"And it is safe to assume that the man who shot you did so on orders from the Tanis Clan."

"Is all of Tanis in on this?"

"No. But it might as well be since the faction in power is definitely against us."

The foursome's conversation suddenly stopped as a little known passageway opened in the corner of the room. A large painting swung aside to reveal a secret passage. The hinges squeaked from disuse. Everyone jumped to defend themselves against whatever intruder was coming into the room.

Kilala stalked into the room covered in blood and dragging the body of a man in her massive jaws.

"By the moons!" Ghaleb drew a blade he kept at his side and started towards the massive cat.

"No, stay calm." Megan laid a hand on Ghaleb's arm as the ghost lion let out a feral growl around the body of her kill. "Kilala wouldn't kill without reason."

Megan calmly approached the growling cat and laid a hand on the animal's head, murmuring soothing sounds. The ghost lion dropped the body with a thump and head-butted Megan.

"I had heard that you had connected with the Tiaret totem animal, but I hadn't really believed it until now." Ghaleb looked at the woman and cat in awe.

"Where are the cubs?" Reijo asked.

"Cubs? You mean there are more?"

"She has three ghost lions at her disposal," Reijo claimed with pride.

"Amazing."

"Yeah, I'm great and wonderful." Megan stood and brushed off her dress. "Now let's find out what this is all about."

*****

They followed the trail of blood back towards the family living quarters. Megan's heart began to race as she realized that they were moving closer and closer to her daughter's room. The guard stationed outside of Abby's room lay in a heap; glassy eyes stared unseeing at the ceiling. Reijo wrapped an arm around Megan, and she realized then that she was shaking. What would they find in Abby's room? Was her baby girl alright?

She heard Reijo let out a relieved breath when they opened Abby's bedroom door. Abby was there in the middle of her large bed. One of the cubs had curled up on the foot of the bed while the other paced the room watchfully. The rise and fall of the child's chest let them know that she was sleeping peacefully. Whatever had happened, Kilala had made a quick and silent kill, leaving the child undisturbed.

The men fanned out in the room, searching for clues. Megan found where the trail of blood began. A puddle had formed at the foot of Abby's bed. That man Kilala had dragged to the study had killed a man and then stood in her child's room. *Thank god for Kilala.*

*****

Megan exchanged a wordless glance with Reijo. He knew what she wanted without even having to be asked. He reached over into the bed and gingerly picked up the sleeping Abby. The child contentedly snuggled into Reijo's arms and his heart stopped. Someone had meant harm to this child in his own home. It was an offense he would not let pass.

Unbeknownst to the person who plotted this little episode, Reijo now had the evidence needed to convince the clan to stand behind Megan. The men of his clan were an honorable bunch, and children above all were treasured things. The simple fact that someone would try to harm or take a child would be the fortifying catalyst to bring the Tiaret Clan together as one.

Reijo carried Abby towards his own quarters. Since Megan had basically taken up residence there with him, he didn't see the point in taking the child to her quarters. Besides, his quarters in the stronghold were probably the safest place for mother and daughter to be. Behind him three large black shadows silently followed.

Reijo caught the attention of one of his guardsmen and gestured him down the hall where his fallen brethren lay. He held a finger to his lips, silently telling his soldier to keep this quiet for now.

Gently, Reijo laid Abby into the center of his

large bed. Tomorrow would be soon enough to make arrangements for something more permanent. Kilala and her cubs nosed their way into the room. One cub paced the floor as they had found it in the child's bedroom; another curled up on the foot of the bed. Kilala sat, watchfully, near the only window in the room and made sure she had a clear view of the door.

Reijo knew Abby would be well guarded as they sorted this mess out, but that didn't keep him from summoning a few of his most trusted men to stand watch outside of their master's bedroom.

CHAPTER TWENTY

Back in the study, Megan paced. She had followed Reijo with Abby to assure herself that her daughter was safe. Once that had been accomplished, her distress had bled away only to be replaced by a burning fury. Someone had tried to harm her child. It was an unforgivable act as far as Megan was concerned. While she was not normally a bloodthirsty individual, part of her kind of wished that Kilala hadn't killed the man because she wanted—no, needed—a target for her anger.

The men sat across the room from the furious woman. It was only their sense of self-preservation that kept them from trying to comfort and protect Megan. Megan snorted. *At least they aren't stupid*, she thought.

Megan whirled around on the men, her gaze laser focused, "What did that man want with my child?"

The men exchanged glances, and Megan could see the wheels turning about how much they should tell her. Men were all the same, thinking they needed to protect the poor defenseless woman. Megan didn't have the patience to deal with misogynistic bullshit right now.

"Tell me now!" Her voice echoed through the study loud enough that the guards outside burst through the door.

Reijo assured the guards that everything was fine and dismissed them. Finally Kavi was the one who decided to address Megan.

"If it is any consolation, I don't believe the intruder intended to kill your daughter." Megan's eyes narrowed and she crossed her arms but said nothing. "We found a dark cloak and restraints. I believe his intent was to smuggle the child out of the stronghold."

"For what purpose?"

"I cannot answer that with any certainty, since the man is now dead."

Megan's fingers played a thoughtful tattoo where she gripped her arm. "What do we know about him? Anything that will tell us clan affiliation? Perhaps a clue as to who hired him?"

"What makes you think he wasn't acting on his own?" Ghaleb inquired.

Megan shrugged. "The timing is too convenient. He came during a time when strangers in the stronghold wouldn't be questioned. Plus the only people we have let in other than those who are regularly here came with the guests and their entourage. Since I know he is not a regular here in the stronghold, that tells me that he had help getting here from one of the guests. My question is, why target a child?"

Reijo put his arm around Megan and drew her into his arms. For a moment she stood rigid against him, but soon she let herself melt into the comfort of his arms. "*Jinaria*, there are many reasons to take Abby.... If nothing else she is female and one day would be able to bear children. But I think this has more to do with you. She is your weakness and you are a threat to many here. If someone controlled your daughter, in effect they could control you."

Reijo's words hit Megan like a stone. He was right; she would sacrifice anything to keep her daughter safe. Her shoulders slumped and she began to cry into Reijo's shoulder. "What am I going to do, Reijo?"

"You aren't going to let these bastards win. That's what you are going to do." Ghaleb slammed his fist on the table for emphasis.

Megan wanted to think of Ghaleb as a friend, but she knew that he was using her as a pawn in a much larger political game. But his statement still resonated with her. She had never been the kind of person to back down from a challenge.

"I will make sure Abby stays safe during the *Mate Avi Keiger*. No one will harm her. It is you I am more worried about. If they cannot get to you through Abby, then I am fairly certain they will strike at you directly." Reijo gave Megan a squeeze. She knew that he was a lot more concerned than he gave off. It was one of the things she loved about him.

Love? Did she love Reijo? She had loved her husband Richard. Theirs was a deep, sustaining love. The fierce want she felt for Reijo was decidedly different; but was it love? When this threat manifested, she wanted Reijo's arms around her comforting her. She needed the touch of his skin to fall asleep at night now. She trusted that Reijo would keep Abby safe in her absence. Trust, passion, want, need…yeah, she was in love with the man.

"I will still perform the *Mate Avi Keiger*, Ghaleb. But right now I just want to go to bed and get some sleep. We will figure this out in the morning."

Reijo stood to escort Megan back to their bedroom. Just as they were about to leave the study, he turned back to the two remaining men.

"Kavi, find out who is behind this. I don't care if you have physical evidence of it or not. I have my suspicions, but I need to know for certain who my enemies are. As soon as Ghaleb leaves tomorrow, gather the clan elders. We are going to prepare for war. I will not let this attack on my house pass unanswered."

"Careful, *Kijani-a*. This will be a war fought in the shadows, not in the light of day."

"So be it."
*****

Ghaleb and his delegation had left without a single individual mentioning a missing person, which told Reijo that whomever that man had arrived with knew exactly what the man was attempting. He tried to console himself with the fact that whoever set this up knew by now that the attempt to take the child had failed, but Reijo knew that may make his enemy even more dangerous.

Reijo forced his attention back to the council of clan elders. They were beating the same dead horse at this point, and no action had been decided on. For the most part, Reijo let the elders of his clan decide how things should be run even though as clan head he had the right to make a judgment and demand compliance—a right that he would exercise now.

"Enough!"

The council quieted almost instantly at Reijo's angry bellow. This was the first time their leader had ever showed his temper within the council chamber.

"You can sit and dicker about protocols and precedence all you want, but I have had enough. I will not let this assault on my house...on my *mate*...pass unanswered."

"Did you say mate?" Elod, the young physician who treated Abby was smiling at his cousin while the rest of the council mumbled about rules and regulations.

"I have claimed Megan O'Connor as my mate and her daughter as my daughter." Reijo leveled his hard gaze at each council member in turn. "Listen well, men of the Tiaret... She is mine. I will not give her up and I will protect them both with my life if necessary."

"You would jeopardize this clan for a

woman?" One of the older clan members voiced the question that many wanted answered.

"She is not any woman…she is the woman I love. Without her my life…this clan…it means nothing. By the god and goddess moons! Why are we even fighting for survival if the best things in life—love and family—are to be denied us?"

Someone in the back of the room spoke up. "These actions could be considered treason against the royal house."

"The *Khalon* witnessed this attack for himself and will stand with us should it come to that."

"You know as well as we do that the House of Ivailo may not stand much longer."

"So you would be willing to bare your throat because it is easiest? Where is the honor and the fight of the Tiaret Clan?"

Elod stood and addressed the clan elders, "Venerable elders, I have personally witnessed Lady Megan's ferocity, honor, and self-sacrifice. She is the living embodiment of the values this clan holds dear. She would willing lay down her life for anyone she considers her family, and I for one want to be counted among that number. In the short time I have known her she has brought grace, beauty, laughter, and most of all love to these ancient halls. It is my belief that she is a gift from the god and goddess to remind us all of what Vukas once was.

"It may not be a popular belief, but when faced with the challenge of declining female numbers, we failed ourselves. Instead of making those things that make life worth living—love, family, honor—a priority, we instead dishonored our wives and daughters in a vain attempt to remain in the universe a bit longer.

"The women of Earth are giving us a second chance to prove to be a people worth saving. The Tiaret have always been great leaders and warriors. Our ancient line produced the heroes that even today our dwindling young still learn about as the pinnacle of what a Vukasin should strive to be. Let us once again be the leaders that forge the way towards the path of honor. Give our daughters the future they deserve by starting with Megan and her daughter."

The elders of the clan were silent. No one knew if Elod's words had reached the hearts of the men surrounding the table until the longest-lived elder responded.

"Well said, boy. We have much to consider about how to proceed. We must also address the charges you have rightfully laid at our feet. Perhaps it is time to right a wrong of many years ago. I say we adjourn until this evening, when you shall present the recent addition to our clan, Reijo."

Reijo's stony face cracked into a smile as the old men left the council chamber. He slapped Elod on the back.

"I think you may be wasted in the medical profession, cos. Perhaps it is you who should take the *Khalon's* council seat."

"My motivations are purely selfish, Reijo. I watched you and Megan. I am envious of what you have found. I want it one day, but I can't have it if things remain as they are now."

"Maybe when this is settled you can travel to Earth and find a woman for yourself."

Elod looked wistfully towards the direction of the capitol city, "I don't need to travel to another star system to find what I want."

With those cryptic words, Elod left the clan's council chamber.

*****

Megan met the clan elders that night, but it took another three days for them to finalize the direction they were going to take. Elod's speech had awoken something within the clan leaders, and they became almost zealous in their plans. It was agreed by all that the clan's plans should remain secret until after the *Mate Avi Keiger*. In the meantime the Tiaret clan would quietly fortify itself, preparing for war.

Reijo found Megan pacing beside their chamber window. For a moment he was struck breathless by her beauty, but she was so much more than her outward loveliness. He must truly be blessed by the divine to be given such a gift. At least he had the good sense to recognize her for the gift that she was.

Megan sensed Reijo watching her. She stopped and held out her hand for him. Reijo crossed the floor and wrapped Megan in his embrace. Laying his chin on the top of her head, he looked out the window with her. Most of the landscape was only illuminated with light from the two moons. In the distance one could just barely make out the lights from the surrounding villages. In the quiet it could be easy to forget the troubles that lay ahead.

"You know this most likely will lead to a civil war, Reijo. As much as I am willing to endure to ensure my right to choose, I worry that you may resent me when your brethren start falling in battle."

Reijo turned Megan to face him. He lifted her chin with a gentle finger and stared into her eyes for a very long time.

"Megan, *jinaria*, I would fight the entire solar system if it meant keeping you by my side. I have come to love Abby like she is my own and I cannot stomach the thought of her being passed around from clan to clan. This is the right decision. If it had come to it I would have walked away from the clan, if they had turned out to not be the men I thought they were; but they made the choice—the right choice—to put what was right ahead of what was expected."

Megan wrapped her arms around Reijo and gently nipped at his chest. "Make love to me, Reijo."

With a growl, Reijo swept Megan up and carried her back to their bed. He laid her on top of the covers as if she was the most precious thing in the world. Reijo wanted to love her gently tonight so she would never doubt how precious she was to him, but Megan and his libido had other ideas.

Soon both Megan and Reijo were lost in a frenzy of mating.

Megan didn't even blink when Reijo began to phase as he neared climax. Megan fell over the edge into her climax. Her body spasming sent Reijo over his own edge. She was so lost in sensation that she barely registered the bite that Reijo gave her over her breast as he emptied his seed into her channel.

Reijo collapsed on top of Megan and rolled to the side, tucking her safely in his arms. It didn't take long for Megan to hear the even breathing of a sleeping man. As she closed her own eyes, her hand reached up to touch the mark Reijo had left. Somehow the dull ache the bite had caused felt right. She was proud to wear the mark of her beautiful Vukasin warrior.

CHAPTER TWENTY-ONE

Reijo paced in front of the fireplace. Kavi sat across from him, watching the warrior work out his nervous energy. Finally the old man had enough.

"By the twin moons! Sit down, Reijo. You are making my old neck ache."

Reijo sat down and heaved a heavy sigh but remained silent.

"What is troubling you, boy? You asked for my counsel. I can't very well give it if I don't know what we need to discuss."

"I've started the bonding, Kavi."

"I knew that. I was there at the inn."

Reijo shook his head.

Kavi studied Reijo and then shrugged.

"I don't think you understand, old man. I have bitten her again. I tried not to, but I couldn't seem to stop." Reijo dropped his head into his hands.

"I don't see the problem."

"You don't see...." Reijo sputtered, "In approximately a week's time she will be separated from me for almost six weeks. The old stories say that bonded pairs die if they are separated for a long stretch of time."

Kavi laughed and held up his hand when Reijo started to launch himself towards his old teacher. "I know this is no laughing matter, but I find it amusing how propaganda has turned to fact over the years."

Reijo settled back into his chair, frowning.

"I've made a study of the history of our people, including private journals of some of our greatest bonded ancestors. The bonding doesn't kill. In fact it makes a couple stronger by linking them. You share both your strengths and some weaknesses. You do feel the absence of a person acutely, but that is because should they be injured or worried you would know through your bond and be in a position that keeps you from aiding them, though you would be able to feed them your own strength until you were able to be by their side. As such, most couples chose to remain together at home and in battle.

"The rumor that death would occur happened around the time that the royal council decided our women would be shared to try and save our race. The Tanis Clan played a large part in that decision generations back. In fact it seems the Tanis have been in the middle of controlling women from the beginning." Kavi stopped as if he just realized something that he should have seen all along. Waving away his wayward thoughts, he continued. "Imagine two people madly in love with each other, connected to such a degree that they could feel what was happening to the other. Take one of them away and force them to become intimate, against their will, with another…both of them would suffer the full abuse. Many bonded pairs opted to kill themselves than to suffer like that for a lifetime."

*****

Megan stretched in the morning light. Reaching out for Reijo, her hand fell on cold empty space. He had left early and evidently been gone a while since his side of the bed was cold.

Megan was wondering where he was when a crash outside made her cover her ears. Slowly she began to notice a myriad of smells and sounds. It was enough to overstimulate her senses to the point of making her nauseous. What the hell was happening to her? Did someone try to poison her? Was this a reaction to some drug?

She knew it was doubtful that this was some drug. Reijo had eaten and drank the same things that Megan did, often from the same cup. He would be here suffering too, if that was the case.

Her heart rate ratcheted up a few notches as she became more distressed. She was going crazy. That was the only explanation. Her mind finally decided it couldn't handle everything and she was losing it.

Her mind started racing. The thoughts jumbled together until it became a roar of sound in her mind. Megan squeezed her eyes shut and tightly gripped her head, trying to make the noise subside. Finally her rational mind took over. "Breathe," She told herself, "….concentrate on one thing, push the rest aside."

Slowly the thoughts in her head faded into the background and she was able to choose a single smell or thought to bring to the foreground. It surprised her to discover that not all of the thoughts were her own; a few were voiced with Reijo's voice. He was distressed, just as she was, but for a different reason. She picked up snippets of his conversation, but not enough to discern what he was upset about, only enough to know it had to do with her.

Megan decided to put her new talents to work. She wasn't sure where Reijo was, but she needed to find him and talk to him about what was happening to her. She quickly dressed and then lifted his pillow to her nose and inhaled deeply. His unique scent enveloped her and she was certain that she could find him anywhere.

Megan stepped out into the hall and scented her way towards Reijo. At first it was difficult because the entire stronghold held his scent, as if he had marked it as belonging to him. Megan concentrated on the strength of the scent and was soon able to discern older scents from newer by how powerful they were.

Megan went down the stairs. She had to take her time because everything seemed more vivid. She heard Abby squealing. For a moment Megan worried that someone was attacking her daughter because she should still be in bed, but the noise didn't sound frightened. Megan cocked her head to the side until she heard her daughter again. The sound seemed to be coming from the window on the stair's landing that overlooked the garden. Megan peeked outside to see her little girl running from Akia. Akia wasn't putting a lot of effort in to actually catching Abby. Knowing her daughter's habit for being an early riser, Abby most likely was wandering the stronghold looking for the kitchen or maybe even Akia, whom Abby seemed to have claimed as her personal playmate. It made her smile to watch her daughter play so happily, and she smiled even more at the care and consideration of Akia.

Turning from the touching scene and following her nose, Megan found herself outside of a door she had rarely crossed. This was the public area of the suite that Reijo had assigned to Kavi. Megan opened the door a crack and caught the gist of their conversation. Evidently her heightened senses were caused by the love bites Reijo had given her during sex. This was also why Reijo was so distressed.

It should have bothered Megan that she could feel his emotion and catch bits of thought, but somehow it felt right to be connected that closely with the man she loved.

Megan took a deep breath and made her presence known.

"Well it's too late to worry about it now," two pairs of eyes snapped to her face, "seeing as how the connection is already forming. Besides, with people trying to kill me, I kind of like the idea of Reijo knowing if I am in trouble during this whole mess."

CHAPTER TWENTY-TWO

The week passed quickly and Tiaret Clan found itself prepared for the journey to the *Mate Avi Keiger*. Once the decision had been made to stand alone against the dictates of the royal counsel, Megan found herself and Abby enfolded into a tight-knit, highly protective family. She had won the respect of several of their celebrated warriors and trackers as she crammed as much knowledge into her mind in preparation for the task ahead.

"Where's Kilala? I haven't seen her in over a week," Megan asked Reijo as the servants loaded their carriage for transport to the slip stream depot.

Reijo wrapped his arms around Megan and gave a squeeze. He knew she was nervous about succeeding. Damn the moons, he was nervous as well. He was trying to decide if he was truly worried or if he was feeling her emotions. He had completed the bonding the day she had discovered him talking to Kavi; now the empathic connection went both ways. It was very intimate, even if it was a little unnerving.

"*Jinaria*, you knew she might return to the

wild once she was fully healed."

"I know…I guess I had just hoped she would go through the jungle with me."

"You can do this, with or without the ghost cats. You are an amazingly strong woman."

"Are you sure I will be able to talk to Himeko before I start the trial?"

"Daray promised she would be there, and his household is supposed to come have dinner with us when we arrive."

"I know, but he could still leave her behind."

"Daray is a man of honor. Besides, I think he is as taken with Himeko as I am with you."

Megan's eyes widened, "Really?"

Banji approached Reijo and saluted before the men gripped forearms in greeting.

"It's good to have you back, Banji. I know Akia has missed your smiling face."

Banji laughed and then looked over at Megan, who was holding Reijo's other hand.

"I see my brother wasn't exaggerating with the tales he has told me since my return, *Kijani-a*."

Megan's hand ventured forth to lay over Banji's bicep. "I'm sorry for injuring you."

Banji smiled. "I'm not. Only a fierce warrior fighting for what is right can change the world. I suspect you will have more than my blood on your hands before this is over." Banji leaned down until he was nose to nose with Megan. "Do you think you can do what is necessary, little Earth woman?"

Megan pulled herself to her full height. "I would slaughter the whole world to protect my daughter."

Banji let out a loud guffaw, causing the servants to turn to see what the soldiers were doing. "Well hopefully it won't come to that extreme, little sister."

Reijo coughed, "Well, let's get back to your assignment. I'm putting you on Abby's protection detail with Akia. We are going into the middle of the viper's nest, and she has already had one attempt on her life."

Banji's cheerful countenance darkened. "Who would dare to harm a child? What happened?" he roared.

Megan slugged him in the arm. "Keep it down you big oaf. Abby doesn't know about it and we don't want to worry her."

"During Ghaleb's visit, someone tried to spirit Abby away. Megan's ghost lions killed the man and stood guard over Abby without even waking the child."

"Really? Megan can truly control ghost lions?"

"Not control them. She has a special bond with a specific set of the cats."

Banji whistled. "Still, that is impressive. Even ghost lions born in captivity have never been tamed as far as I know."

"Anyway," Megan directed the men to the matter at hand, "the lions have returned to the wilds and we don't know if or when they will make another appearance. This leaves Abby vulnerable. The people working against us know that she is my weakness. If they can't get to me, they will try to get to her. So either you or your brother is to be with her at all times until this task is complete."

Banji nodded. "You do know that if you succeed and the clan's plans become known, we are probably facing war and then no one will be safe."

"I know," Megan sighed. "We will deal with each problem as it arises. In the meantime I would like to ask you a favor."

Banji looked surprised. He quickly recovered his composure and bowed low, "If it is within my power, M'lady."

"Teach Abby to be a warrior. We are facing an uncertain future. Abby may be a child, but even a child has a better chance of defending itself if they have the knowledge."

Reijo and Banji both sputtered.

Megan held up a hand and continued. "I know you start teaching your males even younger than Abby is right now. Don't leave her defenseless. Kavi and I started with basic things. I will not be here for over a month, and Kavi is too old to continue the physical lessons. I am asking you to give her a fighting chance. As someone who was once helpless, I beg of you, don't leave her helpless just because she is female."

Megan turned to face Reijo, "And you, my beloved, might want to consider training all of the females within the Tiaret clan to defend themselves because Banji is right: everyone suffers in war. Even if it doesn't come to war, I am fairly certain that there will be those who will seek to steal the women away or worse. Don't let them suffer like I once did. Give them a fighting chance."

Reijo gathered Megan up into his arms, "You know I hate it when you are right, especially when it is something I hadn't even considered."

Kavi called out in the distance and walked towards the trio holding Abby's hand. Behind them Akia walked a respectful distance away until Abby motioned for him to catch up and held out her other hand. The look on the tough warrior's face was priceless and made Megan's heart melt. It was obvious that little girl had him wrapped around her finger.

"Time to head out. Let's get moving so I have some time to soak these old bones in a warm bath before bed tonight." Kavi gestured to the waiting line of carriages. It was a tight fit to squeeze all six of them into a single carriage, but no one complained for the sake of safety.

As the carriages rolled out, Megan pondered the fact that it wasn't that long ago that she had made this journey in reverse. So many things had changed in such a short time, and the gods willing she would change them even more.

CHAPTER TWENTY-THREE

They had arrived in the jungle city of Tilan late the previous night. Normally they would have booked rooms at the local inn, but Ghaleb pulled rank as a royal and the entire party, friend and foe, found themselves housed by the graciousness of the Dyami Clan. Much like the cities governed by the Tiaret, this area had artwork depicting the Dyami totem animal. It was a giant bird of prey, very similar to the eagles back on Earth, though much larger. Reijo called them sun raptors.

The Dyami Clan head was a stately man named Fadri. He was standing by a large stone carving of one of these creatures when he greeted the Tiaret entourage. He kind of reminded Megan of a Buddhist monk. His face was stoic, and he was dressed in ceremonial robes. He was intimidating because he gave the impression of immeasurable knowledge. The fact that he brought Susan, the tall beautiful black woman she met during her time in the woman's wing of the royal palace, comforted Megan. Her irreverent energy allowed Megan to relax.

It seemed like the other Earth woman was being treated well, and despite a nearly constant exasperated look from Fadri, it was obvious the serene Vukasin held affection for the brash Earth woman.

Susan had let Megan know that Himeko had arrived with the Nardo delegation earlier in the day. In fact most of the women had accompanied their various keepers here. It was planned for the Earth women to have breakfast together the next morning.

*****

Megan had barely slept. Nervousness from the upcoming task as well as excitement from seeing others from her home world had made it difficult for Megan's mind to shut down enough to sleep. She jumped out of bed as soon as she spotted the rosy light filling the sky through the window. She kissed a still sleepy Reijo and Abby as she threw on clothes to rush out for her breakfast meeting. She nearly tripped over Banji on her way out the door. Megan waved an apology as she flew down the hall.

*****

Megan enjoyed a companionable hour eating breakfast with the women. So far, nine, including Megan, of the dozen women taken for Earth had arrived. The women who had been given to the Torolf Clan wouldn't be at this ceremony because that clan led the agricultural production on this planet and they were in the middle of their seasonal harvest. The Torolf leader assured Ghaleb that he would bring the women to the closing ceremony in six weeks. So really the only ones they were concerned about were the mysterious first woman and Maria.

Maria had gone to the Tanis clan. She and Sara, the other woman sent to a Tanis household, had traveled together for little while. Sara had been dropped off with Cais, and Maria was supposed to go on to another house. Unfortunately, Maria never arrived at her destination. The carriage had been attacked and her escort killed. No one knew if she was alive or dead.

"I am going to assume that since her body wasn't found with the rest of the escort that she is alive—most likely kidnapped by people within the Tanis, since most evidence seems to point to those bastards being the ones who want us treated like slaves. No offense, Sara."

Sara shrugged. "None taken. The Tanis I have met give me the willies. Honestly, Cais and his friends seem to be the exception rather than the rule. He's tried to protect me from the rest as much as he can, but it isn't always easy." The look in Sara's eyes was a bit haunted, and Megan could guess the kind of treatment she has received from Bel and his ilk. "It isn't just me though. That clan treats their own women horribly as well. In fact I overheard one of the men talk about the auction they have set up to sell off their daughter's virginity to the highest bidder."

"That's horrible." Susan took a sip of her juice to get rid of the bad taste in her mouth.

"They do that in my home," Parvati added. "Well, maybe not an actual auction, but the families arrange marriages and often the woman goes to the man with the most money or highest social standing. Even in the more modern areas of India, the family has a lot of control over who a woman marries."

Megan growled. "My daughter will always have a choice, even if I have to kill to ensure it."

The women at the table were taken aback by Megan's vehemence.

Susan lightened the tense atmosphere. "Too bad we don't have a choice here. I've got to tell you most of these Vukasins are yummy. I mean have you seen the ass on Fadri?"

The table burst into giggles as the breakfast descended into gossip about what makes a man sexy. The women kept up their lighthearted banter for a little while until the meal finished.

Once the servants had cleared their breakfast away, Himeko brought up the need to discuss their plans.

"I know the royal counsel has agreed to hold off making any decision about us until after your trial, but while your success here will help you and maybe your daughter, I'm still unclear how this is going to help the rest of us." Susan asked the question that many of the women had been wondering about.

Megan sipped her juice to collect her thoughts. She wasn't sure how much to reveal to the women, not because she didn't trust them, but because she never knew what spies could be listening.

"Both Himeko and myself have been

studying the laws of this planet to see if there is a way we could work within the system. Frankly, we might as well resign ourselves to living the rest of our days out here. They aren't going to let us go, and I'm not sure I can blame them seeing as they view us as the way to save their planet." Megan paused as the other women murmured. She was surprised to hear many of them say they didn't mind staying as long as they weren't slaves in the process. It seemed that she and Reijo weren't the only ones making a connection.

"Originally I was hoping to succeed in the *Mate Avi Keiger* because it would give me the right to form my own clan. That is one of the reasons that the trail hasn't been attempted in recent memory—well that and its survival rate is quite low. But if I succeed, I would extend to each of you the invitation to join my clan. Since that new clan wouldn't have been conquered by the royal house, it would mean that I could argue that we are not subject to the ruling of the counsel. It would mostly be a political stalling tactic until we could gather allies to help us. But that plan has been kyboshed by my connection to a ghost lion, which makes me a member of the Tiaret Clan by ancient law." Megan paused and took a deep breath. "So honestly, I am not sure where to go from here. I was kind of hoping ya'll would have some ideas."

"Why can't you be a part of Tiaret *and* form a new clan? I have dual citizenship back home," Susan interjected. "What? I was an air force brat born overseas."

Himeko looked shocked for a moment. Megan looked over at the little Japanese lawyer and wondered why they hadn't considered something like that.

"Himeko, you are better with the laws than I am. Would that be possible?"

"I honestly don't know. I don't remember seeing a precedent for that, but even if there isn't one we still might be able to use it. But you would have to act without giving them time to think. Invoke your rights as soon as your return from the trial. But that would only work if there isn't already a precedent blocking this action."

Susan turned to Himeko. "How long would it take you to find out for certain?"

Himeko's head bowed. "A few days of research if I don't do anything else...realistically, a few weeks."

Almost as one the women slumped in defeat.

"So you wouldn't be able to tell Megan before the trial starts tomorrow." Sara sighed.

"And I wouldn't be able to get a message to her either because that action would be deemed interference, which would automatically fail Megan."

"Come on, girls. Don't give up so easily. I'm going to be slugging through that jungle for the next six weeks. That's plenty of time to get the research done, especially if you talk to Kavi, Himeko. That man has a veritable law library in his head. We just need to figure out a way to let me know if I should come back with all guns blazing or not."

The table fell silent as the women thought about what to do.

Parvati was the one who finally spoke up. "We just need to let Megan know to either yes, hit the politics of a new clan now, or no, don't. Correct?"

"Basically."

"So why can't we use some sort of visual signal at the closing ceremony?"

"It would need to be something big to make sure she would notice it," Susan said.

"But it would also need to be something that the rest of the Vukasins wouldn't notice."

"What if we all wore the same color clothes that day if she should form the clan?" Sara looked around the room but lowered her eyes when she noticed the other women gaping at her.

Soon she was engulfed in a giddy hug by Megan. "That is so simple it's brilliant. What color clothes does everyone here have?"

It took a few minutes of discussing wardrobes, but soon the women discovered that each of them had something in red.

"So it is agreed? Himeko will let each of you know if we should push the political agenda. If I am supposed to be the aggressive politician, then I will see each of you in red when I come out of the jungle, right?"

The women agreed with the plan and went their separate ways. Himeko lingered behind with Megan until the other women left. Megan turned to the woman she now considered a friend and let the hope she had plastered on her face fall for a bit.

"I'm worried, my friend." Megan leaned against the door frame. "Even if I somehow survive, it still may not change anything."

"Megan-sama." Himeko added the honorific for a person in a leadership position above her to Megan's name. "Without you we would have retreated into ourselves and let fate decide our futures. You crashed into our lives and gave us the strength to be more than just frightened women. I have faith that the gods would not have given you such strength if it was all for naught. Even if this tactic doesn't work, then we regroup and try something else. We will either change the world or die trying. But even if we die," Himeko laid a hand on Megan's shoulder and gave it a gentle squeeze, "at least we die with honor."

Megan laid her hand over Himeko's, "Thank you." She pushed herself away from the wall and smiled once more. "Now let's go see what that stuffy monk wants to tell me about this mess."

CHAPTER TWENTY-FOUR

Strong arms wrapped Megan in warmth as Reijo nibbled that spot just behind her ear that sent shivers down her spine.

"How was your meeting with Fadri?" His warm breath caused Megan to giggle slightly.

"I have to survive the carnivorous jungle and make my way to a scared temple hidden in the heart of it, even though no one living is really sure of its location. The gods must gift me with some divine weapon at the temple, and I must make it back to civilization all before the two moons separate, which is approximately six weeks, but not exactly. And I have to accomplish it all by entering the challenge with just the clothes on my back. Piece of cake." Megan turned in Reijo's arms and wrapped her own around him. Despite all of her bravado, she was afraid. So much was riding on her completing this task.

Megan knew Reijo could feel her tension. He didn't even need the connection the bond had formed. The man had become an expert in reading her emotions. It made Megan feel cherished. Reijo nibbled and kissed his way down Megan's neck while his hands pushed up under Megan's tunic.

Megan leaned back against Reijo's strong chest. She let her worries slip away for a little while. *Tomorrow can wait, right now is what matters.* Megan blazed her own trail of kisses across Reijo's chest and neck. She had to pull him down from his towering height so she could give him a searing kiss on the mouth. She nipped and sucked, promising the pleasures to come without saying a word.

Megan was reaching down to shuck her tunic when the door of their suite banged open and a small shrill voice yelled, "Momma!"

Megan laid her head against Reijo's chest and sighed.

"Remind me to start locking the door," the big Vukasin growled.

Megan laughed. "Hate to inform you, but that won't keep the children out. I know from experience."

Despite Reijo voicing his frustration, his face still lit up when Abby came running into the bedroom and flung herself into his arms. His love for that little girl glowed from every pore. Megan knew that if something happened to her, Reijo would see Abby safe.

They had even discussed in the dark of night that, should Megan survive but fail this trial, he would find a way to sneak Megan and Abby back to Earth, even going so far as to suggest he desert his own home world to be with the family he loved. Megan knew that it would be unfair to ask him to sacrifice so much; besides, she would never feel right about being safe back on Earth but leaving the other women who have become her friends here to suffer a horrible fate. In either case, her failing at this task was not an option.

Abby bounced up and down on the bed until Megan reminded her that they don't jump on beds.

"I'm sorry for the disturbance." Kavi entered the room at a more sedate pace than his charge. "Abby insisted that she had to give you something right this second."

"What is it, sweetheart?" Megan turned her attention back to her daughter.

"I made you a sur'bible bracelet. So you will sur'bibe and come home." Abby handed Megan a woven rope bracelet. They had learned to make them at a social on the base before her husband had died.

"The little one was very intent on getting a thin piece of rope that was strong enough to hold an adult. You have a very sharp child."

Megan nodded, tears coming from her eyes. She thought that she had sheltered Abby from the troubles going on around them better. She had no idea that Abby had absorbed so much because she seemed like a typical, happy child, even with all of the dramatic changes in their circumstances.

Reijo picked up the woven band from Megan's hand. It looked like a simple child's project. "How will this help you survive?" he asked Megan.

"These were popular back on Earth. The band is made from one continuous rope that is a few meters long and strong enough to hold the weight of an adult. When you are in a dire situation, you unwind the weave and you now have a useful tool. Some of the ones back home even had small knives and fire starters woven into the band."

Reijo fastened the band to Megan's wrist, "I would feel better if this also hid blades and fire, but they will search you thoroughly for that before the trial. But this is ingenious."

Megan looked over at Kavi, "You have no qualms about me cheating?"

"M'lady, I do not consider this cheating, but rather a creative use of the restrictions placed upon you, and to that end, I have my own gift to give you." Kavi presented Megan with a box.

In the velvet-lined box lay a beautiful pair of carved wooden hair sticks, the tops of which had a ghost lion carved into them.

Before Megan could express her thanks for such a beautiful gift, Kavi lifted one of the ornaments.

"You must wear these in your hair when you start your trial. The officials will search you over; but they cannot take from you anything you are wearing unless it is a weapon. When they look these over they will only see a pretty piece of carved wood, but if you know the trick," Kavi depressed one of the carved paws on the hair stick and, with a click, the cat separated from the shaft, "it becomes another tool." Kavi pulled the carving away to reveal that the hair stick was actually a very thin sheath for a needle-like blade. "I'm fairly certain that our ancestors chose their ceremonial clothing just as carefully as we are."

Kavi beckoned Abby back to his side. "Now that you have given your gift, little one, it is time to resume our lessons."

Kavi left the room with Abby, and Reijo heard the lock fall into place so they wouldn't be disturbed again. He smiled; the old buzzard raptor was growing on him.

"Now where were we?" Reijo asked. Megan slid a hand up under his pants to cup Reijo's manhood in response. "Ah, yes of course.... Back to business then."

CHAPTER TWENTY-FIVE

All eyes were on Megan as she made her way to the platform. She was to start the *Mate Avi Keiger* with only the clothes on her back, and her outfit was causing something of a stir.

Megan had asked in the beginning if she would be required to wear some sort of ceremonial garb and was told that traditionally those who took the challenge dressed as warriors. So she had asked the Tiaret weavers to create a few yards for her in a particular pattern. Those yards were now pleated and draped around her like a cloak. She had originally wanted enough plaid fabric to pleat into a kilt, but the weavers had never created a plaid pattern before and were unable to produce enough. She wore a loose-fitting shirt with its long sleeves tied back to expose her arms. Knee-high leather boots covered the lower half of her legs while tight leather leggings covered the rest.

While the Celtic-inspired clothes were odd enough in this place that seemed to prefer clothing that felt more Persian to Megan, it was the swirling blue designs painted on her face and body that had the tongues wagging. Kavi had helped her find a plant that would dye her skin the vibrant blue color while missing the numbing properties that real woad would have inflicted on her skin. Today she wasn't just Megan; she was an ancient warrior released to bring forth justice.

"Are you sure the blue stuff was necessary?" Reijo whispered as he led Megan to the top of the platform where the ceremony would begin. He couldn't help but hear the whispers of the people around him.

Megan lip quirked, "You said to dress as a warrior, so I have added elements to remind me of the warriors my ancestors were. Just be glad I decided not to go completely traditional."

"Why is that?"

"A Celtic warrior, be they man or woman, traditionally went into battle with their sword and the blue woad painted on their body."

"You can't seriously mean…."

"Yup, we went into battle," Megan stepped up on the final step, turned, and grinned at him, "naked."

Megan couldn't help the laughter that bubbled over at his shocked expression. She quickly suppressed it at the glare the Tanis delegation gave her. She took her position at the center of the altar platform while Reijo joined the representatives from the Tiaret Clan.

Each of the six clans had people standing under ceremonial arches. The design and age of each arch was a visible representation of the age and importance of each clan. There were also empty arches from clans that had since died out or been absorbed into other clans. Every arch was allowed a voice on the royal council, though until the last couple of generations, those voices had been more advisor than government, but the declining royal house had seen more power being transferred to the council and away from the royal house. Those that succeeded in the *Mate Avi Keiger* earned the right to form a new clan, if they had those willing to follow them. For that reason, Megan was here to face a challenge that had killed so many of the Vukasin warriors that no one had challenged it in over a century.

Megan surveyed the area. They were right outside the gates of a temple complex. The area was built on a hillside, making it a natural stage. Megan had learned that the Dyami Clan was one of the oldest clans because it had formed long before the clan system had been established. The Dyami were the spiritual leaders of the Vukasins. While not everyone born to the clan became monks, everyone within the clan supported the work of the monks. These monks were not celibate monks like Catholics back on Earth; they were allowed to marry and have children. In fact it was almost expected that they would father children to carry on the family work. She also knew that the Dyami was one of the few clans that had openly spoken against the trading of women between families as well as the breeding program.

The loud ringing of a gong startled Megan

from her thoughts. The sound rippled through the throng of people, leaving silence in its wake. Behind the temple gates, the drone of men chanting rose in volume as the monstrous gates, carved with clan symbols, opened. The opened gates revealed a phalanx of Dyami monks in ceremonial robes.

At the apex, Fadri stood as the master monk for this ceremony. With a loud clap of his hands, the chanting stopped. Everyone paused dramatically, the silence deafening. A loud 'whoop' startled the crowd as men wearing elaborate masks leapt over the stoic monks.

As the performers landed, a deep drum beat was heard in the air. It was like a heartbeat that pulsed through the bodies of the crowd. The bells attached to the feet and wrists of the masked men added a tune to the beat of the drum. More drums of different tones followed. The dancers brandished decorative weapons, but their movements were stylized and meant to punctuate and harmonize with the drums.

The whole effect was energizing as the crowd began to sway and stomp to the beat. Megan knew without being told that this was a war cry and a blessing for the warriors. She could just imagine the Vukasins psyching themselves up before a battle with this display.

As the weapon dancers performed across the stage, the monks marched to the deep bass beat of the largest drum until the dancers split like a stage curtain. The final beat of the drum echoed across the audience.

Fadri stepped forward and stood next to Megan. The tall headdress of his ceremonial robes made Megan look even more childlike next to a Vukasin male. A murmur was heard rippling through the crowd.

"This must be a joke."

"Look at her."

"She is too delicate."

"A woman can't be a warrior."

Megan surveyed the crowd and her heart sank. She had earned the respect of the Tiaret Clan and had thought that would have given her a fair shake with the rest of the population, but old prejudices were deeply entrenched. In the end she didn't have to change the minds of everyone, just the royal council. As Fadri gave the ceremonial speech, Megan let her eyes wander over the delegates from each of the clans. Most were represented by their clan heads and council staff. The Torolf had a young teenage boy standing in for the clan head since they were in the middle of the harvest.

Most of the clan representatives seemed either curious about her or unreadable. But one group stood out: the Tanis. Sara and the household responsible for her were noticeably absent despite the fact that the other Earth women who had arrived for the ceremony were standing beneath the arches for their host's clan.

Bel of the Tanis Clan saw Megan looking over and narrowed his eyes at her. Megan knew the man didn't like her, but she was taken aback by the hate that rolled off of him.

"…As the god and goddess moon join as one and the day creatures and night creatures mingle, we ask that their divine blessings fall upon their children. Under their sacred sight another of their children steps forth to prove their life worthy of leadership.

"Since our creation, we have followed the way of the warrior. The gods created this holy ground and provided trials to test the worthiness of the initiate. The lessons learned on this journey will ensure that a new leader will emerge when the god and goddess separate," Fadri paused dramatically, "or they will not emerge at all."

The crowd's protest of her being a woman and not a warrior started up again as Fadri fell silent. It was during this part of the ceremony that Megan was supposed to make a speech. Megan took a deep breath to begin her part of the ceremony when a loud deep voice from behind her beat her to the punch.

"When will we end this farce?" Bel of the Tanis Clan bellowed, and the crowd loudly agreed with him. Riding high on the public opinion, Bel continued, "What woman could actually claim the title of warrior? It is bad enough that this female doesn't know her place. That could be excused because she is not of this world; however, I refuse to allow her to mock our sacred traditions with her ridiculous appearance."

The crowd roared and Megan knew that she had to speak up.

"How dare you mock me and my ancestors?" Megan let every bit of her anger and frustration roar through her voice. "The noble blood of the Celtic tribes runs through my veins. My people fearlessly rushed into battle with nothing but our swords in hand and sacred designs painted on our bodies, and our enemies trembled."

"You are still but a woman," Bel sneered.

Megan tossed her plaid over her shoulder, exposing more of the blue designs up her arm. She placed a hand on her hip and turned to face Bel, though her voice remained loud enough for the crowd to hear.

"You may mean that as an insult, but I take it as a compliment. Where I come from, women were not only leaders but often feared. We were known as capable and cunning, and were you not so blinded by the illusion of importance that the appendage between your legs gives you, you would realize that each woman faces death for every life beneath her breast. That is the very definition of a warrior: someone willing to give their life for the sake of another."

At this point most of the audience quieted down. They were actually listening.

"If your delicate ego cannot handle such an esoteric thought as the dangers a woman faces with each life she births, then allow me to remind you of the fact that I, after being drugged and kidnapped from my home, defeated a half dozen of your palace guards—your own venerated warriors."

"Propaganda and lies put forth by the house of Ivailo." The dissident voices started up once more at Bel's accusation. It was difficult for them to believe that a tiny scrap of woman defeated so many trained soldiers.

Megan held up a hand to Reijo, who was trying to break free from the grip his family had on him. If looks could kill, Bel would have fallen at her feet right then. When Reijo calmed down, Megan faced Bel once more.

"Really? Well, that is easy enough to test. Bring me a challenger and let us see which of us fares better."

The crowd roared. The worlds may change, but males remain the same everywhere. Get them into a group and they go frantic over watching a blood sport.

Fadri laid a hand on Megan's shoulder, "M'lady, if you do this thing you will still have to enter the jungle for the trial when the moons are high tonight, no matter what injuries you sustain. Otherwise, Bel can rightly declare that you failed the challenge of the *Mate Avi Keiger*."

Megan smiled, but it didn't reach her eyes. "I understand, Fadri, but," Megan let her gaze travel across the masses, "they must believe in me. If they do not, all is lost anyway."

Fadri nodded, accepting her decision, and turned to Bel. "A challenge has been issued towards your house, Bel of the Tanis. Will you choose your champion or concede now?"

"I will choose a champion," Bel growled.

"Then the Dyami will act as arbitrator." Fadri turned and addressed the crowd. "Megan O'Connor has challenged the Clan of Tanis. Bel has accepted this challenge and will choose a champion to face Megan O'Connor in combat. The challenge will take place in two hours in the circle of the valley's amphitheater. The Dyami will stand as judge."

With the declaration, the drums began to beat to disperse the crowd. Reijo rushed to Megan's side, entwining her fingers with his.

"I hope you know what you are doing, *jinaria*."

"So do I, Reijo…so do I."

CHAPTER TWENTY-SIX

"Holy shit!"

Megan's fight or flight instinct had kicked into high gear and she leaned heavily towards flight at this point. The man, if you could call such a beast a man, which walked through the doors at the other end of the amphitheater had to duck and turn sideways just to enter. He was huge, even for a Vukasin warrior.

"He is one of the Tanis Elite. Rumor has it that they are the result of a eugenics project that the Tanis Clan created. They were bred to be bigger, stronger and to feel less pain in battle," Reijo explained to Megan.

"Great…." Megan's sarcasm was not lost on Reijo, "So you are saying I get to have my butt kicked by a super soldier that has been genetically altered to be victorious?" Megan was really regretting issuing the challenge, but Bel just got her hackles up and she wanted to publicly take him down a notch or two. It didn't take much for Megan to realize that her quick temper had walked right into Bel's plans.

"I know that look. You have already lost if your enemy convinces you that you can't win." Reijo wrapped an arm around Megan's shoulders and gave a slight squeeze.

"Reijo, it was one thing to beat off a few men with a spear. I could keep them from getting too close to me. But this is strictly hand-to-hand combat, which means I have to get close, and it looks like just one of his meaty paws would crush me." Megan gestured wildly and her voice rose in pitch.

Reijo grabbed her and kissed her long and hard. He kept kissing until her rigidly locked muscles relaxed and she kissed him back. He broke the kiss and laid his head against her forehead.

"Are you done panicking?"

"If I said no, would you kiss me again?"

Reijo chuckled. "I promise to kiss you every day for the rest of your life when this whole mess is over; but at this moment listen to me. The Tanis Elite are big and strong, but that bulk comes at a price. They can't maneuver as easily as a smaller person. That can give you a tactical advantage. Fadri will call the challenge a draw if there isn't a clear winner before the moons are high in the sky."

"So you want me to just out-wait him?"

"If you can't get in to take him out, then yes I want you to run him ragged. But…" Reijo paused and studied the monster of a man his beloved would be facing, "if you can definitively defeat him, you would turn many of the people to your cause."

"Okay, great and wise *kanji-a*, how do you propose I do that?"

"I noticed that the man hasn't put on a battle collar."

"Yeah, no weapons or armor allowed, according to Fadri."

"That sneaky man." Reijo grinned and pulled Megan into the shadow of the doorway. Anyone looking at them would think Reijo was just getting in one last grope before his female died because of her own foolish boasting.

"Reijo, now is not the time for a quickie." Megan tried to push out of his arms.

"Trust me, *jinaria*, if I thought we had time I would bed you this instant. But Fadri's rules may have given you an advantage." Reijo lifted her hand to his neck. "Do you feel this?"

"Yeah, it's an artery that supplies oxygen to the brain; humans have them too. If I could keep my arms around his neck, I might be able to choke him out, but in the couple of minutes that would take he could do a lot of damage to me. I still need to be able to survive the trial in the jungle."

"While you are correct, I want to you hold your hand there." Reijo phased, and soon her hand was over fur right next to the bony plate that protected his spine. Reijo started speaking again while his clawed hand shifted her hand a little to the right until it was right next to the protective plate. "Right here." His voice was difficult to understand around the lengthened muzzle and teeth of his face.

Megan wasn't sure, but she thought she felt a slight knot under the skin. "A knot."

Reijo nodded and reverted back to his

original appearance. "We wear battle collars because while the phase protects us, it also comes with its own set of weaknesses. One of those weaknesses is that knot. Shifting into the phase causes a bundle of nerves to rise to the surface. A direct hit to those nerves kind of short circuits our system and our muscles freeze, leaving us unable to move for a while. A kill shot is easy at that point."

"I don't have to fight to the death, according to Fadri."

"True, just until one of the opponents can no longer continue. Trust me; we are trained from birth that we are dead if someone hits that nerve bundle."

"Won't that mean he would be expecting that kind of move?"

"Why? You are an off-worlder and a female. As far as he is concerned you are nothing but an annoying insect, easily crushed."

Megan crossed her arms. "Thanks for that."

Reijo smiled and hugged Megan. "I know better, my little virago. I've already seen you in action and I will never underestimate your abilities."

Megan turned when a gong sounded. She heaved a heavy sigh. "Let's get this show on the road. Just in case I don't make it out of this mess, please take care of Abby."

"You know I will."

"And…." Megan's voice trailed off and she bit her lip.

"Yes?"

"No matter what…remember that I love you."

Without waiting for Reijo's response, Megan turned to face her fate.

*****

Megan had removed her survival bracelet and the hair sticks before walking to the center of the amphitheater floor. She didn't want their secrets revealed, nor did she want to chance her opponent using them against her.

Megan considered her opponent as she got closer. She felt like David facing Goliath. Her best bet would be to pull a David and fell this giant with a single blow...quick, with minimum chance of her own injury. But this wasn't a contest just to see who the best was; this was a political game. In this arena, she had to play the crowd, make them love her. Gaining the favor of the crowd takes time. She had a delicate balancing act to perform. More time meant more of a chance for injury.

Fadri stood between the two combatants and raised his hands. The crowd quieted. "Megan O'Connor, faced with the challenged's champion, does the challenge stand?"

"Yes."

The crowd roared and stomped their feet. The whole scene reminded Megan of a wrestling match she attended once.

"Daemon of Clan Tanis, faced with the challenger, do you still accept the role of champion?"

Daemon looked Megan up and down with a lecherous sneer. It made Megan's skin crawl, adding extra motivation to keep this man's hands off of her person.

"Yes."

With that final word, a large gong sounded and Fadri left the floor.

Tease him, taunt him, piss him off...make him phase. The litany of thought trailed through Megan's brain as she ducked and dodged his beefy fists. Megan made good use of her diminutive size by getting under his blows to land a few of her own. Unfortunately, they barely registered to the giant man. Her blows seemed to be doing more damage to herself than her opponent, Megan thought as she sucked on a bleeding knuckle.

Daemon smashed a meaty fist into the side of Megan's head, tunneling her vision. Daemon took advantage of Megan's hesitation and landed a series of body blows that had Megan wondering if she had cracked ribs.

Megan staggered away from the large man's reach. Her fighting spirit was quickly waning. This was a one-sided battle not in her favor. She knew that Daemon could sense her defeat from the sneer he kept on his face.

She must have been projecting her state of mind because the feeling of being wrapped in warm strong arms crept over her, and a strong sense of well-being and love washed over her. She felt her tiredness flee as Reijo used their connection to feed her strength. He whispered in her mind about how much he loved her and believed in her. He reminded her that the battle wasn't over yet and she still had a chance to change the tide.

Megan stood straighter and refocused her mind. She narrowed her world down only to the here and now. She observed her surroundings like a general assured of victory instead of a defeated dog.

Megan could hear the crowd cheering—cheering for Daemon. The masses felt assured of her defeat and were rallying around the victor. If she didn't do something, she knew she would lose the favor of the crowd. She needed something a little dramatic. Her opening came a few minutes after they reengaged when he swung wide, leaving his face open. She had to get in close to take advantage of the opening.

She used the heel of her foot to slam into Daemon's nose, sending him to his knees. Blood spurted everywhere. Daemon lashed out with a fist, knocking Megan to the ground, but she had anticipated such a blow and was able to deflect most of its force, even though she would be black and blue tomorrow. She stood up as the massive man remained down, holding his bleeding nose.

The crowd went wild. While Daemon had been wearing Megan down with crushing bruises, Megan was the first to draw blood, and she did so spectacularly. The scene came straight out of a movie, with enough blood that those in the furthest seats could still tell she landed a telling blow.

The energy that Reijo was sending her pushed all her pain aside. Megan felt fresh while Daemon was noticeably slow in getting back up.

Megan could hear her name being chanted. It was time to play to the crowd. She stood up and sashayed around the floor, waving to the crowd and blowing kisses. The volume increased and Megan knew that if she could just win the match she would reach celebrity status among today's crowd.

Behind her, Megan heard a pissed off growl. When she turned to face Daemon, the Vukasin was finally standing with blood staining the front of his clothes. His eyes held a feverish sheen, but he still remained unphased. Reijo's strategy would only work if she could get the warrior into his phased state.

Megan shifted into a fighter's stance and gestured for him to come at her. "That was just a love tap, sweetheart. The fun is just starting." Megan knew she was playing a dangerous game taunting the man, but the crowd renewed its roaring and chanting for Megan when they heard her taunt.

When the big man charged her, she vaulted over him like a gymnast. Her strategy was to stay out of his reach and piss him off by treating him like a child.

She kicked him in the ass, knocking him off balance and sending him in the dirt once again. She avoided his grasp a few more times, each time hitting him in his backside. Staying behind him was working. He had been unable to grab her, so she didn't suffer further injury. Every time she wondered how much longer she could dance around the giant of a man, Reijo would send her another burst of renewing energy.

The crowd picked up on the game and began to laugh at Daemon. Each taunting gesture, each bit of showmanship on Megan's part, enraged him even more. After Megan used an aikido throw to flip his mass over her tiny frame and she skipped off like a little girl on a playground, something in Daemon broke.

Megan could hear the crowd gasp, and she knew what she would find when she turned around. But prior knowledge did nothing to quell the fear that bubbled up from her stomach. A phased Daemon was nothing short of a nightmarish monster. While the phased royal guards had an animalistic elegance to them, Daemon was strictly a rabid predator. It didn't seem possible, but the man got even bigger in his phased form. His eyes seemed to glow with a red rage.

The people in the stands felt this shift in dynamic. Megan's taunts had been fun, almost playful, but Daemon was a berserker bent on Megan's destruction. The crowd's cries became bloodthirsty. It seemed that the tide of the favor shifted to Daemon, whom they believed would now be victorious against her. No one ever said that the masses weren't fickle.

Megan knew she had to get close to the man to take him out: no more games, no more taunts. This was not the time to play around. She had one shot at this, winner take all. If she succeeded in taking out this monster, she would be legend to those in the stands and they would take the story of today's fight to those who had not been here. By the time she emerged from the jungle at the end of the *Mate Avi Keiger,* she would already be a legend of historic proportions. On the other hand, if she missed this chance, it all ended here because Daemon would most likely kill her once he got his hands on her.

Quit overthinking and just do it. Megan could swear that Reijo whispered those words in her mind, but it was enough to spur her into action.

Megan charged the phased man, sliding onto her back at the last minute so she could use the strength of her legs to take out his knee. No matter how strong a person was, that sudden loss of support always had them toppling to the ground.

Megan felt Daemon's knee pop and he howled in pain. It would be a struggle for him to stand without assistance for awhile. Daemon tried to grab Megan as she scrambled away from him. His claws raked across her bicep, leaving deep bleeding gouges, but she managed to evade his grasp. Megan got behind the man once more to keep away from those deadly claws.

Daemon struggled to turn as she stood up behind him. The man growled and howled like a rabid wolf. Megan knew that if he could reach her she was done for. The time for games was long gone.

It was time to end this. Megan did a roundhouse kick, planting the heel of her foot right against the bundle of nerves Reijo had shown her with as much strength as she could muster. Daemon's body seized and froze. Megan's eyes widened and the crowd suddenly fell silent.

Megan went up to the frozen Daemon and pushed him over. He fell to the ground and didn't move. Fadri made his way to the pair and examined the fallen man. He nodded towards Megan, letting her know that he was still alive. She sighed in relief; for a moment she thought she had killed the man, and while she could justify killing to survive, it went against her moral fiber to kill someone in a simple contest.

Fadri raised her hand and declared her the victor, and the crowd that was moments earlier calling for her blood erupted into cheers. The men who witnessed today's contest would reminisce about the day they saw Megan and Daemon fight, speaking in awe of the little Earth virago who could defeat an elite warrior. The few women who witnessed the fight would whisper behind the men's backs and wonder: if one tiny woman could stand against a warrior, maybe they could too.

Change was in the wind, but Megan knew it would only bring a cleansing storm if she survived this formal trial. Winning the love of the people would help her cause, but the politicians and policy makers were less swayed by showmanship, and she needed a legal leg to stand on to get them to listen to her.

She was already tired from fighting stupid cultural ideas. If it wasn't for Abby and Reijo, Megan would just give up because sometimes the tasks that lay before her seemed never ending.

"I can feel you overthinking, *jinaria*." Megan jumped at the sound of Reijo's voice. She was so lost in her own thoughts that she hadn't realized he had approached her. Reijo wrapped her in his warmth. "Let this just be the victory it is. One challenge at a time, love."

Reijo called for a medic to treat Megan's wounds, but he did not let her go. While he had always been confident that she could win this fight, he would be lying to himself if he didn't acknowledge that his heart was in his throat during the duration of the battle.

Megan turned and tipped her head up to capture Reijo's lips with her own. She could feel his worry and relief, everything that he had shielded from her during her fight washing over her psyche. They both needed a reminder that at least for now they were alive and well. "We have about an hour before I have to enter the jungle. Love me, Reijo…one last time."

Reijo swept Megan up in his arms and took off towards some privacy at a run.

CHAPTER TWENTY-SEVEN

Two weeks—two very long weeks in this *Isle of Dr. Moreau* nightmare jungle, except the experiments all seem to cross plants with beasts. Kavi believed that the carnivorous jungle was a natural anomaly on their planet, despite the lack of anything similar anywhere else in the world. There was no record of its creation or experimentation. The Dyami believed that it was created by the gods for the purpose of discovering a warrior's worth. Whatever its origins, this jungle held significant power within Vukasin society, which is why Megan now found herself slugging through it looking for some mythical temple to be gifted with something from the gods.

Megan didn't really give a damn about the temple at this point; she was just hoping for survival. While her plaid cloak and the rope in her survival bracelet had provided her some semblance of shelter during the jungle's numerous downpours, it was the fact that her hair stick blades were getting a regular workout that kept her on her toes.

They hadn't had time to fully heal the cuts on

her arm. Elod would have needed three treatments to do so, which would have required one and a half days, so in the end she received one treatment that left her cuts scabbed over but still oozing when she pulled them open again. In this place an open wound was like pouring blood into shark infested waters. It made the various plants all the more excitable at her passing. Fortunately for her, most of the plants seemed to have pain receptors along with their appetite.

She quickly got used to the dangers the plants provided. The slightest twitch of a vine had her side-stepping without even consciously thinking about it. She held her breath as a blood red bloom opened a few feet from her. She was glad she remembered that that particular plant poisoned its victims so they decomposed over its root system to feed it from Kavi's lessons, especially after she saw a small rabbit-like creature get caught in its poisonous cloud. It died a hard death, even if it was fairly quick; its tiny body seized with painful convulsions.

There were even a few animals to be wary of in this place. She hadn't come face to face with one of those yet, but she had seen the remains of its kills. This place had a large herbivore that resembled a deer back home, though it was the size of a moose. Somehow it had adapted to be immune to many of the carnivorous plants' various tricks. That and the fact that it was huge would have made few predators an issue for the creature, but Megan had come across two carcasses so far that told her at least one apex predator was in the jungle.

The thick foliage kept much of the jungle in darkness. The dim light and constant state of vigilance was wearing on Megan. If it wasn't for her connection with Reijo, Megan might have snapped. But Reijo flooded her psyche with love and grounded her mentally when things were starting to get to her.

She reached for him now. For the last two days she felt like something or someone was watching her from the shadows. She really was worried that she was beginning to lose it. When she made contact with Reijo, she was surprised to discover that his concern mirrored her own.

"Fucking hell!" Megan barked in the darkened trees while absently slashing at a vine that crept to close. She really wished their bond allowed for consistent telepathic conversation sometimes because she wasn't sure if he was worried because she was cracking up or if he was worried because he heard that someone might actually be following her.

Megan was worrying herself in circles when she heard a branch snap in the undergrowth. She removed the second hair stick blade, giving her a blade for each hand. She crouched down and scanned the area around her. She was at the edge of one of the few open areas within the jungle. The light that filtered through allowed her to see more detail but also created more shadow.

The open glade would make her an easy target without cover, but it was also clear of the deadly traps the plants in this jungle laid, which would make fighting easier since she wouldn't have to think about what the plants were doing to try and kill her.

With a last sweep of the shadows, Megan decided to step into the bright clearing and face down her stalker.

She twirled her blades, getting ready for a fight as she walked to the center of the glade. She turned and faced the direction she felt had eyes on her and shifted into a fighter's stance.

"Come and get me if you want me!" Megan growled loudly in challenge.

In the darkness of the jungle, Megan could just make out three shadows moving. She moved one leg back to put herself into a position that would allow her to maneuver more easily against multiple assailants.

"I see you." Megan's singsong voice was filled with menace.

As one the three shadows burst from the jungle to charge Megan, she raised her weapons to defend herself. Three black streaks of fur bowled Megan over, pinning her to the ground.

"Oomph!" Megan giggled as a rough tongue slathered her face. "Get off of me you fat beast."

Kilala nuzzled the cut on Megan's arm, giving the woman a look. In Megan's mind she got the distinct impression that the large cat felt she couldn't leave her anywhere without her getting into trouble. The feeling was very maternal in nature and made Megan feel like an errant kitten.

Megan rubbed her face along the side of Kilala's. "I was so afraid I would never see you again." Two other wet noses bumped her arms, demanding attention. Megan smiled and wrapped her arms around each of the other cats. She knew these were Kilala's cubs, but they had grown into formidable cats in the weeks since Megan had last seen them.

Megan put her hands on either side of one of the former cubs' face, "Let me see how much you have grown."

Megan had meant to look the cat up and down to see the changes in her friend, but her gaze was caught by the cat's eyes. Her mind felt like it was falling, much like it had with Kilala. This time the fall seemed easier, like he wasn't fighting her the way his mother had originally. He? Yes, this cat's mind was definitely male. Images and emotions were shoved into Megan's mind so quickly that it was hard for her to interpret. The base of everything seemed to be affection and protection. This ghost lion had decided long before it was mature enough to connect mind to mind that it was responsible for Megan's protection.

Megan snapped back to the present moment, breathing erratically.

"You're name is K'ah...." She had thought that her connection to Kilala was a bit of a fluke, but it seemed that something about her own genetics made connecting to the cats easier.

"I wonder...." Megan eyed the last cat. She stood and walked towards the final cat. The ghost lion head-butted Megan's shoulder, nearly knocking her off balance. Megan gave herself over to the joy of sinking her hands into the soft fur of such a powerful creature. She knew she was blessed to have earned the trust and respect of this feline family, but she needed to know if this power within her extended to this one as well.

Megan scratched the ghost lion's ears while guiding its gaze to her own. When their eyes were looking into each other's directly, Megan sent a part of herself seeking the mind of the cat. Megan wasn't sure if this would work because she felt nothing in return. She let her hands go slack and started to turn away when the cat's mind seized her own.

Unlike Kilala's anger and fear or K'ah's protective acceptance, Megan battled Kia for dominance. This little female had a will of iron and would only follow someone she greatly respected. Right now she viewed Megan with the affection of a littermate. And like a littermate, the pecking order had to be established. It gave Megan a glimpse into the workings of ghost lion pride dynamics. While they respected physical strength, they also searched out leaders with mental strength.

Megan knew that she would have to force Kia to submit, otherwise Kia would continue to challenge her and perhaps even convince the other two to leave and follow the stronger cat. Megan didn't want the ghost lions to leave her, not just because she needed them, though Megan was strong enough to admit she needed them desperately, but because she loved them too. She couldn't imagine her life here on Vukas without the cats in it.

Megan poured those emotions into Kia's

mind. She let Kia know how much she was valued and loved, but beneath it all was Megan's immovable belief that she needed to be the one to lead for the good of them all.

Kia gnashed her teeth and growled in the mental images she sent back to Megan. Megan felt the cat's declaration that her body was weak and fragile. Megan countered Kia's arguments by agreeing that compared to the ghost lion her body was fragile. She conceded that she needed Kilala, K'ah, and Kia to act as her teeth and claws but that her strength lay in her mind. She showed Kia that not only did she understand the needs of the pride but she understood the actions of those of other species. She sent impressions letting Kia know that as much as she needed them, the cats also needed her to navigate this changing world.

Kia raised a paw to cuff Megan while she was distracted with the connection of their minds. While it took a lot of concentration to maintain the connection, Megan noticed the cub's underhanded move. Megan promptly bopped the big cat on the nose and reprimanded her for dirty tricks through their connection.

Finally Megan felt Kia concede. It was like the cat had heaved a bratty sigh before agreeing to the logic that finally wore her down. In the end, Kia still had to make sure she had the last word, informing Megan that she was only staying for the hairless cub who gave good ear scratches before breaking the connection.

Megan sagged. Such in-depth connections

were exhausting. In a way she was glad that Kia was more loyal to Abby than she was her. Abby would need a protector, and the love that Kia held for her daughter came through the connection loud and clear.

Megan needed to rest. She decided to sleep in the clearing to keep away from the plants that continuously tried to eat her within the jungle. She motioned for the ghost lions to curl up near her in the long grass while she unfastened her plaid cloak to lie on the ground.

While she curled up in her cloak, pillowing her head on the warm haunches of K'ah, Megan sent reassuring emotions back to Reijo. She hoped that he would understand the joy and affection at the return of the ghost lions into her life. She tried to send a more complicated message, just to test their bond, but she had no way of knowing if it had made it through to him or not.

Megan tried to settle her mind to sleep. She had thought that the feeling of being watched would dissipate after rediscovering the ghost lions, but that spot between her shoulder blades that always told her when someone had eyes on her still itched. She decided to face that problem tomorrow; she was too tired to worry about it now. Besides, if someone tried to get to her now, they would have to make it through a trio of very dangerous ghost lions to do it.

CHAPTER TWENTY-EIGHT

It took another week before Megan found any signs of the temple complex that was supposedly buried deep within this jungle. She had to admit that navigating the dangers of the carnivorous jungle was easier with the ghost lions in tow. Her food situation definitely improved, since Kilala and K'ah made sure to bring her a portion of their kills each hunt. Kia was still stingy with her food stores, but that was to be expected when Megan knew that the person Kia had truly bonded with was Abby.

If Megan hadn't tripped over it, she most likely would have missed the sign that they had finally made it to an area near the temple. It was a carved road marker, long since overgrown by the surrounding jungle. Megan had to carefully cut away the writhing vines she had nicknamed 'the hangman's noose' after an incident where they had nearly strangled her in her sleep. It was one of the reasons she felt safer sleeping out in open areas despite the lack of cover to hide behind.

The stone was carved with images that reminded Megan of pictures she had seen of Mezzo-

American art from the Mayans, Incans, and Aztecs. The fact that the stone was here most likely meant that the temple was nearby. Logically, Megan knew that searching the jungle in an expanding spiral would be the best way to locate the temple, but that could take days or even weeks she didn't have. She was already halfway through the allotted six weeks and she still needed to find her way out of the jungle and back to the Dyami stronghold.

Her frustration must have bled over into her connection with Reijo because she soon was engulfed in a feeling of confidence and strength. Reijo trusted she could do this; she just needed to trust in herself and her instincts.

Kilala had also felt Megan's emotional state. The gentle ghost lion head-butted Megan's shoulder as she sat on the stone marker, trying to figure out what would be the next best move. Megan reached over and absently ran her fingers through Kilala's fur. Since the ghost lions burst into her daily life, Megan found a strange comfort in their presence, like they were meant to be drawn together for some purpose.

An idea so simple it was brilliant dawned on Megan. The ghost lions could cover more ground and at a faster pace than she ever could. If she stayed here with the marker and sent the cats out in different directions to search, they could search more area in a fraction of the time.

It took a little convincing on Megan's part, but she finally convinced the ghost lions to leave her to search for something not natural in the jungle. She was only able to convince Kia to help because she promised the cat that the sooner they found this place the sooner she would be back with the furless cub she loved so much.

It was difficult for Megan to maintain three separate and clear connections. It was stretching the limits of Megan's psychic capabilities and she was exhausted. She estimated that the cats had been searching for a few hours by the position of the shadows around her. If they didn't find some clue soon, she would be forced to call them back and start again in the morning.

Her mind was wandering with thoughts of today's failure and she almost missed the image K'ah flashed into her mind. The looming grey stone was an unusual sight in the overly fertile jungle, where shades of green and bright colors dominated.

Megan closed off her connections to the female cats so she could use the extra energy to sharpen K'ah's visions. She instructed the large cat to circle around the stone structure so she could get a better look. The sides were too uniform to be natural, and when the cat walked away and looked at it from a distance, Megan knew that they had found what they were looking for.

Megan commanded K'ah to return and memorize the path he took so he could show her how to get there tomorrow. Megan also called the other cats to come back to her. As she prepared a fire using the flint-type rocks she had picked up, thankful that she remembered Kavi's lessons on survival, Megan considered what K'ah had found. She was certain it was the temple because the shape was almost a perfect match to the step pyramids built by ancient cultures on her own planet. The thing that puzzled her was how she was going to get in. K'ah had circled around the stone structure twice and she hadn't been able to spot any place that appeared to be a doorway or opening. She hoped that she could figure it out when she saw the place in person tomorrow.

Megan had a cheerful fire going with haunches of the deer-like creature that the cats had killed earlier that morning roasting over wooden spikes. Megan no longer attempted to conceal her presence, despite the fact that she still felt like someone was watching her. It had been three weeks and she had yet to encounter any dangers other than the ones provided by the jungle itself, so she felt justified in deciding that comfort trumped stealth at this point. Besides, she had three ghost lions to see to her safety now.

She smiled as each cat emerged from the shadows of the jungle and head-butted her affectionately before stealing a hunk of meat off of one of the spikes. Megan had learned quickly to provide a separate hunk of food for each cat to prevent scuffles as well as to ensure she actually got to eat. K'ah and Kilala seemed to enjoy the flavor of the roasted meat. Kia groused and sent clear images of preferring her food to still be raw and bleeding.

Once they had filled their bellies, Megan covered herself with her plaid and lay down to sleep sandwiched between the large, warm bodies of the cats. They would take turns prowling as sentinel for the night, watching over Megan.

*****

Deep in the shadows, eyes watched the scene unfold before them. So far he had stayed off the woman's radar, though there were times he wondered if she sensed him like prey senses the presence of a predator. The addition of the cats made his job more difficult, but not impossible. Right now his orders were to observe and report, but he knew that should it look like the woman would succeed, then he would be ordered to prevent that at all cost.

He was kind of hoping that she would force his employer's hand because he had plans for her. He hadn't had a woman in ages. The owners of the brothels of off-world women had long ago banned him for damaging the merchandise one too many times. But one word from his employer and the woman he had been obsessing over for the last few weeks would be fair game for all of his dark needs.

He looked around the small camp that hid his comrades. Perhaps he would even let the other men take a turn with her before they finished her off. He often fantasized about carting her off and keeping the woman for himself until he broke her. She was a strong one despite her delicate appearance. He bet that she would last a long time and he could have a lot of fun with her. Too bad his employer wanted proof of her demise if it came to that. Oh well, he could still play for a little while and make it as rough as he wanted to in the process.

He continued to watch the woman through

his long-range lens as the rest of the small crew bedded down. It gave the man a sense of power to know that he watched her sleep and she was oblivious of the fact that he held her life in his hands.

*****

As dawn filtered through the canopy of trees, Megan set about dividing the remainder of last night's meal. She wanted to be up and moving as soon as possible. As the cats scarfed down their portions, Megan packed up her meager camp.

Before long, K'ah was leading the rest of the group down a barely visible animal trail. Megan knew her presence was slowing the ghost lions down, but the cats dutifully remained near her, doubling back a few times to keep her in their sights.

The jungle writhed and grasped at the living flesh that passed through it. More than once Megan sent up a prayer of thanks to Kavi for the gift of the hair stick blades. After being on the trail for a couple of hours, Megan and the cats came upon a particularly nasty trap. It was a brightly colored giant blossom that blocked their path. When one looked closely, the small petals at the center of the structure weren't petals at all but thorn-like teeth built to rip and shred the flesh of its victims. Most people would just attempt to circle around such an obvious danger; but that was actually part of this plants ruse. The obvious danger distracted from the subtle trap surrounding the main blossom. This plant had sentient vines and roots that radiated out from the central blossom. If you stepped on or sometimes even just drew near them, the vines would wrap around you, constricting like a great snake. The more you fought, the tighter it would squeeze until you passed out or died. Then the vines would drag your prone body to the grotesque blossom where it would grind and crush you into decomposing food.

The ghost lions took to the trees, easily avoiding any of the seeking vines. Megan wasn't so lucky. The path to the tree tops was blocked by a mass of vines; she would have to find a different way across. She briefly considered trying to circumvent the plant by forging a new path through the jungle but found a chain of these vicious blossoms on either side of her present obstacle. She needed to get into the tree tops, but she didn't have the leaping ability of the cats. She did have her survival bracelet. She unwound the bracelet and discovered she had about five yards of thin rope. It wasn't long enough to swing across the entire blossom, but it might provide her a way to get up into the first tree. Megan searched the ground until she found a sturdy piece of broken branch that was about three inches thick and a foot long. She secured the branch to one end of the rope and swung it in a circle, testing its weight. It was a little more awkward than the bolos she played with in the dojo, but she didn't have to tackle a man with it. She just needed to get the rope to wrap around a branch and be secure enough to bear her weight.

Megan gave the makeshift bolo an experimental toss. It wrapped around the branch below the one she was aiming for. This branch was much thinner, and Megan doubted it could bear her weight. This was confirmed when she gave a tug on the rope only to have the branch in the tree snap. The vines shivered and undulated at the disturbance. They attempted to drag the broken branch back to the blossoms deadly maw. Megan quickly gathered her rope and tried again, putting a little more strength into her throw.

All together it took three attempts before Megan was able to secure the rope. Once it was secure, Megan wrapped the rope around her forearm just in case she got caught by the vines and needed leverage to extract herself. She then took a running leap and sailed over the deadly blossom blocking her path.

Megan hit the tree trunk and it knocked the wind out of her. She gripped at the bark as her body attempted to slip down. Finally her fingers and toes found purchase and she strained to lift herself up inch by inch until she could wrap her arms around the branch her rope was wrapped on.

Megan unwound the rope and stashed it on her belt, in case she needed it on the return trip. She looked around from her new vantage point. From here it would be easy to transfer from tree to tree within the thick canopy. Megan could also see the pyramid in the distance. Once she figured out the secret of the pyramid, all that would be left was the return home and this portion of the plan would be completed.

She really hoped this trial was worth it. Kavi and Ghaleb seemed to think this ritual was essential for the success of their plans. Not having grown up in a society with such ironclad traditions and laws, it was difficult for Megan to think that this kind of thing was so necessary for political maneuvering.

Megan took a deep breath and carefully balanced herself as she walked across the tree branches. She carefully noted which branches the cats took. If they could hold the ghost lion's massive weight, that branch should easily hold her own meager weight.

Megan lost her footing and grabbed a branch above her to keep from falling. The motion had her looking down into one of the bloody blossoms. The shredded remains of some hapless animal oozed around the teeth-like thorns. Megan said a quick prayer of thanks that she had not fallen to the same fate.

The branch supporting her weight creaked and dipped. K'ah had backtracked to check on her when she cried out in fear. Megan tried to wave the cat off as it mounted the same branch she was currently standing on. The wood popped ominously.

"Get back."

K'ah ignored her frantic gestures and came right up to her to head-butt her thigh. The ghost lion had to reassure himself that Megan was alright. Her continued distress agitated the large predator.

A loud crack had Megan wrapping her arms and legs around the branch above her. She watched in horror as the branch that held K'ah fell away. The ghost lion's quick reflexes saved it. Unfortunately, it clawed at the nearest hold, which happened to be Megan's back.

CHAPTER TWENTY-NINE

"Ghaleb, I tell you that Bel is up to something. He is too damn smug and so certain that Megan will fail the *Mate Avi Keiger*." Reijo paced the study of the suite of rooms that the Dyami had procured for the royal house. "I know Megan feels like someone is watching her. I would be willing to bet my life that Bel sent some muscle to make sure Megan failed."

"Reijo, you have been pacing the stronghold like a caged ghost lion. Megan is the toughest person I know. She will survive." Ghaleb poured a glass of rare moon liquor and handed the swirling liquid over to his friend.

Reijo reached for the glass but it crashed to the ground, shattering, as Reijo contorted and screamed in pain. The large warrior was brought to his knees with such force that the shocked Ghaleb froze for a moment before calling the servants to fetch a medic.

"Megan…." Reijo hissed her name through clenched teeth. "Something is attacking Megan." He forced himself to stand. "I have to get to her."

"You can't. If you interfere then this whole mess will be for nothing and Bel will make sure the council rips her and Abby from you as soon as she returns."

"He can bloody well try." Ghaleb tried to restrain the man that was both kin and friend, but Reijo was frantic. Megan was hurt and it wasn't a simple scratch or sprain, judging by the pain, it was a life-threatening injury. Reijo's basic instincts told him he needed to get to her now. He didn't care about politics or saving their race. All he cared about was making sure Megan was safe.

Elod along with three other medics burst into the room at the royal summons. They stopped short at the sight before them. Their *Khalon* had pinned his writhing *Kijani-a* to the ground. The sight of two such important men wrestling like schools boys might have been amusing if not for the deadly serious expressions on both their faces.

"Sedate him, now!" Ghaleb was losing his fight to keep the distraught Reijo contained.

The royal command snapped the medics into action, each grabbing a limb to immobilize the enraged warrior. Elod injected a quick-acting sedative into Reijo. It took only a matter of moments for him to fall into unconsciousness. His last word before falling into his forced slumber was, "Megan…."

Ghaleb dismissed the medics, but Elod remained behind.

"Care to explain why I just dosed my cousin?"

"In a moment. First I need Kavi." Ghaleb sent a missive to his old teacher telling him his presence was required. He then turned back to the young physician. "I don't know much, but something has happened to Megan."

"How do you know this?"

"Reijo felt it through his bond and lost control."

"Of course he did. The woman he loves more than life itself is in danger and you expected him to remain calm." Elod snorted at Ghaleb. "You might be a political genius, but when it comes to the individual there are times you are a real dunce."

"You know you Tiarets have gotten into the habit of criticizing your ruler."

"No, we are just honest."

The men situated Reijo on the couch in the study, not an easy feat considering the size of the warrior. Both turned when Kavi entered the room. The old man surveyed the scene, and his piercing gaze settled on Ghaleb.

"So what are we going to do about Megan?"

"One of these days you are going to tell me who all is in your network of spies, old man."

Kavi just smiled.

CHAPTER THIRTY

Megan collapsed on the ground as soon as they were clear of the deadly blooms. That damn cat had nearly killed her. She was fairly certain that the claw marks on her back would leave a nasty scar, and her tunic was shredded.

K'ah licked at the wounds and mewled at Megan. She knew he was seeking forgiveness for hurting her. Megan sighed and sank a hand into the ruff of fur around his neck. She hurt and was losing quite a bit of blood, but she still wouldn't wish death on her ghost lion companion. If he hadn't grabbed a hold of her he would have fallen into the bloody blossom's mouth and been devoured by the plant. It wouldn't have been an easy death.

Megan struggled to her feet. She still had a ways to go to get to the temple, and she wanted to be there before nightfall. Kilala, K'ah, and Kia surrounded her, each cat taking turns to support Megan's battered body as they moved quickly over the trail.

The group only stopped once when a horrendous scream filled the air and was suddenly silenced. The sound had come from behind them, and Megan knew that some hapless creature had fallen victim to the trap she had narrowly escaped. She shivered at the thought because the sound had been frighteningly human. She hoped that once her business at the temple was concluded, she could find a different trail out of the jungle.

Twilight was just beginning to fall as Megan stepped into the shadow of the temple. Despite the massive overgrowth of jungle around the ancient temple, not a bit of moss or vine covered the gleaming structure. The building reminded Megan of pictures she had seen of the step pyramids in Central America, except this one seemed to be carved from hematite.

Megan laid her hand on a carving of a stylized face. No, not hematite. The temple wasn't made of stone but of some sort of metallic substance. Its construction seemed out of place on this planet where they used only natural materials in an eco-friendly manner.

With a gesture, Megan sent the ghost lions to help her inspect the structure. She needed to find a way in to complete the ritual. Unfortunately, Kavi or even the Dyami monks had no knowledge of what awaited her here. All they knew was she needed to enter the temple and receive a gift from the gods. In all of the ancient writings, it appeared that the gift was usually some sort of blessed weapon that helped to direct the course of history.

The wall appeared to be seamless; there was no obvious door. Megan stood back and studied the carvings. At first glance, the carvings seemed almost random, as if the artist just created whatever they chose on any given day. The longer Megan examined them, the more she realized that the carvings weren't random but a story pattern. The stylized figures made the story difficult to recognize at first.

The artist was actually a bit of a genius, Megan decided. Up, down, diagonal…it didn't matter what direction you 'read' the story in, it would make sense. It wasn't just a single tale, but numerous ones all interwove together to form a great tapestry of many stories.

Megan read through a few of the tales: stories of war, some of peace, of joy and hardship. The temple was a shrine to the human condition, or should she say the Vukasin condition. Yet all of the tales began and ended in the same spot.

About halfway up the pyramid on the side that would face the rising sun was a carving that depicted the temple itself. Each tale seemed to start in that spot and would wrap around to end there as well. The beginning and the end….Alpha and Omega. In many ways, humans and Vukasins were very similar, so it didn't really surprise Megan that similar religious concepts appeared.

Megan was certain that the pyramid carving was important to finding her way inside the temple. It was too symbolic not to be.

No stairs lead up the pyramid. Megan placed her hands on the cool metal, searching for purchase to make the climb towards the carving she had set her sights on. The smooth surface made the journey difficult.

She pulled herself up and over the first base. Her heart was pounding and she lay down to catch her breath. She looked up and counted six more sections before she would reach the area she needed. She wasn't sure she would make it. Even if she did, there was no guarantee that she had solved the riddle of getting into the temple. She was basing her idea off of Earth ideologies and gut instinct.

Megan pushed herself up and stood. "Onwards and upwards."

Her progress was painfully slow. She slipped and fell twice, each time slamming her battered body onto the hard surface of the temple ledge she just left. Thankfully she didn't fall over the ledge. That fall might have killed her. At the very least, the thought of starting all over again would have broken her spirit.

Megan's extremities trembled as she pulled herself up in front of the pyramid carving. She leaned her back against the metallic wall. The wind ruffled her hair, and the ghost lions raised their heads to scent the surrounding area.

Kilala gave a distinctly big cat cough and wrinkled her muzzle. The ghost lion's eyes focused on the treeline of the surrounding jungle. Megan crawled to the edge, trying to see what had disturbed her feline friend.

The unmistakable rapport of a gunshot echoed through the jungle. Megan instinctively ducked when the shot ricocheted off the pyramid behind her, nicking her skin. The small graze would have hurt if her body hadn't already been overloaded by the pain from K'ah's claw marks.

Damn it. She didn't have a weapon to defend herself with at this distance.

"Come out, little girl. We want to play."

The voice was filled with amusement and violence. Megan knew if they got their hands on her she would be going down hard. She had no illusions that these men would let her live; they had been sent to keep her from completing the *Mate Avi Keiger* at all cost.

Megan silently directed two of the ghost lions to circle around. If these men had been watching her, they knew the animals traveled with her. She hoped that by keeping at least one visible, the others might be able to sneak around.

"I only play with real men, and they seem to be in short supply in the jungle," Megan taunted the men as they emerged from the jungle. She kept a restraining hand on a growling Kilala.

The man that Megan assumed was the leader stopped two of the others who tried to rush forward at her taunting.

"This will go much easier for you if you cooperate. You might even find pleasure in the end."

Megan snorted. "Your pick up lines need some work, mister. I'm not stupid; your orders are to make sure I don't come out of this alive." Megan's hands frantically searched for some sort of switch to get into the temple. It wasn't a perfect solution, but it would give her some cover. "Come and get me if you can!"

Megan could barely see Kia's shadow as she stalked the enemy from the rear. She pounced on a straggler, cutting his scream short as she crushed his neck in her powerful jaws from behind; even the man's battle collar couldn't withstand the force of a full-grown ghost lion's bite.

One down, four to go. Megan watched as three of the startled men phased into their warrior forms. Only the leader remained in his human form. He ignored everything that was going on around him, his eyes fastened to Megan.

That unblinking stare caused Megan to shiver. For all of her bravado, she was afraid. She could feel it in her soul that if this man got his hands on her she would end up brutalized and raped long before blessed death.

Megan felt a calming influence roll through her psyche. The touch of Reijo's mind steadied her as nothing else could. She was not facing this danger alone. She would never be alone again. Megan projected her overwhelming love for the man waiting for her to complete this task.

Her enemy started stalking towards the pyramid. K'ah rushed the man, but his comrade saw the giant cat and fired. Megan felt the bullet's impact through her bond with the cat. It hit him in the shoulder. The wound wasn't fatal but was painful enough to put him in grave danger with armed enemies circling around him. Megan recalled K'ah and Kia, though Kia protested leaving her kill.

The cats withdrew to circle around to

Megan's position; their powerful leaps made their progress up the pyramid much easier than it had been for Megan. Unfortunately, it was an advantage that their enemy somewhat shared. The men were quickly gaining ground, their leader out-pacing the rest. He made it to the second tier while the others were still on the ground.

Desperate, Megan turned her back on the men with guns and frantically started searching for the key to open the door to the temple. She was tired and she was weak from blood loss. If she had to fight now, she would lose.

Nothing seemed to work. There were no levers or switches. She couldn't even see a seam that she might pry open. She could hear the grunts of her enemy as he hauled himself closer to her position.

She was so close. The weight of her failure overwhelmed her and tears began to fall. This wasn't just about her and her survival; it was about Abby and all of the other women brought from Earth. Hell, it was even about the future of the Vukasin women.

The man was on the ledge below her, taunting her. He laughed at her tear-stained face. The only things keeping him at bay were three very angry ghost lions. Megan spotted a hand gun in his hand and knew that he would kill the lions as soon as he could get a decent shot.

Megan directed the lions to keep out of his line of sight, but it was simply a stop gap. She didn't have the strength to climb higher, and as the cats became more agitated, eventually one of them would make a mistake and get shot.

Megan screamed her frustration and started beating on the immovable door with her fist. The action left her knuckles raw. Blood was flowing freely down her back and arms from her unhealed wounds.

With the last rush of her strength, Megan slapped her palm on the door, leaving a bloody handprint behind, and collapsed to the ground. Her body was leaning against the door. At first the sounds of various mechanisms engaging seemed to be wishful thinking, but as the door vibrated, Megan looked up.

The handprint was gone. In its place several panels had lit up. With a whoosh, Megan tumbled into the open passage way. Without thinking twice, she whistled for the ghost lions. The three cats ran after her.

Megan watched as her enemy leapt up to the final ledge and raised his gun in the frame of the door. The ghost lions circled around Megan protectively and Megan waited for the gunshot that never came.

CHAPTER THIRTY-ONE

"Well you are unexpected."

Megan ventured to open her eyes, even as Kilala emitted a low growl. The doorway to the outside was firmly shut and darkness surrounded Megan and her ghost lions. She turned her head towards the unfamiliar voice.

"Who are you?" Megan continued to scan the darkness as her eyes adjusted.

"I am the Keeper, and you are a genetic anomaly." A figure materialized in the shadows. The voice sounded male, and the silhouette was of someone quite tall and thin. "Forgive my rudeness." Megan blinked back tears at the sudden illumination. "It has been many generations since I have had guests here. Though you are completely unexpected. Tell me, how did a member of the control subject end up here?"

Megan stood, wincing in pain, "I have no idea what you are talking about."

She was finally able to get a good look at her host. His features were human, though something seemed off about them. He had the Vukasin height, though he was totally devoid of their dark coloring. She wasn't sure why, but Megan doubted his origin was from this planet.

"You are injured; we must treat you." The man abruptly turned and walked away without even checking to see if Megan followed. Megan hurried to keep up, Kilala and K'ah on either side of her with Kia bringing up the rear. Megan prayed that this person truly wanted to help her because if she was honest, she wasn't going to make it back without some help; her injuries were too severe and she had pushed herself to her limit.

"Can you explain to me what is going on?" Megan called after the man's retreating back.

"In time. In time." He waved off her question and continued to move quickly through a maze of corridors. Megan wasn't sure she would be capable of finding her way out. She should feel uneasy following a strange man in a strange place, but for some reason she didn't. For most of her life Megan was a decent judge of character; she hoped her intuition wasn't failing her now.

She was so lost in her thoughts that she almost ran into her host's back. He had stopped in the doorway of a large room. He stepped to the side to allow her to pass. As she stepped up next to him, he took his large hand and placed it on Megan's back, urging her to enter the chamber. His touch was electric, literally sending a tingling sensation across her wounded skin.

He guided her to a raised table in the center of the room. Megan sat on the table and studied the man as he bustled around the chamber that she now realized was some sort of laboratory. Everything seemed to be made of the same metallic substance that the entire pyramid was made of. Her host was easily as tall as the Vukasin, but his skin was almost silver in color. His hair was white, and his eyes were amethyst with a hint of gold and large enough to seem out of proportion with the rest of his face. While his basic features looked human, something in his overall proportions screamed otherworldly. He was alien looking even on this planet.

"What is your name?" Megan asked as he came close with a device she had never seen before and a container of some sort of salve.

"I was not assigned a name; my function did not require it."

"Function?"

The Keeper gently spread the salve across the claw marks on her back before applying the device he held in his other hand. A stinging warmth spread across Megan's injuries and she couldn't help the painful gasp that escaped.

"Easy now. This will only take a moment, and then you will feel much better. I'm still curious how a control subject ended up here?"

"You've said that before." Megan stretched when he put the medical device away. Her back did feel better. "I don't know what you mean by 'control subject.'"

The Keeper ignored her comment and began watching her intently. His direct gaze was very disconcerting because he didn't blink. It was as if he was scanning her deep into her soul.

"If you aren't going to tell me what you mean, then at least tell me how to complete the *Mate Avi Keiger*."

Again her demands were met with silence. Megan growled and hopped down from the table. While she was grateful to this man for treating her injuries, she had little time to waste. Her sudden movement seemed to jolt the Keeper out of his intense stare.

"Subject cataloged and anomaly recorded." Megan watched as the Keeper shimmered like a T.V. station not quite in tune. She soon realized that this wasn't an actual person at all but some sort of programed computer system.

Armed with this new realization, Megan changed tactics. "What is your primary function?"

"Observe and guide genetic experiment designation 5387." Finally a direct answer.

"What are the parameters of experiment 5387?"

"Evolution of species and culture when guided by a basic set of moral laws from a perceived 'divine' and interactive source."

"How long has this experiment been ongoing?"

"10,000,000 generations so far, though experiment shall terminate soon."

"Why?"

"Outside contamination facilitated by some of the subjects has corrupted the genetic material. Subjects will die out within a limited number of generations."

"Why experiment?"

"We were alone."

"Clarify that statement."

"Our society advanced to the point of interstellar travel, but everywhere we went was devoid of sentient life. Our scientists decided to salt our genetic material in various suitable locations. Trying to discover the best way to raise a civilization, observation facilities such as this one were created to introduce and record various stimuli and their effect. One planet in a distant system was allowed to evolve without interference. Each experiment's genetic code changed based on the level of intervention and the environment surrounding them. Those codes have been carefully logged. You are a control subject and should not be here."

"Your experiment has moved beyond the bounds of its original intent. What happened to the race that created you?"

"I do not know."

"When was the last time you were contacted by them?"

"Five hundred thousand generations ago."

Megan suspected that the original species who began this experiment had died out long ago, leaving their program behind to continue with its basic function. Megan had always wondered if life was just one big cosmic experiment, but it was rather disconcerting to have her fanciful musings confirmed.

This information would shake the very foundations of Vukasin culture. Their civilization was struggling to maintain its integrity. Megan didn't want to know what would happen if the core tenants of their belief system and honor were called into question. People like Bel would use it as an excuse to push forward with their own experimentation, regardless of the rights and feelings of their subjects. No one had visited this place for hundreds of years, and with the established clans and government, it was doubtful there would be much of a need after Megan finished the trial.

In the end, Megan decided that it wasn't her place to destroy the foundations of an entire planet's culture.

"Keeper, why are the Vukasin dying out?"

"A subject introduced an engineered virus that attacked the genetics that controlled gender identity in a developing fetus. It was introduced to the genetic line the society considered royal. It triggered a chain reaction that caused the majority of births to result in functionally male offspring. At first the effect was minor, but within just a few generations the virus had spread to epidemic proportions."

Megan gasped; the clan of Tanis was this world's doctors and scientists for the most part. Ghaleb had said that their scientists couldn't find the cause of the lack of female births. In their research they should have at least figured out that some of the males born were genetically female, but Megan hadn't heard any whispers about that. Her gut was telling her that Tanis knew what was happening and perhaps even caused it in a misguided attack against the Ivailo line.

Megan made a promise to herself to inform Ghaleb of the information she had acquired here.

"One more question…when your test subjects make the journey here, what is your programmed response?"

*****

Megan spent the next hour arguing with a computer program. The irony wasn't lost on her considering how many times she had threatened to throw her antiquated laptop through a window back home.

She learned that the carnivorous jungle was an engineered trial, meant to ensure that only the strongest and most cunning members of society were able to advance to a position of leadership before a centralized government had developed. From there the Keeper would further shape the society by bestowing a symbolic gift. The meaning of each type of gift had been duly integrated into both the political and religious systems of the Vukasin people.

The Keeper took his programming literally and was refusing to hand over the gift Megan needed to prove that she was successful. However, his programming didn't keep him from expanding upon the various items that could be gifted. Each one raised the level of leadership and prestige, but certain ones ensured sweeping changes such as the forming of a new clan.

It was the last item the Keeper spoke of that got Megan's attention. It had only been gifted once to a member of the Ivailo clan many generations ago and that had been the catalyst to unify the clans. The Keeper referred to it as The Spear of Authority. It had been laid down in Vukasin mythology that this spear denoted a person as an emissary from the gods. It gave them the divine right to guide the affairs of state, even if that meant changing the whole governmental system.

It was the perfect solution to Megan's problem. If she made it back with that spear, then the royal council had to listen to her and the other women. She wasn't naïve enough to think that just having the spear would make things easy, but it would definitely get her voice heard.

All of this was a moot point if she couldn't get the spear to take back with her. It was impossible to argue with a computer program. The very nature of its existence prevented it from moving outside the bounds of the parameters of its program.

Of course getting the spear was only half the problem. The Keeper had made it clear that her presence would further disrupt the evolution of the experiment and as such she would not be allowed to leave the temple. He also would not send her back to Earth because she would contaminate that experiment as well. She was a prisoner of a computer left by a long-dead race, albeit a well-treated prisoner.

Megan allowed the Keeper to show her to some quarters so she could get some sleep. The ghost lions followed, being completely ignored by the computer system. Megan supposed they weren't evolved enough to warrant the Keeper's attention.

When the door to her room closed behind the Keeper, she heard the click of a lock fall into place. So much for wandering around tonight.

The cats paced nervously, picking up on Megan's agitation. Megan walked around her gilded cage. The room held a bed and seating area with a small table. The only decoration was the strange carvings on the metallic walls.

Megan reached out and ran her hand across one of the carvings. She snatched her hand back when the space above the carving lit up. Was it possible that she could access parts of the computer from here? Megan wasn't a hacker by any means, but she could search for information with the best of them.

Megan settled into one of the chairs and started going through anything the systems would let her access. Knowledge was power and she was going to learn as much as she could about her present situation. Hopefully come morning she would have a better idea of what to do.

CHAPTER THIRTY-TWO

Kilala nosed Megan awake. *Damn.* She had fallen asleep while looking through the systems. Megan wiped the little bit of sleep-induced drool from her face. Hours of reading and searching had left her head aching.

She had discovered maps to this facility, notes about the experiment and more. Unfortunately it seemed that her access was limited to 'read only' mode; she hadn't been able to change anything. One useful bit of information she did discover was an entrance to the facility hidden in the jungle away from the main pyramid. If she exited from that entrance she would not only avoid the people who attacked her, but it would cut her trek home considerably.

Her major obstacle was the Keeper. That program was determined to keep her in the facility and flatly refused to give her the Spear of Authority. The controls to change any of the Keeper's programming were locked with a DNA locking mechanism. Megan's DNA wouldn't open them. More likely than not, the ancient aliens had set up the facility in this manner to keep their experiments from being able to change the function of the pyramid and the Keeper.

The Keeper arrived bearing food for Megan. It was not in his programming to kill her or let her suffer needlessly.

Megan's stomach growled and she took the food from her jailor. She had to keep her strength up, and emotional pleas would fall on deaf ears.

Between bites, Megan talked to the Keeper. "When are you going to release me?"

"You are not a prisoner here. However, I cannot allow you to corrupt the experiments further."

"I have to return; my daughter needs me. Besides, they have brought other women from Earth as well."

"I will make adjustments for a few outliers and, if given the opportunity, they will be removed from the equation."

Megan stopped mid-bite. While the Keeper's appearance made it difficult not to forget that it was just a computer program, hearing him speak about living beings as if they were no more than numbers on a page chilled her. She pushed the remains of her food away, no longer hungry.

The Keeper collected her dishes and retreated from the room without even commenting on her lack of appetite. When the door slid shut behind him, Megan didn't hear the tell-tale click of the lock like she had the night before. Even if she could move freely around the facility, it didn't solve the problem of needing the spear or all of this would be for nothing. She also doubted that the Keeper would let her just quietly walk out of the pyramid.

This would be so much easier if that stupid computer program didn't exist.

Oh my god! Could the solution be that simple? If she just shut down the computer systems, she could take the spear and escape. The question was, how could she do it? Destroying the computer console in her room would accomplish very little. She was fairly certain that the Keeper was integrated into the entire facility, considering he moved freely from one place to the next. She couldn't spare the time of going from room to room destroying the computer consoles; besides, the Keeper would quickly figure out what she was doing and most likely confine her.

No, she had to find a way to knock out the systems with one act. Megan trolled her memory for anything about her experiences with computers that might help. Unfortunately, her experiences were rather limited. She had worked as an office assistant for a large corporation that had all of their computers networked together. That office job and watching videos on the internet were pretty much the extent of her computer knowledge. At her job, if anything went wrong, the IT people were the ones that dealt with it, not her, even that one time when all of the computers went down because of a fire in the control room that housed the actual hardware for the office's network.

A light bulb went off in Megan's head. She pulled up the map of the pyramid facility. The laboratories, sleeping quarters, galley, even restroom facilities were all clearly labeled. Megan realized that each level was specifically marked except for the lowest level. On that level, only the outer ring of space was labeled. Right in the center was what appeared to be a big open courtyard. Megan knew that the pyramid was a solid structure with no openings. So why leave such a large area unmarked?

There was only one way to find out. Megan went to the door and laid her hand on the plate next to it as she had seen the Keeper do when opening the door. She exhaled a breath she hadn't even known she was holding when the door slid open to the darkened corridor. Kilala and K'ah pushed their way in front of Megan as she began working her way to the stairwell that should take her to the lower levels. Kia snarled but followed the other three.

Megan was having difficulty navigating the dark passageways, but she didn't want to alert her presence to the Keeper by turning on lights. If that space was what she hoped it was, she would only have one chance of making this work.

Down two levels, Megan had to pass through the large laboratory the Keeper had treated her in to make her way to another set of stairs. She paused for a short while in the lab, searching for something that she could use as a weapon.

Most things seemed to be medical equipment. She pocketed a few scalpels for possible use later, but she still needed something a little more destructive. In a cabinet off to one side of the room, Megan found a multitude of different tools. She had no idea what most of them were for. She picked up and discarded a few because she couldn't get them to work.

She was about to consider this cabinet a bust when she picked up a cylindrical object that had a ninety-degree bend in it. Along the shaft were several rubber-like pads that fell about where her fingers did. Not seeing a switch, she shook the device, her hands squeezing the shaft.

Megan jumped when a concentrated bright blue flame erupted from the device with a pop. She nearly dropped the device, and as soon as she let up on the pressure in her grip, it shut off. She squeezed it again….pop, blue flame.

On and off over and over. "Cool." Megan tucked the little flame thrower into the waist of her pants. This was exactly what she needed.
*****

Megan O'Connor, by the moons you better answer me! Her bond with Reijo had obviously grown. Emotions and general feelings had morphed into a very loud and angry voice tinged with fear inside her mind.

Megan fell to her knees clutching her head. She had finally made it to the lower level that housed the room she suspected was the control center for the facility. She didn't have time for conversations with Reijo, even if hearing his voice gave her comfort like nothing else.

I'm a little busy here, Reijo. So if you could get out of my head that would be great.

Her mind was swamped with a feeling of

relief so strong that her own body sagged in response.

Damn it! I love you but get out of my head. I can't afford the distraction!

I don't think so, jinaria. I felt your pain and fear of death a scant two days ago and have lived in dread ever since. I am right here until you come home to me. Otherwise I won't survive the wait.

Megan smiled, of course he was going to be stubborn about this, but despite the inconvenience his insistence presented, it also made her feel cherished and important.

You are the most important thing to me, Reijo whispered into her mind.

Megan got up and continued to creep down the hall. If she remembered correctly, there should be a door leading to the area she was curious about just up ahead.

Fine, but I need you to keep quiet for a bit, Megan sent back to Reijo.

Megan found the door locked with a DNA-encoded locking mechanism

"Fuck." Megan examined the area around the door. There had to be another way in.

Ventilation system. They are always a nightmare to secure and if this room houses the central computer systems, then it would need good ventilation to keep the room from overheating. Reijo had stayed a shadow in Megan's mind and saw her dilemma. He was a security expert and offered his knowledge freely to the woman he loved.

Megan looked above her head; sure enough,

there was a perforated panel that allowed airflow. It was made of the same metallic substance as everything else but it was covered in tiny holes which gave a screen-like effect. The holes were so tiny that it nearly blended into the rest of the structure. She would have overlooked it had she not had Reijo's help pointing it out.

The walls were too slick to climb, so the real question became, how was she going to get up there? Megan looked around; there were no chairs or even boxes. The pyramid provided nothing that she might use to hoist herself up to the screen.

Her eyes landed on the ghost lions. On all fours they weren't tall enough to get her to the ceiling. Megan mentally calculated the distance from the wall to the opening. She just might be able to reach it if the cat was raised up on its hind legs and she was on its shoulders.

Megan called K'ah over to her. She sent the cat impressions of what she was asking. He briefly balked at the idea of her using him as a ladder until Megan reminded the cat of how he had shredded the flesh of her back. K'ah groused a bit but dutifully raised himself as tall as he could against the wall. Megan climbed up the cat, which gave her the needed height to reach the ventilation opening.

Megan pushed against the screen, but it wouldn't give. She looked all around and couldn't find bolts or screws to hold it in place. It seemed to be molded from a single piece of the strange metal that the whole pyramid was constructed of.

Could nothing be easy on this whole

escapade? Megan pulled the small blow torch she found in the lab from the waistband of her pants.

"If this doesn't work, K'ah, I don't know what else to try."

She squeezed the device, activating the small blue flame. She raised the flame above her head to the grate. She was surprised to find that the flame adjusted itself to cut through the material it touched. Slowly the flame cut through the metal.

Her arms were beginning to shake and had started going numb by the time three of the four sides had been cut through. It would be dangerous to try and continue cutting the final side, so Megan released the torch and shut off the flame. Amazingly, the torch cooled almost instantly.

Megan tucked it back into her waistband and reached up to grab one of the cut sides of the ventilation grate. Megan leapt from K'ah's back, putting all of her weight on the metal she was holding. For a moment she was afraid that it wasn't going to bend. Then the metal swung back until it was perpendicular to the ceiling.

Megan swayed back and forth with the forced of the sudden drop until she lost her grip.

"Oomph!" Megan couldn't breathe as the air was knocked out of her lungs. She inhaled sharply as she assessed herself for damage. Nothing was broken, as far as she could tell. Her mangled back was throbbing again, but the Keeper's healing seemed to be intact. The thought flashed through her mind that she wondered if Reijo would still find her attractive with all of the scars.

You will always be beautiful to me.

Megan snorted as she stood up. This mind-meld thing was going to be a pain in the ass when it came to privacy. She wasn't sure she wanted Reijo to see all of her thoughts and insecurities.

We will figure it out. Besides, you are as much in my mind as I am in yours. You are just too busy at the moment to uncover my secrets.

Quit distracting me. I have work to do, Reijo.

Megan mounted K'ah's back once more, launching herself at the opening she had made. She grabbed the edges of the opening and dangled there. Using her arms, she turned her body so she would be facing towards the room she was trying to access. Megan's martial arts training came in handy, as she doubted a typical woman would have had the upper body strength to haul themselves up just by their arms. As it was, Megan was barely able to accomplish it.

She shimmed into the tight space of the ventilation shaft. She could see lights glowing through another screen about ten feet in front of her. She belly-crawled forward to peer into the next room. Sure enough, it was filled with banks of equipment. This had to be the control room for the facility.

Megan used the torch once again to cut through the grate. It was much easier to push out the grate from above than it had been to access from below. She dropped from the ceiling to the center of the room. The lights were not on, but everything around her emitted a low-level glow, casting the entire room into an eerie twilight.

Megan walked around the system and nearly cried. This looked nothing like the computer systems found back on Earth. It was full of crystals and glass-like panels. Even the wiring seemed to be made of a flexible glass. Even without computer knowledge she could have fried the systems by destroying motherboards if this had been a familiar computer system. But she didn't have any idea which component of this crystal-based system worked in the same fashion as a motherboard.

She hurt; she was tired and frustrated. Nothing had gone right on this whole mess. Tears welled up in her eyes, but she refused to let them fall. Wallowing in despair and frustration never accomplished anything. She didn't have time to fall apart now.

Your idea to destroy the control center is a sound one. This looks similar, though more advanced, to our computer systems. If I am correct, the data and programs are integrated into the crystal's structure. Destroy the crystal and you destroy the program.

Megan walked over to the nearest bank of crystals and pulled one from its housing. As she slipped it free, an alarm sounded and lights began flashing. She threw the crystal on the ground, shattering it. There were hundreds of crystals in this tower alone and there were dozens of towers. She would never have the time to finish the job before the Keeper found her and hauled her off. If she knew which set of crystals controlled his program, she could buy herself some time, but she had no idea which ones controlled which.

Megan pulled and smashed as many as she could get her hands on while she contacted Reijo.

I could use a little help here. They know I am in here, and smashing these damn things is taking too long. I need another way to shut it down fast.

Reijo paused before answering, *Find the power supply. There would be a series of cables that connected to each of the towers of crystals.*

Megan searched for what he described. *I see a glowing set of cords. It looks like ropes of light, but it is connected to each tower before converging into a single large tube of light.*

That's it! Reijo exclaimed.

Megan heard the ghost lions bellow a warning. The Keeper was in the hallway.

Megan knelt beside the large tube of light. She tried smashing it, but unlike the crystals it wouldn't break. It was flexible like plug wires. Shit, if it wouldn't break, how the hell was she supposed to destroy this thing? She put her hands on her hips to think and her fingers wrapped around the blow torch still tucked into her waistband.

Megan heard one of the cat's growl before a heavy thunk hit the wall and she felt the pain of Kia's ribs cracking. She winced in sympathy. It was now or never.

Megan pressed the flame to the tube of light and she watched as it dripped and melted like molten glass.

She had cut halfway through the power

supply connection when the door to the control room opened and the Keeper stalked in. His program was glitching, and he faded in and out like an analog television show with bad reception. He stopped to examine the shattered pieces of crystal, dropping the shard he had picked up when his glitch took away his solid state.

"Come on, com on..." Megan willed the torch to cut through the cable faster because the Keeper spotted her. If it was possible for the computer program to feel emotions, Megan would swear that it hated her right now. She saw death in that unblinking stare.

The Keeper rose and started stalking towards Megan. Megan kept the flame to the tube of light, but her eyes were glued to the distorted image coming closer.

Kilala attacked the Keeper and was able to keep him occupied for a moment until he once again became insubstantial. The ghost lion fell to the floor with a thud, shaking its head in confusion. Kia limped in behind K'ah, and all three circled the Keeper warily, but none of them tried to attack him again.

The efforts of her ghost lions to block the Keeper from getting to her failed easily, as he took the opportunity to glide right through them when he glitched once more. It appeared that the more she cut of the power supply the more difficult the Keeper was finding it to stay solid.

The Keeper reached out and grabbed Megan, hauling her away from the power cord right before she had completely cut it through. It was only another glitch that saved her. She scrambled back to the power cord as soon as she fell through his insubstantial hands. She applied the torch one more time, praying that it would do its job before he became solid again.

With a final hiss of heat, the torch cut through the last of the cord. The Keeper disappeared and darkness fell everywhere. Megan could hear doors opening all over the pyramid as all the systems shut down. The pyramid was effectively dead. The gods of Vukas were no more.

CHAPTER THIRTY-THREE

Megan sprinted through the darkened halls, thankful for the Keeper's minimalist tendencies that kept her from tripping over objects. She slowed down on the stairs, feeling for each step as she went. She used the torch as a makeshift flashlight in the lab before heading to the weapons room.

Just like every door she had encountered so far, the weapons room was no longer locked. The warrior in Megan wanted to admire each of the weapon choices and find the best one for her personal use, but this was about politics, not the weapons. She scrounged around until she found the weapon she was looking for: the Spear of Authority.

Once the spear was located, she couldn't help herself; she picked up a set of knives and found the edges dangerously sharp and the balance perfect. She debated about taking another set of weapons since Kavi and the Dyami never mentioned anything about a person being gifted with more than one set of weapons.

"Little girl...little girl...come out and play." The sing-song voice of one of the men who had attacked her outside of the pyramid echoed through the halls.

Damn it. When all of the interior doors opened, the exterior door must have opened too. She knew what these men had planned for her, and she sure as hell didn't want them to get their hands on her.

Suddenly the decision to take the knives wasn't such a difficult one.

I feel your distress. What is wrong?

Bel sent a goon squad after me. They are back on my trail. According to what they said at our last encounter, I'm not supposed to make it back alive.

Ghaleb and Kavi have me under house arrest to keep me from getting to you. They are worried that my interference would jeopardize their political mechanizations.

Good news is I have found a shortcut back. So get the masses gathered and I should be there within two days, if all goes well. As for politics, I've got a few things up my sleeve for the political bullshit.

You better come home alive, jinaria.

Just be ready and be armed. I don't know what Bel and his faction within Tanis will do, especially after the information I have becomes public.

Kilala gave a low growl that signaled the men pursuing her were getting close. Megan cut off her communication with Reijo and strapped the knives to her thigh. She grabbed the spear and eased her way into the shadows of the hall. The underground tunnel that led through a good portion of the jungle was on this level according to the schematics she had memorized earlier. She just had to make it through her attackers and she would be home free.

The ghost lions' black fur blended into the shadows. Megan would not have known they were there if she wasn't connected to them. Kilala stalked ahead to make sure the path was clear while Kia limped slightly to the rear. As soon as they were back in civilization, Megan would get Kia's ribs bound to relieve some of the pain the cat felt. K'ah remained close to Megan, using his body to gently guide her around obstacles that he was able to see in the dark with his superior night vision.

The tunnel would shave off days of travel, as it was practically a straight shot towards the Dyami compound and ritual site. Unfortunately, there was no place to hide in the tunnel. Megan's only hope was to stay far ahead of the men who pursued her until she could get out to open ground.

*****

"I'm telling you, Ghaleb, Bel is interfering with the *Mate Avi Keiger*."

"What proof do you have, Reijo? I cannot act without proof."

Reijo slammed his hands on Ghaleb's desk. "I already told you that Megan told me about the men Bel sent to kill her. Do you call her a liar?" Reijo's eyes flashed and his nose flared. Ghaleb instinctively backed up to give himself room to defend himself if his *Kijani-a* snapped.

"Of course not, Reijo. But no one in our lifetime has been bonded. Do you really think that the council is going to believe that your connection to a woman who isn't even Vukasin is strong enough to give that kind of information over such a distance? They would remove me from the throne for attacking a noble house with manufactured lies."

"Do you think I care about the fools on the council when the woman I love is being hunted?" Reijo growled.

"You have to understand, cousin…as much as I like and respect your mate, I have an entire population to consider. We are dying, Reijo. The Earth women have allowed me to dare hope that we may yet survive, but I do know this…a civil war would ensure our extinction."

Reijo sank into the chair in front of Ghaleb's desk. He knew the *Khalon* was in no position to help him, but he had hoped the blood ties they shared would have moved Ghaleb into action, politics be damned.

"Perhaps you should let us go extinct, Ghaleb. The gods know there is little good left of our people and our society at the moment."

Ghaleb stood and walked around his desk, laying a hand on Reijo's shoulder. "I will make this concession, Reijo. You said that Megan should be back before the moons separate."

"If all goes well she should be here tomorrow near sunset."

"Fine. I will have a battalion of soldiers on hand

and alert those I know are loyal to Clan Ivailo to be ready. It is the only thing I can do for now." Ghaleb took a chair next to his cousin and gave a half-hearted smile. "Megan is one of the toughest people I have ever met. She will come back to us. Trust her to return to you, even if you can't trust anything else."

Reijo stared off into the distance and Ghaleb wasn't even sure if he had heard him. Ghaleb couldn't imagine knowing that the one you loved was facing danger but being unable to do anything about it. He knew the sacrifice he was asking of Reijo was a tremendous one. He also knew that if push came to shove, Reijo's loyalty was no longer his but Megan's. His cousin was a great man of honor, but the love he had for the fiery little Earth woman outweighed any cultural ideals of honor. Reijo would willingly lay down his life to keep Megan safe. For that reason, Ghaleb knew he had to tread lightly with him.

Reijo turned his gaze back to his cousin and ruler. Ghaleb saw something dark and dangerous within Reijo's eyes. He suddenly wondered if he had taken his political chess game too far. Sometimes Ghaleb forgot that the pieces he moved around the board were living, breathing people. Reijo reminded him that he was not all powerful and his pieces had minds and desires of their own.

"I will tell you this only once, Ghaleb, and I give you this warning only because of the blood that bonds us and the love we have shared as brothers in arms. If Megan does not return safely to me there will be blood. You will have to kill me and you and I both know that will not be an easy task. Until someone accomplishes my death, I will rain terror and pain down upon everyone I deem responsible for the loss of my mate, including you, *Khalon.*" Reijo practically sneered on Ghaleb's title. For the first time, Ghaleb actually feared the man who was considered the deadliest warrior on the planet.

Reijo pushed himself up from the chair and marched out of Ghaleb's private study. Ghaleb watched him leave.

"You better step carefully with that man, Ghaleb."

Ghaleb had been so intent on Reijo's departure that he jumped at Kavi's words.

"What have you uncovered, Kavi?"

"Reijo was correct. A death squad of a half dozen clanless mercenaries was dispatched into the jungle shortly after Megan. My contacts traced the money back to the Tanis clan, though nothing was officially recorded."

"So we have no proof still and we are gambling with Megan's life."

"All moves are a gamble one way or another. You just must decide if the possible win is worth risking the possible loss."

Ghaleb looked towards the door that Reijo just exited and sighed. "It is too late for me to question the risk, though I admit I miscalculated this gamble. Let us pray that somehow we get the winning hand because all is lost if we do not."

"You miscalculated because you forgot to

account for one of the variables," Kavi stated as he sat down in the chair Reijo had vacated.

Ghaleb stood and walked towards the far wall where a small selection of the Dyami's finest liquors was located. He raised an empty glass at Kavi, silently asking if his old teacher wanted a drink. When Kavi nodded, Ghaleb poured them both a generous serving of the deep blue whiskey. Ghaleb rarely indulged in such powerful alcohol, but today his nerves needed the extra numbing.

He handed Kavi his glass and returned to his seat behind the massive desk. He threw back the whiskey in a single gulp despite Kavi's raised brow. He stopped himself from slamming the glass down in front of him. He gently placed the delicate crystal cup between his hands and slid it back in forth while he thought.

Kavi quietly watched his best pupil turned ruler as the man worked out the issue going through his head. It was a pattern they had fallen into many times before. Ghaleb would think through his issue, meditate on something Kavi had expressed, and then... "Which variable do you believe I missed?" Ghaleb would ask for clarification.

Kavi sipped his own glass of whiskey and considered how best to explain. Ghaleb was an extremely logical man and, as such, expected things to progress in a logical manner. Kavi knew that logic alone wouldn't win the day because people were only logical to an extent. It was in the nature of creatures that experienced emotions to act on those emotions. This was something Ghaleb often forgot when forming a strategy.

In the end Kavi decided that the simple approach was best. "Love."

Ghaleb coughed and sputtered. "What do you mean by love?"

"Reijo loves Megan and Abby. He would do anything to ensure that the ones he loves are safe. In fact, I would keep an eye on him to make sure he doesn't find a way to slip into the jungle to try and protect Megan."

Ghaleb frowned but called in one of his most trusted observers and gave him orders to keep an eye on Reijo.

"So Reijo loves Megan…. Why would that change our plans?"

Kavi frowned, "You may have been a brilliant student, Ghaleb, but there are times you really are an idiot. When someone is in love, they are a loose cannon. You can't control them; you may be able to manipulate them somewhat, but their actions are unpredictable."

"So I have lost an ally to the Earth woman."

"Not entirely…but I do think you have the potential of losing many allies to the Earth women if you do not tread carefully over the next few days."

"What do you mean by that?"

Kavi shook his head and placed his half empty glass on the desk before rising from his chair with his bones creaking.

"Open your eyes, Ghaleb. Look at the people around you as people and not just pieces to be maneuvered and maybe you will finally learn something about human nature and motivation." Kavi left through the hidden panel, leaving Ghaleb to ponder the message his old teacher was trying to impart.

CHAPTER THIRTY-FOUR

Megan's side burned and every breath caused pain, yet she continued. She felt like Pheidippides running from Marathon to announce the Greek victory, but her battle had not been won yet. The exit from this tunnel should be only a short distance up ahead. She dared not attempt to rest until she could find cover in the dense foliage of the carnivorous jungle.

Megan could hear her pursuers calling back and forth behind her. They didn't seem to be in much of a hurry. Of course there was no place for Megan to hide from them while in the tunnel.

"There is nowhere to hide, little girl. Let's have some fun before you die. I promise to give you pleasure and a quick death."

The voice sounded closer than before, which had Megan gripping the spear tighter and forcing air into her burning lungs as she picked up the pace. Fear of death could be a powerful motivator.

The damp, earthy smell of the jungle wafted

across her senses. Megan looked up sharply, but the way before her still appeared to be the dark mass of the tunnel. The scent could just be wishful thinking.

As she continued to run forward, the smell of plant life and earth became stronger. She was nearing the end of the tunnel. If she could just make it to the jungle before the men caught up with her, she may have a chance. She pushed her tired body to move even faster. The closer she got to Reijo, the stronger their connection became. He was a silent shadow in her mind, pouring strength into her tired limbs. Without him, Megan wasn't so sure that she wouldn't have collapsed before getting out of the temple complex.

Megan burst through the darkness; the only indication that she had left the tunnel was the different flooring beneath her feet. The blackness surrounding her was all consuming, leaving her disoriented. It took Megan a moment to realize that the tunnel emptied into a cave. Relief washed through her; she made it out.

K'ah nudged Megan's leg, reminding her that she still needed to find somewhere to hole up and rest. If her calculations were correct, it should be a couple of hours until sunrise. She needed that time to sleep if she could. She still had a day's hike to cover in the morning. Megan told the cats that they needed to find someplace to hide. The cats' vision was much better than hers in the darkness, so she had to trust them to guide her. What they found was a small chamber off the main trail of the cave. Without the cats, she would have missed it, as the opening curved around a rock formation. It was a tight fit with Megan and the three ghost lions inside. Megan settled behind the dark furry animals, hiding the spear behind her own back. Thanks to the cats, if someone stumbled upon the alcove and looked in, they would just see darkness.

Megan could hear the men pursuing her pass by her hiding place. She held her breath for a moment, fear gripping her that they would turn around and discover where she is. When her body forced her to take a breath, Megan connected with Reijo.

Reijo?

Is everything alright, jinaria? Are you hurt? I didn't feel any pain, but I have felt your distress and maybe that—

Megan interrupted his panicked ramblings. It was nice to know that there was someone who worried about her well-being again. *No, I'm fine for now. I just wanted to hear your voice.*

Megan felt warmth and love envelope her soul.

You are everything to me, Megan. You and Abby have become my whole world.

The men pursuing me have passed me for the moment. I've hidden in a cave for now. I'm hoping to rest a bit before heading home.

Be careful, my love. The men will soon realize that you have not made it back to the stronghold ahead of them.

I know. I have a battle ahead. I wish you were here with me.

I am with you. If you can elude them until you are within sight of the stronghold, Ghaleb has

promised soldiers at the ready to help. If not, call
me, the trial be damned. I will not lose you.

How's Abby?

Megan could feel Reijo's heart soften as he thought of her daughter. In his thoughts he didn't think of Abby as Megan's child; she was his daughter as sure as any child who carried his blood in their veins.

She is becoming the little terror. She has taken to her training with a ferocity only matched by her mother…. Sleep, jinaria. I can feel your fatigue beating at me.

I love you, Reijo.

And I you, Megan.

*****

A rough wet tongue swiped across Megan's face. She batted it away, trying to remain in blissful sleep, but Kilala wasn't having it. The mother cat swatted Megan's shoulder, careful to keep her claws retracted. Even without the deadly claws, the powerful swipe got Megan's attention.

"Fine, I'm up." Megan frowned at the cat through squinted eyes. Light was filtering into the cave opening. They had hidden much closer to the mouth of the cave than Megan had realized last night. "You could at least have brought me coffee." The cat huffed a warm breath in Megan's face and gave the distinct impression of calling the woman lazy. "Fine…no coffee, but don't expect me to be cheerful about it." The ghost lions turned and padded out of the cavern, Megan had no choice but to follow.

Kilala scouted ahead. Megan had informed her feline companions to keep a watchful eye out because the men who had been chasing them still were a danger. K'ah kept his post at Megan's side and Kia took up the rear once more.

Kia seemed to be moving a bit better this morning, so hopefully her ribs had just been bruised rather than cracked. Still, they were tender, as the snarl she gave Megan attested, when Megan ran her hands along her side to check for injuries.

Hours passed without any indication of her pursuers. Megan wondered if perhaps they had made it all the way to the compound and decided to stay there. It would make things much easier for her if she could just walk into Reijo's arms this evening.

Of course she had no such luck. It was past noon, judging by the shadows cast among the trees, and the thought of a warm bath and a soft bed had her mind wandering. Kilala called out a warning and Megan nearly tripped over K'ah as he moved into her path to force her to stop. She was about to reprimand the cat when she heard voices nearby.

Thankfully they were close enough to the Dyami stronghold that the carnivorous plants had begun to thin. Megan hid herself in the dense foliage. She mimicked the ghost lion's patient advance, a freeze-frame movement much like the leopards of earth. Creeping up on the voices, she recognized one of the men who had attacked her at the temple, looking worse for wear just like she was for his time in the jungle. She didn't recognize the other man with him, but he wore a uniform she did recognize.

Bel must be getting desperate if he was willing to chance sending identifiable Tanis Clan soldiers to stop her.

"You will not receive payment until Bel is positive that the woman is dead, *Mercenary*." The Tanis soldier sneered the last word like it was distasteful to him.

"Careful, *Kijani*, I would hate to slit your throat before the night is over." The man who had threatened to rape and kill her spat on the ground in front of the soldier.

"Don't be so cocky. After all my squad was ordered here because your team lost the woman."

"We haven't lost her. We just overtook her to lay this ambush."

The soldier snorted his disbelief. "I hope for your sake that the woman doesn't slip through, but then again if she does at least I will have the pleasure of killing you."

Megan had heard and seen enough. She carefully moved into a more hidden position so she could think about her next course of action.

The ghost lions could take out a couple of the men each probably before someone realized what was happening, but with an entire squad of armed soldiers as well as the four or five mercenaries that were left, it was doubtful that they could take out enough to clear the way.

If you could stay hidden and sneak around them for another couple of miles you would be close enough that we at the stronghold would hear the sounds of battle. Reijo broke into Megan's thoughts.

Ghaleb has us stationed outside of the wall with soldiers. I have spoken to Fadri and he says that it wouldn't count as interference if we can hear you being attacked.

That's all well and good, Reijo, but I still have to get through those couple of miles in an area crawling with Tanis's soldiers.

Take a trick from Kilala; go to the tree tops. Soldiers rarely look up. If you can travel quietly through the trees you might have a chance.

Megan looked up at the trees surrounding her. The canopy here wasn't as densely packed as it was in the heart of the jungle. It could be done, but she would be in the open for a moment moving from tree to tree. Oh well, it wasn't like she had any better plans.

I'll give it a shot, Reijo. If this doesn't work, remember I love you.

It will work; just get a little closer and I will be there to make sure it does.

Megan melted into the shadows of the surrounding forest, moving away from the men hunting her. When she felt like she was far enough away, she climbed high into the branches of the trees. As quietly as possible, she maneuvered through the tree tops.

The going was slow. Megan had to carefully balance as she crossed from branch to branch. More than once she had to freeze as soldiers searched for her below. Reijo was right, hardly any of the soldiers looked up as they searched the forest for her. Unfortunately, the trees began to thin and it was becoming more difficult to find a path between the trees.

Megan climbed higher in the tree she was in. She had reached the end of the line in her tree-top trail. She hoped she could see above the tree line so she could figure out how far from the stronghold she was. The sky was beginning to turn pink as the sun set. The twin moons looked like a shining infinity symbol. If she could survive the soldiers hunting her, Megan would complete this task with almost two weeks to spare. It was an amazing feat by Vukasin standards. In the twilight, Megan could just make out the stone walls of the Dyami fortification. She still wondered if she was close enough for them to come to her aid, but at this point she didn't have much choice; she had to descend to the forest floor to continue. Once there she would be a sitting duck for the soldiers searching for her.

CHAPTER THIRTY-FIVE

"Get ready, Ghaleb. She's close and we are about to have a battle on our hands." Reijo's grip on his clan blade tightened. He was dressed for battle with both firearms and close combat weapons. Ghaleb had lived up to his promise and stood among the squadron of palace soldiers. Fadri and Dayan were also there with men of their own. Amazingly, no one questioned Reijo's knowledge that Megan would be arriving early, though Bel of Tanis scowled at his declaration. Still, the odious man insisted that he remain to see if the Earth woman succeeded.

The soldiers startled at the terrifying scream of the ghost lion. Reijo would have dashed off with that confirmation that Megan was near if Ghaleb had not put a restraining hand on his arm.

"You must wait, Reijo. You and I may know that was the call of one of Megan's cats, but if we leave before Fadri gives the word then all of her trials are for naught."

Reijo's fist clenched and released as he tried

to reign himself in. "She is being attacked. I should be at her side protecting her."

"You will have a lifetime of that once we get her home, Cousin."

Gun shots were heard in the distance, and Fadri gestured for silence. More shots sounded along with a ghost lion's roar. The sound came from the forest leading into the carnivorous jungle. Fadri's eyes narrowed when he spotted Bel's smirk. The bastard was giving himself away with his over confidence. Fadri wouldn't let the Tanis poison go any further and signaled the troops to advance.

"Remember your instructions, men." Earlier, Fadri had briefed the troops that they were allowed to remove the interference of others but could not offer help or aid to Megan. She still had to return to the ritual space on her own.

At the signal, Reijo took off at a run, pushing far ahead of any of the other soldiers. He knew Megan was alive but felt through their connection that she had a new injury. She was ignoring him, but Reijo was able to discern snippets of a bloody battle.

Reijo felt his connection to Megan grow stronger the closer he came to her. He used it like a homing beacon to find the woman he loved. Bursting from the forest into a clearing, Reijo phased, blade and claws ripping apart the nearest target in his path. Behind him the reinforcements did the same, joining the battle.

The sight they beheld was the stuff of legends. Megan was at the center of a pitch battle, wielding her spear with the skill of a born warrior tempered by the flames of battle. She was an avenging goddess of ancient times come to the mortal realm once more. Her long, fiery hair had come loose and billowed around her with every move she made. Her pale skin still held faint traces of the blue symbols she adorned herself with at the beginning of the trail, giving her an otherworldly appearance. Blood stained her face and clothes. She was retribution. She was death.

The troops stood in awe of the woman before them. For a moment, the men forgot their purpose and just stood there watching. They all knew of the spear she carried. Three ghost lions surrounded her. They protected her back and attacked at her direction. It soon became clear that while the troops could clear out the stragglers, Megan hadn't really needed their help. The soldiers knew that the legend of this battle would grow with the retelling. Their own stories would be embellished when they spoke of how they helped the warrior queen as she vanquished her enemies. Once the soldiers leapt into action, it didn't take long to finish off the mercenaries and soldiers surrounding Megan.

Bel burst through the forest into the clearing after everyone else, his immense size hindering his progress. He leaned over his knees, huffing. He squealed and fell on his ass when the head of his *Kijani* rolled to his feet.

Bel scrambled up as Megan advanced on him with murder in her eyes and ghost lions growling next to her. With a simple hand gesture from Megan, one of the cats tackled Bel, saliva and blood dripping from its deadly fangs. One word from Megan and the cat would snap the clan leader's neck with a single bite.

Reijo wrapped his arms around Megan and whispered, "*Jinaria....*"

"You would not be so quick to stay my hand if you knew what I now know, Reijo."

"I don't doubt that, beloved, but now is not the right time for swift justice."

Megan shrugged out of her lover's arms. Planting the Spear of Authority into the ground, Megan marched toward Bel, who was still pinned under the weight of a ghost lion. As she got closer, she scooped up the head of Bel's commander who had been ordered to kill her. Already, the fat politician was trying to spin the fact that members of his soldiers being in the forest had been for her protection. It was a plausible excuse, and most likely the royal council would buy it, only giving the Tanis a slap on the wrist for disregarding Fadri's orders. Megan wasn't the council, however, and Bel had sealed his fate as her enemy. She would kill him one day, even if that day wasn't today.

"K'ah," Megan barked. The ghost lion growled and swiped at Bel, cuffing him on the head before moving off of him with a snarl. The rotund man struggled to sit upright when Megan replaced the cat. She planted a boot square on his chest, forcing him back down on the ground. She held the severed head of the soldier sent to kill her nose to nose with Bel. Blood had begun to congeal instead of flowing free. Some of it plopped onto the shirt of the man who had been a thorn in Megan's side since arriving on this planet.

Megan lowered her voice, hissing with menace. "I swear to you, upon all that is holy, if you target me and mine again I will have your head on a pike outside my stronghold gates so the carrion birds can feast on your flesh." With a final shove, she stood and placed the decapitated head upon Bel's chest.

Fadri retrieved the Spear of Authority and bowed before Megan, presenting it to her. "M'lady, you must still reach the ceremonial site with what the gods bestowed upon you for this trial to be declared won."

"Your gods have forsaken you, Fadri. I'm just the messenger to tell you as much." Megan's fingers turned white as she gripped the spear, taking it from the Dyami monk. The Dyami just nodded before standing and moving back away from Megan.

Megan turned to Ghaleb and held the spear in front of her. "Do you know what this is?" she demanded.

"I do."

"Go then and gather the council. The time for pointless bickering is done. We will see to this tonight!" With that proclamation, Megan turned on her heel and marched out of the forest flanked by her ghost lions.

The stunned men of Vukas just stood there as the woman, by her very presence, commanded respect from all she passed.

"I believe, Cousin, that I might have just lost

my throne."

Reijo slapped Ghaleb on the back and laughed. "Perhaps and perhaps not…either way, I do believe you will be dancing to her tune for a while."

Ghaleb shook his head before taking off to gather the royal council. He had set the pieces in motion; the least he could do was see the gambit to the end.

CHAPTER THIRTY-SIX

Word spread quickly that the challenger for the *Mate Avi Keiger* had returned. A rumor had started that the soldiers dispatched earlier were just bringing home a body. Many of the men found that easier to believe than Megan completing the trial. It didn't take long for every person within the city of Tilan to make their way to the ceremonial grounds.

Reijo wanted to stay by Megan's side but he knew that this was a moment he needed to remain in the background. He followed at a stately distance with Fadri. Both men continued to scan the growing crowd for any sign of trouble; neither trusted the Tanis Clan to leave well enough alone.

"Your mate wishes to speak with me alone after she has spoken to the council." Fadri looked sideways at Reijo and tensed when he made that statement.

Reijo chuckled slightly, "If you worry about me being jealous, monk, you can rest as ease. I knew she wished to speak with you."

Fadri nodded. The two men continued in contemplative silence until they stood along with the soldiers who witnessed the scene in the jungle. Megan had earned the awe and respect of the warriors who stood as a phalanx behind her as she stepped into the scared circle. The soldiers raised their weapons as the crush of people surged forward. Reijo prepared to defend Megan from the mob.

He shouldn't have worried. Megan's ghost lions circled around to flank the woman they had bonded with. Three full-grown lions let out a roar that echoed across the ceremonial grounds. The advancing crowd skidded to a halt, knocking a few of the people in the front to the ground. Megan stood tall and planted the Spear of Authority firmly beside her. She gave off the air of regal rule even with blood and dirt covering her body and tattered clothing. She stood taller than anyone there despite her petite frame.

Reijo could see Megan scowling and scanning the crowd for something. Her face relaxed when she saw the rest of the Earth women.

A horn sounded at the back of the crowd and the masses parted. The royal council marched forward. Bel was noticeably absent. Reijo wondered if he had turned tail and run away or if he was just retreating long enough to regroup and attack again.

"We are here by the *Khalon's* command," the oldest council member announced to the crowd. His disdain for Megan rolled off of him as he stared down his nose at her. Reijo shook his head and smiled. Megan had stared down angry ghost lions; one old man would not intimidate her.

Megan turned her gaze to the council

member. She watched him, unblinking. The crowd surrounding them shifted and murmured about her examining his soul. The other council members lowered their eyes, but to his credit, the old man tried to match Megan's steadfast gaze. Sweat glistened across the man's brow and his body trembled until he too was forced to look away.

Megan simply nodded and then raised her voice for all to hear. "You are wrong, Council. You are called here at my command."

That statement caused the council to clamor all at once, their denial that a woman would dare command them.

"Enough!" Megan grabbed the spear and advanced on the council members. In a bit of showmanship, she twirled it before planting the spear in the ground at the feet of the closest council member, a young man newly appointed. "Do you know what this is?"

The young man's eyes dilated and color drained from his face as he stammered. A weathered hand on the man's shoulder calmed his babbling as the older member of the council took up his role as speaker once more.

"Yes, we do. We acknowledge the feat you have accomplished, though there are questions still to be answered." The old man took a deep breath, intending, Reijo suspected, to barrel through with a mass of words that said nothing. "We will be glad to discuss the implications of such a gift bestowed upon you the next time the council is in session. Now is obviously not the time as the people," the old man gestured to the gathered crowds, "would like to celebrate your successful return. I'm sure that as a woman you would prefer to come before the council in appropriate attire." The old man continued to talk despite the anger that flushed Megan's face. "If the Tiaret Clan has not provided for you, am sure the Dyami would be more than gracious to—"

"Tonight," Megan said the word through clenched teeth, breaking the rambling train of speech the old council member spewed.

"What?"

"This will be resolved tonight. Your clan representatives will be in attendance or I will disband any clan that is not there," Megan announced with a clear voice that carried over the masses.

The speaker for the council attempted to cajole Megan into reconsidering. He mumbled about how it just wouldn't do to gather so soon because preparations needed to be made first. Megan silenced him with a wave of her hand.

"What is your clan, old man?"

"Torolf, Madame." The old man stood straighter as he declared his clan name.

Megan nodded. She remembered that in their numerous discussions with Kavi, the Torolf clan seemed to be the most sympathetic with the Tanis.

"That explains why I do not recognize you since you remained with your clan at the beginning of this trial. So I will forgive your ignorance at assuming that I am like the women you have dealt with in the past. However, do not think that my fairness implies any weakness, Council representative of the Torolf. If your smiling face is not before me when this council meets in one hour, your clan will be the first I decimate." Megan's face darkened and the smile on her lips became twisted and feral. The ghost lions growled low in their throats, advancing on the now trembling old man.

The representative of the Torolf Clan took a step back and noticeably swallowed before he answered. "Yes, M'lady."

Megan turned, grabbed the Spear of Authority, and walked towards the temple at the heart of the Dyami compound. Her cats lead the way. They easily cleared a path for Megan as they snarled and cuffed those who did not move out of the way fast enough.

The rest of the Earth women left their escorts and fell in behind Megan, creating a royal procession of women. The various shades of red worn by the women emphasized the blood that still adorned Megan's body.

As the women passed from sight into the temple, Kavi smiled from the shadows. Megan's exit couldn't have been more perfect if he had planned it himself. Now to report to his new mistress.

CHAPTER THIRTY-SEVEN

Megan slumped into a chair. She was in a large chamber that acted as the Dyami Clan's meeting space. It was similar to the council chamber at the Tairet stronghold, in that it contained a large table with plenty of comfy seating. Megan supposed that comfortable chairs were a must when debating for hours straight.

"Megan-sama, could you please explain what just happened?" Himeko took a seat next to Megan. All of the women were gathered together with the exception of the mysterious original woman who started all of this and Maria, who disappeared on her way to the Tanis household she was assigned to.

Megan knew that at some point they would have to discover what happened to the missing women, but there were other things that needed to be addressed first.

She was so tired, but her task wasn't yet complete.

"What happened was a woman just turned our entire government and I suspect culture on its head."

The women jumped at the unexpected sound of a male voice. The women surrounded the exhausted Megan with fists raised, prepared to defend their friend. All of them had spent enough time in this world to know that Megan would be in danger, especially after what they witnessed at the sacred circle, even if they didn't understand the implications of all of it.

"It's all right. Kavi is a friend." Megan waved the old man over as the women parted to let him pass.

Kavi patted a wrinkled hand on Megan's shoulder, careful to avoid most of her injuries. "You did well, child. Though I must admit, I didn't expect you to return with such a vaulted prize."

"Could you explain what is going on here?" Susan crossed her arms and narrowed her eyes at Megan and Kavi.

"Megan returned with a symbol that, on the surface, gives her the divine right to rule this planet."

"So she did it? She somehow managed to give all of us the right to choose? We can go home?" Sara asked.

"In a manner of speaking. Her spear will give weight to her decisions and declaration that they wouldn't have had before, though I doubt the council would agree to any of you returning to Earth. She is a ruler of Vukas in name only right now. But even with the historical precedence, she still has to win the respect of the people and leaders, otherwise she could be disposed like any ruler."

Megan laid her head on the table and heaved

a massive sigh, "I don't want to rule, Kavi. I just wanted us to be able to choose."

"I know, Megan, but that choice comes with a price, and this is it. You are the rallying point for the cause of the women. You are the only voice that can overshadow the voices like Bel of Tanis. Today you will make great strides, but the journey is far from over."

"Isn't there some way to let Ghaleb keep his crown? Maybe I could just be a representative on the council or something," Megan implored.

Kavi shook his head, "Council members have very limited powers alone, and you would face an uphill battle as only a council member. Before Ghaleb's grandfather transferred the governmental power to the council, the *Kholan's* power was absolute. The good rulers listened to the advice of the council, but the king's rule was law. Ghaleb can no longer return us to that, and honestly a single man's rule could wreak havoc depending on the man."

"What makes you think a single woman would do any better?" Kilala butted her head against Megan's hand at the distress in her voice.

Parvati coughed, drawing attention to herself. "I have an idea." She gave Kavi a sideways glance. "But I would rather discuss it among just the women. No offense."

Kavi smiled and made his way to the door, "None taken, M'lady." Kavi opened the door to leave before turning to address Megan. "Best foot forward, child. What you do today will have far-reaching consequences. I suggest you take the next half hour or so to look like a queen."

Megan watched the door until it closed fully. She then turned towards the women. "All right, ladies; let's come up with a plan."

*****

Megan had forgone cleaning up before the council representatives arrived and refused to relinquish her ghost lions. She felt that the blood and gore, as well as the cats, served as a stark reminder to the men of the council that she was a battle-hardened warrior and not just a woman.

Today was all about presence and intimidation. Megan wasn't normally one for theatrics, but she knew the role she had to play today. She had to convince these men she was untouchable, not matter how untrue the reality was.

Megan intentionally sat at the head of the table so she could watch as the men filtered in. Reijo seated himself to her right as the head of the Tiaret Clan. Behind him stood Elod. Since this was a formal meeting of the council, each clan had a senior and junior representative. The senior representative sat at the table while the junior representative stood, waiting to fetch whatever was needed.

The men filed in. Dayan was representing the Nardo. Fadri sat in the seat for the Dyami. Ghaleb was at the other end of the table as both *Kholan* and the representative of the Ivailo Clan. The old man from yesterday, whom Kavi had informed her was named Dracen, sat in the Torolf seat to Megan's left, half way down the table. A young man who introduced himself as Reyn of the Torolf stood behind him.

Megan signaled to her ghost lions and they began to prowl around the now full meeting chamber. It was purely an intimidation tactic as the big cats circled with low growls and the occasional snarl before returning docile to Megan's side.

As the host Fadri called the council session to order, Megan watched as the meeting descended into chaos. Everyone tried to out-speak everyone else, each man vying to be heard. The opinions ranged the entire spectrum, especially where Megan was concerned.

Megan quietly observed until she had her fill of such nonsense. She sent the impression of a pack challenge to Kilala to explain what was happening, and the cat responded in the way Megan hoped she would.

The ghost lion's roar rattled the walls of the meeting room, and the men had to cover their ears when the other two joined their mother. Megan sat quietly with a slight smirk on her face as many of the men paled and trembled.

As the roars subsided, Megan had what she wanted…silence.

She stood and addressed the councilmen. "M'lords, today is a turning point in this planet's history. By this spear," Megan laid the Spear of Authority on the table in front of her, "your gods have declared their favor for me. I do not wish to destroy the pride and culture of this planet…."

Megan was interrupted mid-sentence as a

group of heavily armed men burst through the door. None of them wore clan colors, so it was impossible to tell who had orchestrated this attack. A smoke bomb was thrown into the room, shrouding everything in a haze. Violence erupted everywhere. Members of the council battled the intruders, though a few councilmen turned to battle their fellow councilors, accusing them of setting this ambush.

Megan's cats didn't hesitate and quickly pounced on the attackers nearest them, dispatching them quickly before moving on to the next. Megan worried that the cats might start attacking their allies; she tried to see their movements in the smoky haze. She was concentrating so hard on the cats that she almost missed the movement next to her.

Dracen had raised a dagger into the air and charged Megan. The old man's eyes held a murderous gleam.

"No woman shall rule here!"

Reyn tried to restrain the older representative, but despite the man's age, years in the fields and training as a warrior had left him very agile.

The smoke was clearing but the rest of the men were occupied with their own battles. It would be ironic, Megan thought, to die here at the hands of an old man after everything she has survived.

Reyn was knocked aside with a gash on his arm from Dracen's dagger, and the old man once more charged Megan. Megan was left with no choice but to defend herself. The ghost lions were across the room and would be of no help. So Megan grabbed the only weapon she still had at hand: the Spear of

Authority.

With an ease that surprised the old man, Megan used the Spear to knock the dagger from his hand, only to have Dracen pull another knife out of his tunic, which he sent flying towards Megan with a flick of his wrist.

Megan ran him through with the spear just as the knife imbedded into her shoulder—another scar to add to her collection.

The smoke cleared and silence fell. Reijo ran to Megan to pull the knife from her shoulder. She batted his hand away and growled, "Leave it."

Megan shoved the body of Dracen to the ground and removed the spear, her body vibrating with anger.

"This…this is why the gods have cursed you. You have lost your honor. When you treat your own citizens as property…." Megan had to stop and calm herself before continuing. She pointed a finger at every male in the room. "You need to get your shit together and fix this…because so help me, if you don't…I will!"

A few of the men tried to cut in to spin whatever bullshit politicians spin in this situation, but Megan had had enough. She hurled the spear, still dripping with Dracen's blood, at the end of the table where Ghaleb sat.

"By this spear, I am the Goddess who walks the land. If you cannot rule the way the people, both male and female, deserve, then I will cut you down like the weeds you are and find someone who will to fill your place.

"You are cursed by your own pride and arrogance, and you will die unless you change. Your gods have given you yet another chance to redeem yourselves. Don't fuck it up." Megan's complexion paled, but she refused to show weakness in front of these men. "Today's attack has only proved that we are on the brink of civil war. You can be like Dracen and fight the divine will of the gods, but know that if you walk that path I will cut you down. You have until the next joining of the moons to make your choice. Send out your messengers, call your clan councils, think of solutions to fix what your chauvinistic ideals have broken. I strongly suggest that you listen to the women, both Vukasin and from Earth. Remember what makes life worth living: family, home…love; make choices based within those things and perhaps the gods will smile on Vukas once more."

Megan walked out of the meeting chamber followed by Reijo and her ghost lions, with the knife still imbedded in her shoulder. She only made it halfway down the hall before collapsing into Reijo's arms.

CHAPTER THIRTY-EIGHT

"I can't believe you went before the council covered in gore, with your ghost lions still bloody from battle," Kavi snorted in laughter while Reijo recounted what had happened earlier.

Megan had just entered the study, finally having been able to clean herself. Who knew a hot bath could make her feel like she was in heaven. Now she was being cosseted by Elod and Reijo to get her injuries looked at.

"I would have loved to see the looks on those pompous politicians' faces when you walked out like a conquering warrior."

"Knowing you, you were probably hidden away in some alcove watching the whole thing," Megan teased before wincing when Elod prodded the area where the knife had stabbed her shoulder.

Kavi laughed harder, but the twinkle in his eye told Megan that she wasn't far from guessing the truth.

"Megan was amazing." Reijo took a seat next to her, placing a possessive hand upon her thigh. "She has the majority of the council convinced that their own actions against women called down the gods' wrath, which is why our race was dying."

"Clever girl."

"It was a stroke of genius on my part," Megan smiled. "Though having the Spear of Authority definitely greased the wheels. Perhaps if we are lucky the council will actually have some real solutions in the next few months." She didn't mention the other plan, despite the fact that all the Earth women wore red when she got back. With the spear she hadn't needed to form a new clan.

"How is Ghaleb taking all of this?" Elod asked, "I haven't seen him since that meeting."

Reijo sighed. "About as well as can be expected. Half the council wants to raise Megan as *Khala* despite her refusal; they believe a 'living goddess' needs a title. The other half are still debating the merits of the Tanis breeding program, albeit with input from the women of Earth."

"I have no desire to rule, Elod, but I do want a voice in what happens to me and any other women brought here." Megan looked up at the young physician. "Do you think you will be able to remove the scars on my back?"

Elod shrugged. "I'm not going to lie to you, Megan. They are deep and have already healed quite a bit. I can lessen their appearance, but I honestly don't know if I will be able to remove them."

Megan's shoulders slumped and Reijo wrapped his arm around her, pulling her into his lap.

"*Jinaria*, you are beautiful…scars or no scars. They are a symbol of your strength, and I will kiss every one thankful that you returned to me."

Kavi cleared his throat and turned the conversation to things less personal. "How did Fadri take the information you gave him about the temple?"

"Surprisingly well. I've come to find out that the knowledge that the 'gods' were alien ancestors has been handed down from leader to leader within the clan for generations. He did ask that I not spread the knowledge around because for many, their faith is all that keeps them going from day to day. It also allows an avenue to teach the next generation how to have a moral compass." Megan tapped a finger against her chin, thinking. "I agreed with him. I think culture and tradition are important. So I saw no reason to destroy it."

Elod handed Megan a series of antibiotics to keep infection from her various wounds at bay. He kissed her forehead and told her to call him if she needed him before exiting the room.

"I thought he would never leave."

The other occupants jumped at the sound of someone near the far wall. Ghaleb was coming out of the hidden panel that Kavi favored using.

"Now, little sister, tell me what I really need to know." Ghaleb sat in a chair across from Megan. She noticed that there seemed to be more lines around his mouth and his eyes were tired. This was the main reason Megan had no desire to rule; the stress just wasn't worth it in her opinion.

"Where do you want me to start?" Megan had already given Ghaleb the short version of her adventure.

"What did you find out from the Keeper?"

All eyes turned to Megan as she took a deep breath. It was going to kill the men to hear what she had to say.

"Well, I learned that both your planet and my planet were long-term genetic experiments by an ancient alien culture. That is probably why the women of my planet are genetically compatible with the men of yours: we started with the same basic genetic code.

"I can't be certain, but I believe that the alien race somehow died out long ago. The Keeper was simply a computer program that kept performing the function assigned to it, even though it hadn't had contact from its creators for eons."

"What was its function?" Kavi asked curiously.

"Mostly to monitor the experiment and record results. It also played the role of emissary from the gods when necessary."

"You said that you learned something important there." Ghaleb looked her in the eye without blinking.

"I learned that your declining female population wasn't an accident…at least not entirely."

"Explain." Kavi leaned forward, his eyes intent.

"The Keeper said that a part of the experiment introduced an outside variable…a virus to be exact. This virus affected gender assignment in utero, effectively making babies that should have been born female male instead."

"Who would do something so stupid?" Ghaleb growled

"Actually, it was a fairly smart move if I am correct." Kavi leaned back in his chair. "Please continue, Megan."

"Kavi's right...originally the virus was introduced only to the royal line. They were trying to have you die out over time. Unfortunately, the virus spread until it became pandemic."

"How could our scientists have missed this? A virus can be cured."

Reijo gave Ghaleb a look that conveyed that the ruler of a planet should be smarter than this.

Ghaleb swore violently when his train of thought caught up with the rest of them. "By the gods—Tanis...the Tanis are behind this. They have to be; most of our scientists are from that clan. It would be easy for them to cover up findings of a virus, and they have the most to gain from Ivailo falling."

"The good news, according to the Keeper, is that since the virus was introduced a few generations back, the population now has a natural immunity built up to it. Unfortunately, that immunity came after the breaking point. Left as you are now, the Vukasin population will die out in just a couple of generations."

Ghaleb leapt from his chair and grasped Megan's hands tightly. "But you can save us...you said women of your world are genetically compatible with us, we just need more women."

Megan shook her head and extracted her hand from Ghaleb's grip. "It's not that simple, Ghaleb. I would never condone kidnapping, even to save you. I believe that many women would willingly take a chance at coming to this world of their own volition, but only if they were certain they would be safe and cared for."

"We are dying, Megan. How can you condemn us to such a fate?" Ghaleb slumped in the floor defeated.

"I'm not condemning you. I'm telling you that we women deserve a choice in our own fate. Make this world a place where women could be happy and I will do whatever I can to bring them here. But it will always be their choice."

Kavi laid a hand on his old student's shoulder and quoted an old Vukasin proverb: "You must first clean the vipers from the bed before lying in it. We have a battle to fight, my boy. There are still enemies among us, even if we know some of their names. It is time for you to be *Khalon* in more than name only. Destroy your enemies, bring order to your land and pray the gods bless us for it. Besides, you are going to have more on your hands to worry about soon."

"What have you heard, you old buzzard raptor?" Reijo sighed.

"Not everyone is willing to go quietly into the new world order. Bel's disappearance was no accident. He left to rally his support in the southern hemisphere where the Tanis once held power. Rumor has it that there are many willing to follow him."

Ghaleb sighed. "So this means war is on the horizon."

Kavi nodded. "You can no longer afford to placate the politicians, Ghaleb. It is time to be an Ivailo ruler."

Megan stood next to Reijo. The pair wrapped their arms around each other, and Ghaleb felt a pang of jealousy at the support they offered each other.

Reijo extended his hand. "Make the right choices, Cousin, and you will always have the support of the Tiaret."

EPILOGUE

Megan gazed out the window of their bed chamber. It was good to be back home in the mountains. She smiled to herself. Yes, this was now home. Reijo had offered to take her and Abby back to Earth before they had left the Dyami. He even claimed that he would stay with them there on Megan's planet. Megan knew he wouldn't be happy there, and truth be told, she didn't really have a reason to return. Everything she wanted was here on Vukas. So she had kissed him and told him to bring her home to the Tiaret.

She had spent the last few hours playing with Abby. The child seemed almost afraid that her mother would disappear again, and it took a long time before she succumbed to sleep. Megan had left the Abby's room with Kia curled up at the foot of her bed. The ghost lion hadn't left the child's side since they returned from the jungle. Megan wouldn't be surprised to hear soon that Abby could feel Kia's bond.

Megan reached down and affectionately scratched K'ah's ears. She had arranged for him and Kilala to have free reign within the walls of their stronghold, yet one or the other rarely left her side.

Megan felt strong arms wrap around her shoulders and she smelled the unique scent of the man she loved.

"You look pensive, *jinaria*. Are you regretting staying here with me?"

Megan turned in his arms and laid her head on his solid chest. "I could never regret being with you, Reijo. I was just thinking."

"About?"

"The past, the future…."

Reijo smiled and leaned down to kiss her softly. "We cannot change the past."

"This is true."

"We will shape the future."

"This is also true."

"So we only need to worry about the present." Reijo tilted her chin up to look at him and gave her a wolfish smile.

"Why do I get the impression that you have very definite plans about our present?"

"Because, my love, you can read my mind."

Megan kissed Reijo's chest, nipping at him with her teeth and soothing the bite with her tongue. "And an interesting mind it is…." Megan pushed Reijo back towards the bed. When his knees hit, he lay back, pulling Megan on top of him to straddle him. "I think maybe we should try this idea I see floating around in your head." Megan sent him erotic flashes and smiled when it obviously aroused him.

It was time to start living her life—because life right now was very good.

ABOUT THE AUTHOR

B.D. Snowden is a Texas native living in the Great Plains with her children of both two-legged and four-legged varieties. She is a voracious reader whose book habit literally brought a small town library to life. One day, when she was unable to get something new to read, she started turning the stories floating through her head into concrete concepts on paper. Find information about new releases and appearances at:
Geekygothblog.wordpress.com
Facebook.com/BrandiceSnowdenWriter